"It's not that you can't," Chase said. "It's that you don't want to."

She hadn't expected him to force her hand. "Well," she started, "you're my patient. It wouldn't be professional."

"So I'm your patient. I'm also the brother of friends of yours. There's nothing unprofessional about you staying at my house. I won't even be there," he argued.

Eyeing her tightly crossed arms, he reached toward her and slipped his fingers around her exposed wrist. As he did, his knuckles brushed the soft undercurve of her breast. At the intimate contact, their eyes locked, something electric happening between them. Her breath hitched.

No, he wouldn't be there, but how she wished he would be....

Dear Reader,

Happy 20th Anniversary, Silhouette! And Happy Valentine's Day to all! There are so many ways to celebrate…starting with six spectacular novels this month from Special Edition.

Reader favorite Joan Elliott Pickart concludes Silhouette's exciting cross-line continuity ROYALLY WED with *Man…Mercenary… Monarch,* in which a beautiful woman challenges a long-lost prince to give up his loner ways.

In *Dr. Mom and the Millionaire,* Christine Flynn's latest contribution to the popular series PRESCRIPTION: MARRIAGE, a marriage-shy tycoon suddenly experiences a sizzling attraction—to his gorgeous doctor! And don't miss the next SO MANY BABIES—in *Who's That Baby?* by Diana Whitney, an infant girl is left on a Native American attorney's doorstep, and he turns to a lovely pediatrician for help.…

Next is Lois Faye Dyer's riveting *Cattleman's Courtship,* in which a brooding, hard-hearted rancher is undeniably drawn to a chaste, sophisticated lady. And in Sharon De Vita's provocative family saga, THE BLACKWELL BROTHERS, tempers—and passions— flare when a handsome Apache man offers *The Marriage Basket* to a captivating city gal.

Finally, you'll be swept up in the drama of Trisha Alexander's *Falling for an Older Man,* another tale in the CALLAHANS & KIN series, when an unexpected night of passion leaves Sheila Callahan with a nine-month secret.

So, curl up with a Special Edition novel and celebrate this Valentine's Day with thoughts of love and happy dreams of forever!

Happy reading,

Karen Taylor Richman,
Senior Editor

Please address questions and book requests to:
Silhouette Reader Service
U.S.: 3010 Walden Ave., P.O. Box 1325, Buffalo, NY 14269
Canadian: P.O. Box 609, Fort Erie, Ont. L2A 5X3

CHRISTINE FLYNN

DR. MOM AND THE MILLIONAIRE

Silhouette®

SPECIAL EDITION®

Published by Silhouette Books

America's Publisher of Contemporary Romance

To my editor, Debra Robertson,
with thanks for her insight and patience

 SILHOUETTE BOOKS

ISBN 0-373-24304-9

DR. MOM AND THE MILLIONAIRE

Copyright © 2000 by Christine Flynn

This edition published by arrangement with Harlequin Books S.A.

Visit us at www.romance.net

Printed in U.S.A.

Books by Christine Flynn

CHRISTINE FLYNN

admits to being interested in just about everything, which is why she considers herself fortunate to have turned her interest in writing into a career. She feels that a writer gets to explore it all and, to her, exploring relationships—especially the intense, bittersweet or even lighthearted relationships between men and women—is fascinating.

IT'S OUR 20th ANNIVERSARY!
We'll be celebrating all year,
continuing with these fabulous titles,
on sale in February 2000.

Special Edition

#1303 Man...Mercenary...Monarch
Joan Elliott Pickart

#1304 Dr. Mom and the Millionaire
Christine Flynn

#1305 Who's That Baby?
Diana Whitney

#1306 Cattleman's Courtship
Lois Faye Dyer

#1307 The Marriage Basket
Sharon De Vita

#1308 Falling for an Older Man
Trisha Alexander

Intimate Moments

#985 The Wildes of Wyoming—Chance
Ruth Langan

#986 Wild Ways
Naomi Horton

#987 Mistaken Identity
Merline Lovelace

#988 Family on the Run
Margaret Watson

#989 On Dangerous Ground
Maggie Price

#990 Catch Me If You Can
Nina Bruhns

Romance

#1426 Waiting for the Wedding
Carla Cassidy

#1427 Bringing Up Babies
Susan Meier

#1428 The Family Diamond
Moyra Tarling

#1429 Simon Says...Marry Me!
Myrna Mackenzie

#1430 The Double Heart Ranch
Leanna Wilson

#1431 If the Ring Fits...
Melissa McClone

Desire

#1273 A Bride for Jackson Powers
Dixie Browning

#1274 Sheikh's Temptation
Alexandra Sellers

#1275 The Daddy Salute
Maureen Child

#1276 Husband for Keeps
Kate Little

#1277 The Magnificent M.D.
Carol Grace

#1278 Jesse Hawk: Brave Father
Sheri WhiteFeather

Chapter One

Dr. Alexandra Larson had a fantasy. It was decidedly tame, as fantasies went, but she'd never regarded herself as terribly creative or adventurous. She didn't even have what she considered any real sense of style. She just played it safe. She wore her dark hair short, her make-up soft and her clothes either simply tailored or loose, depending on her mood or what was handy. And she always shied away from the extravagant, the outrageous or the truly indulgent.

She considered her little daydream the ultimate indulgence.

In it, she was alone. In a hot bath. The kind of bath a woman had to carefully ease into while aromatic steam fogged the room, beaded on her chest and filled her lungs. The kind where skin pinked and knotted muscles relaxed in the liquid heat, and the mind emptied of everything but the knowledge that all she had to do was…soak.

She savored that image, lingered over the details, letting

her mind drift to it as she ran between surgery, hospital rounds, clinic appointments, day care and, occasionally, the vet.

She'd been caught indulging in it when her pager had gone off as she'd pulled into her driveway forty minutes ago. It was her thirty-second birthday. She should have been able to toy with the thoughts a little longer. Instead, she was scrubbing in for surgery with barrel-chested Ian Whitfield, one of the trauma doctors from emergency, and the fantasy of aromatic steam had given way to the reality of antibacterial scrub.

"What can you tell me?" she asked, working lather from her fingertips to beyond her elbows. "I was only told that we have a thirty-four-year-old male with a compound femur. Are we dealing with anything else?"

"CT shows no concussion or other internal injuries. The compound break in the left leg is the worst of it. That's why I asked for the orthopedic surgeon on call."

Between the green cap covering the man's receding hairline and the band of white mask obliterating the bottom half of his ruddy face, only his bespectacled eyes were visible. They narrowed, light bouncing off his lenses, as he shook his head. "That's one lucky man in there. According to the paramedics, a truck blew a light and nailed him full on the driver's door."

"He was driving?"

"Apparently."

That meant the victim had borne the brunt of the impact. Alex stored that detail as she reached for a brush to work under her short, unpolished nails. The force of that impact also explained how such a strong bone had penetrated the lower thigh.

She'd already seen her patient's X-rays. The femur, the long bone of his upper leg, had fractured in two places. The distal break, the one closest to the knee, had also splintered into a jagged spike.

The good news was that she'd seen far worse. The bad news was that this sort of break often led to nasty complications.

"Was anyone able to get a medical history from him?" she asked.

"They had him full of morphine when they brought him in, but we got enough to determine that he's never had any medical problems. Except for his injuries, he appears to be in excellent shape."

"Excellent is an understatement." A gowned and masked surgical nurse with an awestruck look in her heavily made-up eyes rustled through the bright, white-tiled room in her paper booties. "That has to be the most gorgeous hunk of muscle and testosterone to ever grace an operating table. No man that rich should look that good."

Alex glanced up. As a surgeon, the emergency patient's identity made no difference to her. She helped where she could, in and out of the operating room, and this man definitely needed her assistance. But the female part of her— the part she tended to neglect the most—was suddenly curious to know who she was about to put back together.

The X-rays had been labeled C. Harrington. Beyond that, all that had registered was the damage done to an otherwise impressively healthy bone.

Rita Sanchez, one of Alex's favorite scrub nurses, approached the door of the surgical suite. "He may be gorgeous, Michelle," she conceded, her tone disapproving, "but he'll walk over anyone to get what he wants. That's what I read in the papers, anyway." Her back to the door to push it open, her hands in the air to keep them sterile, she paused. "I wonder what he's doing in Honeygrove."

"There can only be one reason Chase Harrington would

be here.'' Pushing forward on the horseshoe-shaped knee handle to turn off the water, Whitfield snagged a sterile towel. ''The man lives, eats and breathes mergers and take-overs. We've had a couple of manufacturing facilities take off here in the last couple of years. I'll bet my golf clubs he's after one of them. I just wish I knew which one it was,'' he muttered. ''The stock is bound to go up.''

''What about you, Doctor?'' the matronly nurse asked Alex. ''Why do you think he's here?''

''I haven't a clue.'' Alex flashed her a smile, taking a towel herself. ''I really don't know that much about him.''

All she did know was that Chase Harrington was one of those people whose name popped up on newscasts and in print because what he did and what he owned set him apart from the masses. As she understood it, the man's lust for multi-million-dollar mergers and trades was as legendary as his drive, his ambition and his tendency to run over anyone who stood in his way. Since his image routinely graced the covers of *Time* and *Newsweek* in waiting and exam rooms, she even knew what he looked like. She wouldn't go quite as far as the early-twenty-something Michelle had in her sighing description of the man, but he was rather attractive—if one was drawn to the lean, chis-eled type.

As for the body the impressionable nurse had described, when Alex, gowned and gloved, backed through the door of the surgical suite, all she could tell was that it was… long.

The familiar beep of the heart monitor underscored the quiet murmur of conversation as she approached the blue-draped form on the operating table. The trauma doctor and the anesthesiologist hovered at the head. At the other end, the surgical nurses and another assistant were setting up stainless-steel trays of barbaric-looking instruments that appeared more suitable for torture than healing.

The only exposed parts of the patient were the facial laceration Whitfield had already starting suturing and the thigh she would repair.

The thigh was what had her attention.

It was a mess.

"Ouch," she whispered, and reached for the large plastic bottle of clear antibiotic wash Rita had anticipated she would want.

"Was he alone?" she heard Michelle ask.

Rita clamped a gauze pad with a hemostat, holding it ready. "You mean, was there a woman with him?"

"This suture's too big." Metal ticked softly against metal when the curved needle Whitfield tossed landed on a tray. "I need a one-point-three."

Michelle was the float nurse, the one who moved about the room taking supplies and materials to and from the team members at the table. "I'm just curious," she defended on her way to the supply cabinet a few paces away. "If he's alone, he might appreciate a little extra TLC when he wakes up."

"I'd give up that idea right now," Alex's assistant chided. "I'm sure he has someone waiting to give him all the TLC he needs. The man dates models."

Paper crackled as Michelle peeled a small packet open and held it out. "Maybe so. But no one's been able to get him near an altar yet. Maybe he's tired of male-fantasy quality women and rich society types."

The bushy-browed anesthesiologist snorted. "I doubt it."

Whitfield held up the fine-threaded and curved suture, eyed it, and went back to work. "I don't think he spends as much time running around as the press says he does. I read an article in *Forbes* that said he puts in sixteen-hour days. His latest thing is the high-tech market. And sailing,'' he added, as he methodically stitched. ''It's his passion. That same article said he's putting together a team to race in the next America's Cup.''

Checking his patient's vital signs on the monitors, the anesthesiologist tweaked the flow of gas keeping the man under discussion…under. ''I thought it was rock climbing he was into. Didn't he climb Mt. McKinley last year?''

''I'd heard that, too.'' Reverence entered Whitfield's voice. ''The man never slows down. I don't know which I envy more. His investment portfolio or his stamina. I hiked the Grand Canyon a few years ago, but I can't imagine climbing a mountain.''

Michelle sighed. ''I wonder what he'd planned to do next.''

''I hope it wasn't anything he had his heart set on,'' Alex murmured. ''The only thing this guy's going to be climbing for a while is the training stairs in the physical therapy department.''

Looking from the four-inch gash in his thigh, she critically eyed the X-ray on the monitor beside her to judge the position of the upper, unexposed break. The team was still talking, their voices low, but everything they said only made Chase Harrington sound more and more like a man who played as hard as he worked and who wouldn't have anything left for a relationship even if someone did slow him down long enough to snag him.

No woman in her right mind would want to fall for a man like that. A woman needed a partner, someone to share with. Someone who cared enough to be there even when things got rough. Someone who wouldn't walk away, leaving her to handle everything alone just when she needed him most.

She jerked her glance toward the head of the table, annoyed with herself for becoming distracted, displeased with the unwanted direction of her thoughts.

"Move that retractor higher. Perfect," she murmured, pointedly turning her attention to debriding the open wound. "I need to cauterize these bleeders."

Ian took his last stitch. "I'm ready to assist."

"Would you like your music, Dr. Larson?" Rita asked her.

Alex usually liked to have music while she worked, preferably classical and mostly to keep from inadvertently humming whichever Disney tune her four-year-old son had plugged into the car stereo. But she declined the subliminal diversion tonight. As she set about the painstaking task of manipulating, drilling and pinning to stabilize the breaks, her only other thought was that Chase Harrington was going to slow down for a while, whether he liked the idea or not.

The surgery took over two hours. It took Alex another half hour to dictate nursing instructions and the surgical notes chronicling the procedure that, given the hour, she probably could have put off until morning.

She never put off anything when it came to her patients, though. It was the personal stuff she let slide—which was why her washing machine still leaked, why she hadn't started the renovations on the potentially lovely old house she'd finally plunged in and bought last year. And why, she remembered, grimacing when she did, she was always running out of milk at home.

She'd meant to go to the grocery store after she'd picked up Tyler from child care, but they'd stopped at Hamburger Jack's for dinner because Tyler had really, really needed the newest plastic race car that came with the kiddy meal and she'd flat forgotten about the milk.

Hoping she wouldn't drive right past the Circle K on her way home and forget it again, she headed for the recovery room. If she hadn't been up to her eyebrows in student loans and house and car payments, she'd have hired a personal assistant. Someone to tend to details like picking up the dry cleaning, paying bills and keeping the kitchen stocked with SpaghettiOs and Lean Cuisine.

She'd bet Chase Harrington had one.

She'd bet he had a whole bloody staff.

His long, lean body lay utterly still on one of the wheeled gurneys in the curtainless, utilitarian room. Tubes and monitor lines ran every which way, his body's functions converted to spiking lines and digital numbers on screens and illuminated displays. The surgical drapes that had helped make him more of an anonymous procedure than a person were gone, replaced with a white thermal blanket that covered everything but one arm and his bandaged and braced leg.

Nodding to the nurse in green scrubs who'd just administered the painkiller she'd ordered, Alex stopped beside the gurney. A white gauze bandage covered his upper left cheekbone and a bruise had began to form beneath his left eye. Even battered, broken and with parts of him turning the color of a bing cherry, he was an undeniably attractive man. His features were chiseled, his nose narrow, his mouth sculpted and sensual. Dark eyebrows slashed above curves of spiky, soot-colored lashes. His hair was more brown than black, cut short and barbered with the sort of precision she supposed someone with his wealth might demand of those he paid to tend him.

"Mr. Harrington," she said quietly, knowing he couldn't yet focus but that he could hear her well enough. "Chase," she expanded, offering him the comfort of hearing his name, "you came through surgery just fine. You're in recovery. You'll be here for a while before they take you to a room. Everything went really well." She knew many patients emerged from anesthesia unaware that the procedure was already over. Some returned to consciousness worrying about the outcome. Either way, she never hesitated to relieve whatever anxiety she could as soon as possible. "Are you with me?"

His eyes blinked open, but she'd barely caught a glimpse of breathtaking blue before they drifted closed again.

"What time is it?"

His voice was deep, a low, smoky rasp made thick by drugs and raw from the airway that had been in his throat.

"After eleven."

Once more he opened his eyes. Once more they drifted closed.

"Morning or night?"

"Night. You've just come from surgery," she repeated, thinking he was trying to orient himself. "You were brought up here from Emergency. Do you remember what happened?"

His brow furrowed. "I was in an accident," he murmured, trying to lift his broad hand to his forehead. An IV was taped into place in a vein above his wrist. From beneath the open edge of his blue-dotted hospital gown, EKG leads trailed over the corded muscles of his wide shoulders. "I need a…phone."

Too drugged to master the effort, his hand fell. "I missed a meeting. It was…where was it?" he asked, sounding as if he were trying to remember where he was supposed to have been. "Why can't I think?"

"Because the anesthetic is still in your system," she told him, rather surprised he sounded as coherent as he did. It took a while for such heavy anesthesia to loosen its grip. Normally, all a patient wanted to do was sleep. Yet, he refused to give up and let the drugs carry him off again. "That's perfectly normal. Just forget about the phone for now.".

"Can't. It was important," he stressed thickly.

"Nothing's as important right now for you as rest."

His hand lifted once more, this time to stop her. "Don't go. Please." The word came out as little more than a whisper. "Don't."

The metal siderails were up on the gurney. Catching his arm to keep him from pulling on a lead or bumping the IV, she lowered it to his side.

His hand caught hers. "I need to let them know."

"Let them know what?" she asked, as surprised by the strength in his grip as by the urgency behind his rasped words. Given the sedation he'd had, that urgency totally confused her. It was the same sort of frantic undertone she'd encountered when accident victims came out of surgery worried about someone who'd been in the accident with them, an overwhelming need that reached beyond any immediate concern for themselves.

But he'd been alone. And he was talking about a meeting.

"They need to know I didn't...stand them up."

The soft click and beep of monitors melded with the quiet shuffle of the nurse moving around Alex as she stood with her hand in his, studying the compelling lines of his face. She couldn't begin to imagine what sort of deal he had going that was so important to him that he'd fight through the fog of drugs to keep from jeopardizing it. It was none of her business anyway.

He was her business though. And she definitely recognized signs of an iron will when she saw one. Right now, that will was definitely working against him.

Shelving an odd hint of dread at the thought of encountering that will when he was conscious, she curved her free hand over his shoulder. She wanted him calm. Better yet, she wanted him sleeping. "What time was your meeting?"

Over the blip of the heart monitor, he whispered, "Seven-thirty."

"As late as it is, I'm sure your party has already figured out that you're not showing up tonight. You can talk to your secretary in the morning and straighten out everything." Practicality joined assurance. "You wouldn't be able to carry on a phone conversation anyway. Your voice is barely audible."

His brow furrowed at that.

"Try to let go of it for now," she urged. "Get some rest."

The muscles beneath her hand felt as hard as stone, but she could feel him relaxing beneath her touch. He said nothing else as she stood there watching the furrows ease from his brow and listening to his breathing grow slow and even.

Letting her hand slip from his, Alex stepped back, her glance cutting to the nurse hanging a fresh bag of saline for his IV. She didn't believe for a moment that he'd accepted her logic or her suggestion. The painkiller he'd been given had just kicked in. With the sedatives still in his system, he couldn't have stayed awake no matter how hard he'd tried.

She glanced at the institutional black-and-white clock high on the wall.

Her day had started nearly twenty hours ago and she was tired. Not exhausted the way she'd so often been during her residency. "Exhausted" came after forty hours with no sleep. But those days of honing her skills in the competitive battlefield of a teaching hospital were over. She had a normal life now. As normal as any practicing surgeon and single mom had, anyway. This kind of tired was a piece of cake.

"I don't imagine any of his family is here yet. Did they want me to call?"

"His family wasn't notified," the soft-spoken nurse replied. "His chart says the only person he wanted contacted was his lawyer."

"His lawyer?"

The nurse shrugged. "That's what he told them in Emergency. Some guy in Seattle. The only other thing he wanted was to make a phone call about a meeting. The one he was talking about just now, I guess. They told him they'd call anyone he wanted for him, but he apparently insisted that he had to make the call himself.

"He was in no shape to use a phone," she continued, checking the monitors and noting the readings. "From the notes in his chart, the paramedics already had him full of morphine and all anyone downstairs cared about was getting his bleeding under control and getting him into CT and surgery."

Alex slipped off her cap, threading her fingers through her short dark hair as she cast one last glance at the still and sedated man on the gurney. Even with the morphine, if he'd been conscious, he'd been in pain. Even then, in pain and bleeding, that meeting had haunted him.

Unless he was negotiating world peace or working on a deal to cure some disease, she still had no idea what would have been that important to him. But Honeygrove was hardly the Hague, there were no big medical research facilities that she knew of in town, and she was shooting in the dark. Her concerns tended to remain very close to home. It was people she cared about. Her family. Her friends. Her patients. There was no way to know what really mattered to a man like Chase Harrington.

She couldn't relate at all to him. Yet, as Alex told the nurse to call her at home if there was any change and headed for the locker room, she actually felt bad for the guy. For all his wealth and notoriety, when he'd been hurt and in pain, when he'd just come through what had to be a horrific accident, there hadn't been anyone he cared to call except the person he paid to look out for his interests. No wife. No girlfriend. No parent. No friend. Just his lawyer.

She found that incredibly sad.

It wasn't long, however, before it became apparent that she was the only one inclined to feel compassion toward him. It had literally taken general anesthesia and a walloping dose of narcotic to end his insistence about needing to make his call. And while use of a phone no longer seemed to be a problem, Alex had the distinct impression when she left another emergency surgery the next morning that at least one member of the hospital administration and part of its staff would love to have him re-anesthetized.

Or, maybe, it was euthanized.

Chapter Two

"I'd appreciate it enormously if you'd see him and get back to me as soon as you can, Doctor. He's not cooperating with me and I've been getting calls all morning from reporters and wire services wanting to know his condition and what he's doing in Honeygrove. I simply can't release the statement he gave me," Mary Driscoll, the dedicated assistant to the hospital's administrator, implored Alex over the top of her silver-rimmed half glasses.

Dressed in a dove-gray business suit with slashes of black that somehow managed to match her bobbed hair, Mary looked perfectly coordinated, as always, and enormously capable of handling the myriad crises she intercepted for her boss. Alex knew the administrator, Ryan Malone, personally. The dashing and diplomatic man who'd gone out of his way to make her feel welcome at Memorial had just married one of her friends. And she knew he trusted Mary's judgment implicitly.

If Mary was finding Chase Harrington difficult, Alex thought uneasily, then he was definitely presenting a challenge.

"What did he tell you to say?" she asked, her voice low so it wouldn't carry beyond the corner of the hallway Mary had cornered her in.

"He told me to say nothing about him other than that he's in excellent condition following a minor accident."

"Excellent?" Alex repeated, stifling the urge to laugh. "I don't think so."

"My point exactly."

"I wouldn't call it a minor accident, either."

Looking vindicated, Mary murmured, "Thank you, Doctor. I tried to tell him that it's hospital policy to issue the truth about a patient's condition, even if it's just a statement like 'guarded' or 'stable.' Or we could go with 'no comment.' His response was that rules are bent all the time. That was when I offered to let him discuss the matter with Mr. Malone," she continued, as Alex's eyebrows arched, "but he informed me that he'd already given me his statement, and that the hospital administrator was the last person he wanted to see. He doesn't want anyone in his room other than necessary medical staff."

The murmur of voices drifted toward them when the wide doors of the surgical department swung open. Stepping back so the gowned attendants could bring out a patient on a gurney, Alex could practically feel the weight Ryan's assistant carried shift to her own shoulders. It was something in the woman's eyes. The encroaching relief, probably.

"If that's what he wants, we'll do our best to maintain his privacy," Mary said confidently. "I just need something I can give the press. You'll call me after you've seen him to give me his official condition?"

Alex had been on her way to the med-surg floor to do her rounds when Mary had intercepted her. Mentioning that, she then assured her she'd call as soon as she could and started down the beige-walled hall.

She hadn't made it a dozen steps when Mary paused at the stairwell door.

"I almost forgot," she began, looking apologetic now. "He asked for a fax machine. A plain-paper one. Not the kind with thermal paper. He said he doesn't like fighting the curling sheets. Anyway," she continued, having dispensed with the details, "I told him I'd have to defer to you on whether or not he could have one. Since we have no specific policy regarding office equipment in patients' rooms, I believe that decision would be entirely up to the physician."

Alex thought the woman looked entirely too cheerful as she opened the door and disappeared. But then, she'd just unburdened herself of any further dealings with the man Alex was now on her way to see.

The med-surg unit was on the opposite side of the floor from the surgical suites. Working her way through the labyrinth of halls with her lab coat thrown on over her scrubs, Alex could hear the whine of a saw grow louder the closer she came to her destination.

A small crew was framing a doorway near the third-floor elevators, presumably to lead to the roof garden on the new wing presently under construction. The noise was awful but unavoidable, and undoubtedly contributed to the agitation of the nurse who bore down on her the moment she stepped through the unit's doors.

Everyone knew Kay Applewhite. And everyone knew the irascible nurse hated disruption. When she was on duty, she ran the floor as tightly as any sea captain ever ran a ship, and she didn't tolerate anything that upset hospital routine or her patients. Despite her grandmotherly appearance, she was a stickler for schedules, did everything by the book and had little compassion for whiners, slackers or malcontents. With her family grown and gone, her work was her life and she didn't hesitate to let everyone know that forty years of nursing had taught her that those who helped themselves, providing they were capable, healed far faster than those who were coddled.

The nurses called her General Sherman behind her back.

She took it as a compliment.

Figuring she was about to get a reminder to shut out the noise, Alex leaned against the heavy door to get it to close faster while Kay, her gunmetal-gray curls permed too tightly to move and elbows pumping, kept coming down the wide, door-lined hall. Below the cuffs of her white scrub pants, her orthopedic shoes squeaked like a pack of chattering mice.

"I'm so glad you're here, Dr. Larson." Lowering her voice when she reached Alex, she turned with a squeak to accompany her to the nurses' station. "I need to talk to you about the compound femur that came through Emergency last night," she muttered, referring to the patient by injury the way staff often did. "But before I forget, Mr. Malone's assistant has been looking for you. She needs to talk to you about him, too. That woman's the epitome of patience and tact," Kay said, speaking of Mary Driscoll, "but when she came out of his room, I could tell he even has her exasperated."

"We've already spoken." Looking as unruffled as she sounded, Alex stopped at the nurses' station with its computers and banks of files. "What kind of trouble is he giving you?" she asked, watching the short, stout woman slip behind the long white counter and hand over a chart.

"Beside the fact that he's demanding and uncooperative," the woman said, her tone as flat as the metal cover of the chart Alex had just opened, "he's now refusing his pain medication. He was due for it over an hour ago."

Alex's head came up.

"He says he doesn't want anything but aspirin," Kay continued, seeming gratified by Alex's swift frown. "We tried to explain that he needs something stronger, and that even if we wanted, we can't give him anything his doctor hasn't ordered." Her expression pruned. "He also wants some financial newpaper I've never heard of and a fax machine for his room."

Ah, yes, Alex thought, the fax machine. "I heard about that," she murmured, not sure which feeling was stronger, displeasure or dread. "What room is he in?"

"Three-fifty-four."

"How are his vitals?"

"Better than they should be. I took them myself. Blood pressure's a little high, though."

A rueful smile touched Alex's mouth. "Now there's a surprise. I'll take care of him," she promised, feeling her guard go up even as she stood there. She hated confrontations. Especially when her reserves were low. And they were now. She'd managed exactly five hours of sleep between Harrington's compound femur and an impacted radius and ulna. Some idiot had actually tried to catch a safe his accomplice had dropped from a second-story window.

"I also need to see Brent Chalmers and Maria Lombardi. And Dr. Castleman's and Dr. McGraw's patients, too," she added, pulling a slip of paper from her pocket on which she'd written their patients' names. Castleman and McGraw were the other two doctors in the orthopedic clinic that Alex had joined two years ago. Whoever was on weekend call from the clinic checked on all the clinic's patients.

"I'll pull their charts for you right now," Kay assured her. "I know you're anxious to get out of here today. I heard you and Dr. Hall talking in the cafeteria yesterday," she explained when Alex, clearly puzzled by her comment, glanced back at her. "You were telling her how you hoped things would be quiet this weekend because the Chalmers boy will be staying with you while he goes through his therapy and you need to clean your guest room.

"I know it's none of my business," she continued, her keen hazel eyes softening, "and I won't say a word about what you're doing if you don't want me to, but I think it's really nice the way you take in some of these kids. That Brent's a sweet boy," she pronounced, speaking of a shy sixteen-year-old Alex had operated on two weeks ago. "He deserves a break."

The sharp ping of a patient call light echoed over the clatter of a lunch cart being wheeled by and a page for an orderly to report to Three G.

"I can't say the same for that man, though," she muttered, noting on the panel behind her that the light for room three-fifty-four was lit.

Alex didn't bother telling Kay not to repeat what she'd overheard in the cafeteria. Her plans for Brent were hardly confidential and if Kay had overheard her talking with Kelly, her obstetrician friend who'd talked her into taking her *last* houseguest, someone else had probably overheard, too. But finding time to put sheets on the guest bed wasn't the only reason Alex hoped the rest of the weekend passed quietly. She and Tyler had plans with friends for an early dinner that evening. And tomorrow, she needed to take him to the mall for new shoes.

"Give me a minute with Mr. Harrington," Alex said, wanting the nurse to hold off answering the light as she headed for his room herself. She wasn't going to be any more rested when she finished her rounds, so she might as well face the showdown now.

The image of a long hot bath flashed, unbidden, into her consciousness.

Practically groaning at the delicious thought of it, she paused outside his door, indulging herself a full two seconds before drawing a breath that pulled her five feet, five inches into the perfect posture she'd learned from Miss Lowe's School of Tap and Classical Ballet. Releasing it the way she'd learned in Lamaze class, knowing a person could get through anything if she just kept breathing, she walked into the room.

Her first thought was that the man had no concept of the word *rest*. The ceiling-mounted television was on, the volume muted. Stock quotes ran in a continuous ribbon beneath a talking head.

Her patient wasn't watching the television, though. The head of his bed was partially raised and the upper half of his body was hidden by an open newspaper.

Walking past the empty bed by the door, her glance skimmed from the metal external fixation device stabilizing the breaks in his elevated leg, over a long expanse of sheet and settled on the headlines of the *Wall Street Journal*.

He didn't move, but it was apparent he knew someone was there. Presumably, the nurse he'd rung for.

"I just need the blinds adjusted. If you don't mind," he expanded with far more civility than she'd expected. "It's too bright in here to focus."

His deep voice still held a rasp from the airway, but there was strength to it now and the smoky undertones sounded as if they belonged there.

"You can't focus because you're barely twelve hours out of surgery and your eyes are still affected by the sedatives. Give it time."

Her tone was conversational, her manner deliberately relaxed as she walked over to the window and dimmed the buttery glow of the mid-June sun filling the room. She itched to get outside in all that warmth and brightness. Cloudless days were a rarity in Honeygrove. "How are you feeling this morning?"

She'd heard the faint crackle of newsprint as he slowly lowered the paper, but her focus wasn't on his face as she turned from the window. It was on the round metal rods above his knee that formed a double H on either side of his leg and the four pins that went through it. At least, that was what had her attention until his silence drew her glance and she met his impossibly blue eyes.

Last night, she remembered thinking the color breathtaking. The observation had been purely factual, rather like the way a person would describe velvet as soft and rock as hard. Now, she actually felt her breath stall in her lungs. The phenomenon was disconcerting enough. What made it downright unnerving was the unabashed way he held her glance before his own moved slowly, boldly over her face.

The man was cut, broken and battered. He looked every bit as tired as he undoubtedly felt, and he needed a shave. His dark hair was rumpled and the burgundy bruise along his high cheekbone had bloomed to contrast sharply with the stark white bandage and his faint pallor. Yet, even looking as if he'd come out on the losing end of a bar fight and stripped of any trapping that might indicate status or power, the aura of masculine command surrounding him was unmistakable.

So was the sensual tug low in her stomach before his glance settled on the embroidered *Alexandra Larson, M.D.* on her pristine white lab coat.

It didn't matter that she'd seen him before. Until the moment his eyes locked on hers, he'd been more procedure than patient, more media myth than man. Before that moment, too, she hadn't been the subject of his attention. Being the sole subject of it now, unnerved by the fact that she hadn't moved, Alex forcibly reminded herself he was on her turf and held out her hand.

"I'm Dr. Larson," she said, jerking her professional composure into a subdued smile. "When we met last night, you were pretty groggy. I'm your surgeon."

She rather expected him to go a little chauvinistic on her. With his reputation and considering what she'd heard of his attitude so far, a little alpha-male behavior wouldn't have surprised her at all. Or so she was thinking when his hand engulfed hers and the heat singing up her arm made her feel more female than physician.

"I remember your voice." His glance narrowed as it fell to their clasped hands. A hint of memory glimmered in his expression, as if he might have recalled the feel of her hand in his, too. "I'm sorry, but I don't remember what we talked about."

Feeling strangely disadvantaged, Alex pulled back, letting her hand slide from his firm grip. "Mostly we discussed whether or not you were in any shape to make a phone call," she replied, deliberately ignoring the tingling in her palm as she slipped her hands into her pockets. "I assume you've placed it by now," she added, since a phone was within convenient reach on his bed table. "It was about a meeting last night that seemed rather important to you."

Hesitation slashed his features. "Yeah," he murmured. "I made it. Thanks." Looking uneasy and not at all comfortable with the feeling, he nodded toward the bed. "So what's the deal with the leg?"

It was as clear as his water glass that something about his business still disturbed him. It was equally clear that he wanted to change the subject.

"My question first," she countered, more curious about his reaction than whatever his call had been about. "How do you feel?"

"Like I was hit by a Mack truck." Moving gingerly, he set aside the paper someone had obviously gotten for him. Just as carefully, he eased back against the pillows. "Actually," he muttered, looking paler from the movement, "I think it was a Ford."

She'd expected antagonism from him. She'd been braced for bluster. She hadn't anticipated raw sensuality or a dry humor that had somehow managed to survive obvious discomfort.

Feeling her guard drop, she eyed the wicked bruise edged beneath the left sleeve of his gown. She knew there was also one on his left hip. His thigh would be rainbow-hued for weeks. "I understand you're refusing pain medication," she said, reaching for the edge of his gown to lower it from his shoulder. "Why?"

"Because I don't like the way it makes me feel."

"You'd rather be in pain?" she asked mildly.

"I'd rather be able to think." He hitched a breath when her fingers moved over the tender joint. "I just want my mind clear. I have things to do and I can't do them if I can't concentrate."

Trying to concentrate herself, she made a mental note to have the nurses ice his beautifully muscled shoulder, then clinically ran her hand over his rock-solid trapezius muscle to the strong cords of his neck. The tension she felt there could easily have been a normal state of affairs for him. Her neck was definitely where she tended to carry her stress. But the impact would have strained his muscles, too.

"You're going to be sore everywhere for a while," she told him, frowning at the way the heat of his skin seemed to linger on her hands as she slipped the gown back in place.

"I was the last time, too."

"You've done this before?"

"Not this way." There was an edge in his voice that hadn't been there a moment ago, a heavy hint of frustration that almost overrode the discomfort. "I broke my other leg skiing a couple of years ago. It's an inconvenience, but it isn't anything I can't function with if I'm not taking anything that messes up my head. And as long as I can move around," he pointedly added. "So let's get rid of that scaffolding and just put a cast on it. I need to get out of here."

"I'm afraid that's not possible."

Looking at her as if she couldn't possibly have said what he thought he'd heard, he muttered, "Why not? All you have to do is take that thing off and wrap my leg in plaster of paris. It'll probably take a couple of days to dry completely, but I don't have to stay in the hospital for that."

He was rubbing his temple. The one without the bandage. She didn't doubt for a moment that he had a headache. She was also beginning to see why he seemed to be giving everyone else one, too. Especially Kay with her regimented routine and Mrs. Driscoll with her hospital regs. She seriously doubted that any man who'd accomplished what he had followed other people's rules. He did things his way.

That was how he wanted them done now.

Unfortunately for him, he wasn't in a position to call the shots.

Unfortunately for her, she was.

"You may have had a broken leg before," she patiently allowed, still more concerned with the way he winced when he moved than with his obstinance, "but there are different kinds of breaks and this particular one can't be casted. At least not yet. Your mobility is a priority but not our first one. The bone penetrated the skin and our biggest concern is infection. You'll be able to get around with the scaffolding," she assured him, referring as he had to the external fixation device. "But right now, you need a three-day course of IV antibiotics. As for letting you out of here, we'll talk in a few days about how long you need to be hospitalized."

"A few days isn't acceptable. If I can get around on this thing, you can give me a prescription for whatever I need to take and I can get out of here now. I need to reschedule a meeting and I can't hold it here."

The man was clearly under the impression that it would take more than a speeding truck to slow him down. He also seemed to think her medical opinion of his treatment was negotiable, which, given his injuries, it was not. He held her glance, his carved features set and the furrows in his forehead speaking as much of pain as of impatience. He had work to do and he clearly intended to do it.

He seemed to overlook the fact that, at the moment, he couldn't make it from the bed to the bathroom without help.

"You don't seem to understand," she said, every bit as determined to get her point across. She didn't doubt for a moment that the man had a few dozen irons in the fire and that any number of them needed tending. Especially the meeting he was obsessing over. She understood career pressure. She was intimately acquainted with job stress. But she also knew that people in pain could be irritable, unreasonable.

"What you need right now are antibiotics. If you don't get them, you could get an infection and, trust me, that's the last thing you want. If you do get one, we're talking six weeks of IV therapy. If that doesn't work, you could lose your leg. It gets bad enough and we can't control it, you could lose your life.''

He didn't seem nearly as impressed as he should have been with the consequences. "Scare tactics, Doctor?"

"I'd be happy to bring you a few case histories to back up my conclusion.''

"I'd rather have a copy of the *Financial Times*.''

"Fine. You can cooperate and be back on your feet in a few months, or do it your way and have it take longer. And by the way,'' she added, in that same velvet-over-steel voice, ''you might not be acting like a wounded bear if you'd take what I prescribe. The pain is only going to get worse. Especially when they get you up in a few minutes so you can move around. I guarantee you're not going to want to stand up without it.''

Pulling a small, rubber-tipped reflex hammer from her pocket, she swallowed her irritation at the deliberate challenge in his eyes and moved to the end of the bed. ''Can you feel this?'' she asked, refusing to let him bait her any farther as she ran the instrument over the top of his foot.

The relief Chase felt at the faint tickling sensation was buried as promptly as the fear he'd denied when he'd first seen the metal pins protruding from the bandages on his leg. Aching everywhere, trying desperately not to think about it, he purposely waited until his doctor glanced toward him before he acknowledged her.

"I feel it,'' he finally said, trying to decide if he was impressed with her aplomb or just plain annoyed by it.

He did know he was intrigued.

With her attention on her exam, his glance skimmed the feathered sweep of her hair. It was too short for his taste, barely enough for a man to gather in his hands. But the color was incredible. Shades of ruby and garnet gleamed like lines of fire in rich, dark cinnamon. And it looked amazingly soft. Almost as soft as the skin of her long, graceful neck and the delicate shell of her ear.

A pearl stud gleamed on her earlobe. Simple. Understated.

Her profile was as elegant as a cameo.

Alexandra Larson looked nothing like someone who would replace hips and knees and piece together broken bodies for a living. With her delicate features and doe-soft brown eyes, she looked more like some advertiser's idea of a kindergarten teacher. Or a dancer. He'd always been under the impression that orthopedic surgery required a little muscle. If he had to guess, there wasn't a whole lot beneath the narrow white coat covering her scrubs.

He had no problem with her not looking like his idea of a doctor. He had no problem with her being female. His problem was with needing a doctor in the first place—especially one who seemed to think she knew his body better than he did.

Shelving that little annoyance, he settled back, mentally whimpering as he carefully let his body relax against the mattress he was certain had been constructed of concrete. As sore as he was, the surface felt as hard as a slab and was just about as comfortable. He tried to overlook that, too.

What he couldn't overlook was how he could so easily recall her from last night. He'd been too drugged to fully comprehend much of anything beyond the pain and the need to get to a phone. But, somehow, he could still remember the soothing tones of her surprisingly sultry voice and feeling strangely calm when she'd rested her hand on his shoulder.

That feeling completely eluded him now. As she continued her examination, his thoughts flashed to the accident that had landed him on her operating table. A couple of seconds one way or the other and he wouldn't have been in the intersection when that idiot had blown the red light. If he'd called to confirm his appointment from the airport rather than heading straight for his meeting, it wouldn't have happened. If he'd taken an earlier flight instead of eking every possible minute out of the afternoon, he would already have been at the hotel.

The accident hadn't been his fault, but that didn't stop him from being angry with himself for not preventing it. He knew he'd been preoccupied. He'd been thinking of the two men he was to meet in the hotel's lounge, worrying about what he would think of them. Or, more importantly, what they would think of him. He had no idea how he'd be received and the uncertainty had him feeling more unsettled and uneasy than he'd felt in his entire life.

He was thinking he'd give up half of everything he owned just to get that meeting over with when he felt his doctor's hand rest on his bare calf. Small and soft, its warmth penetrated his skin, mercifully drawing his attention from his thoughts and focusing it on the one part of his anatomy that hadn't been throbbing until he caught her scent and felt her touch when she'd checked his shoulder.

He'd had no idea that surgical soap could smell so appealing. He didn't know either what she wore with it that made it so seductive. Or, how she could lower his blood pressure even as she raised it.

"I understand you're from Seattle. If you'll give me the name of your personal physician, I can start arranging a transfer to a hospital there, if you'd like."

"I'm not leaving Honeygrove until I've done what I came to do."

She hesitated. "Fine," she said, again, when he was pretty sure what she actually thought was "great." "We'll just keep you here, then."

"I need a fax machine."

Something like resignation washed over her delicate features. Or maybe it was annoyance. The way she schooled her features as she crossed her arms made it hard to tell for sure.

For some reason he couldn't begin to identify, her forced calm annoyed the daylights out of him.

"I heard," she informed him, all business. "Unfortunately, we're not equipped to set up an office in a hospital room. If you need something sent, I'm sure Mrs. Driscoll would be happy to take care of it for you."

"I'm not asking to use your personnel or your equipment." Curbing the quick flash of exasperation, he closed his eyes, fighting for the calm she seemed to manage with such exasperating ease. "I've already explained that."

"You haven't explained it to me."

She had a point. She also actually looked willing to listen, which was more than anyone else had done so far. "I'll buy a machine if someone will just get me a phone book so I can have one delivered and set up. I have a meeting in Chicago on Tuesday and I'd planned to finish the contracts this weekend. The drafts are in my briefcase, which no one can seem to locate," he pointed out, trying hard to hold back his frustration but pretty sure he wasn't succeeding. "If I had them, I could work on them instead of lying here doing nothing. Since I don't, I'll have my attorney fax me a copy. I'd have my secretary do it, but she's at her son's wedding this weekend.

"I know I won't be going to Chicago myself," he countered, sharp claws of frustration gripping hard when she pointedly glanced at his leg. "My attorney will represent me. That's what I pay him to do."

His terseness caused the soft wing of her eyebrow to jerk up. Looking a little cooler than she had a moment ago, she picked up the chart she'd dropped on the end of his bed. "I'll get you the number for the fax at the nurses' station," she said, sounding as if she were willing to be reasonable even if he wasn't. "You can have them sent there."

"That won't work." There were changes he needed to send to his attorney and his attorney would have to send the documents back once the changes were made. Aside from the fact that he'd prefer his business dealings to remain confidential, he had other projects he needed to stay on top of, and he knew as sure as stocks rose and fell that the hassle with the head nurse wouldn't be worth the trouble. "Attila out there has already pointed out that the nurses aren't secretaries—"

"It's General Sherman... I mean Kay," his suddenly fatigued-looking doctor hastily corrected. "The woman's name is Kay."

"Fine. I'm sure General *Kay* isn't going to like having her precious routine interrupted. I can do everything myself if someone will just get me a phone book." His voice was low, partly because he had no intention of losing control to the point where he raised it; mostly because his throat felt as if he'd swallowed sandpaper.

That frustrated him even more.

"I also need to have the meeting I missed last night," he muttered. "But that's something I can't do until you let me out of here."

And that's what bothered him most, he thought, and shoved his fingers through his hair.

Alex saw him wince, then heard him hiss a breath when the suddenness of his movement caught up with him and pain radiated from his shoulder. She didn't doubt for a moment that his agitation had only increased the pain in his head. Strain dulled his eyes. Except for his bruises, the sheets now had more color than his face. She didn't know if he was the most stoic man she'd ever encountered, or the most masochistic. She would concede that he was the most driven.

She truly didn't care about his wheeling and dealing. Her concern was getting him well and keeping him comfortable while she was doing it.

"I realize you have obligations," she conceded, certain he wasn't coping with the pain anywhere near as well as he wanted her to believe. "But I don't think you appreciate how much trauma your body has sustained. I'll have your nurse bring you a phone book and I'll change your pain medication to something that will take the edge off and leave your head clear. But you might as well call whoever handles your schedule and have them cancel everything for the next couple of weeks."

She turned to avoid his scowl and headed for the door. "Oh, yes. One more thing. Your condition right now is, officially, stable. Do you want that released to the press, or do you want no comment."

"I already gave my statement to the woman from the administrator's office."

"And you overstated your condition and understated the accident."

For a moment, he said nothing. He just watched her with his brow furrowed while frustration warred with the pain that undoubtedly frustrated him, too. "I'm not going to argue with you, Doctor. Go with your call on the condition, but leave my estimate of the accident alone."

He'd been there. She hadn't.

He didn't say as much, but that was the message she got as challenge slipped once more into those disturbingly blue eyes.

"Good enough," she told him, wondering why he

couldn't have piled up his car when someone else had been on call. "Get some rest."

She stepped into the wide hall, feeling more as if she'd escaped the room rather than merely left it. She'd dealt with demanding type-As, the chauvinism prevalent among some of her male colleagues and her son's terrible twos. All of which, she felt, qualified her as something of an expert when it came to handling difficult men.

But a woman didn't handle Chase Harrington. She worked around him. Still, she hadn't lost her cool when he'd lost his patience. Or when he'd so cavalierly informed her of how she could handle his leg and his medication. And she thought she'd done a commendable job of ignoring the way his glance kept moving to her mouth as she spoke. All he'd done was make her forget to ask if he had any more questions about his condition, which was something she rarely failed to do with a patient.

Irritated with herself for letting him get to her, refusing to go back and let him do it again, she headed for her next patient intent, for the moment, on putting the man from her mind.

Her intentions were honorable. But Brent Chalmers axed them within ten seconds of her walking into his card-and-mylar-balloon-filled room. The gangly blond teenager with the shy smile had heard that Chase was there.

He'd never actually heard of Chase before. Until a few weeks ago when his throwing arm had been mangled in a thresher, the boy's life had centered around sports, a car he was saving to buy and the little farming community of Sylo a hundred miles away. If he'd ever read the business section of a newspaper, it was only because he'd been required to write a report on it for class. He'd just overheard the nurses whispering about some rich guy who'd climbed Mt. McKinley and his ears had perked up.

Brent was usually serious and quiet, and whenever he saw Alex he worried aloud about his ability to ever use his arm. Today, though, as she examined his nicely healing wounds all he wanted to talk about was how awesome it must feel to reach the top of the world.

"Man," he mused. "Can you imagine the shape he must be in to do something like that?"

The question was rhetorical, but she could easily have answered it. Even as she marveled at the boy's excitement, a mental picture of a beautifully muscled male intent on conquering a mighty mountain flashed in her mind. She couldn't begin to imagine the determination, the endurance, the sheer strength of will such a challenge required. But Chase apparently went after what he wanted, claimed it, then moved on.

The thought disturbed her, almost as much as the odd jolt she'd felt when she'd first met his eyes.

What disturbed her more was that he'd distracted her from her patient.

"Do you, Dr. Larson?" Brent asked, shaking his stick-straight blond hair out of his eyes.

"I'm sorry." Pulling the top of his gown back up over the muscles developing in his bony shoulders, she blinked at his narrow, expectant face. "Do I what?"

"Think you could ask him how long he had to train before he made his climb. And maybe you could ask how long it took. I mean, that would be so cool. Climbing like that, I mean. Wouldn't it?"

"Actually, I can think of about eight hundred things I'd rather do than struggle for oxygen while I freeze my backside over a mile-high drop-off." Smiling easily at his unbridled interest, she nodded to the nurse to replace his elastic bandage and sling. "Tell you what. Now wouldn't be a good time, but if you'd like, I'll ask Mr. Harrington if he feels up to having company tomorrow. If he does, you can talk to him about the mountain yourself before I release you on Monday.''

The mix of emotions flushing his face was fascinating. ''Oh, don't do that,'' he begged. ''I couldn't talk to him. I mean not, like, to his face,'' he explained, sounding as if she'd just suggested a personal audience with the Pope. ''But, thanks. Yeah, really.'' The onslaught of discomfort gave way to a smile. ''I'm getting out of here?''

''You sure are. There's something I haven't told you, though. I haven't had a chance to redo the room you'll be staying in since I bought my house. It's sort of pink.'' Wendy, the pregnant teenager who'd lived with her until she'd delivered and moved out last month, had called it rose. It reminded Alex more of antacid. ''And you have to share a bathroom with my four-year-old.''

His expression suddenly shifted, concern moving into features sharpening with the first angles of budding manhood. ''I don't mind, ma'am,'' he murmured, his voice cracking. ''I'm used to my little brothers and sisters.''

She hadn't meant for him to go shy on her. But that's how Brent usually was. It had only been the prospect of the extraordinary that had breached the adolescent self-consciousness and quiet manners she normally saw.

''I know you are,'' she told him, rather wishing she could see that enthusiasm again. He was such a neat kid. And his family was salt of the earth. She'd met all four of his brothers and sisters. They and his parents had held vigil while she and a team of vascular surgeons had reconstructed his arm. Their prayers and his doctors' skills had brought him this far, but it would take months of daily physical therapy for him to regain use of the limb. The problem was his parents' insurance. It wouldn't cover a live-in rehab facility and his family's circumstances and distance from town made outpatient treatment impossible.

Alex had figured that two more weeks of intensive therapy would give him enough of a start to continue on his own at home. His beleaguered parents had been thrilled, and embarrassingly grateful, when she'd offered to have him stay with her during that time. Since she was used to having someone borrow her spare room, she told them, it wouldn't be an inconvenience at all.

Alex left Brent a few moments later to move on to her next patient. But as she headed for elderly Maria and her shiny new knee, she couldn't help wondering if Chase had ever known what it was like to truly need something and not be able to get it.

She was thinking about him again. Irritated with herself for not being able to get him out of her mind, she started down the hall, deliberately humming a repetitive tune from one of Tyler's tapes. Once that melody got started in her head, she knew it would take forever to get it out. It drove her positively nuts. But she figured even that was better than wondering what it was that drove the compound femur in three-fifty-four.

Chapter Three

The mind-numbing melody had been replaced by the theme from *Tarzan* by the time Alex and Tyler arrived at Granetti's for dinner at six o'clock that evening. Parking her sedate silver Saturn in her spot at the hospital, since the restaurant they were going to was across the street, she explained to her son for the third time that she wasn't going to work, that they were going to dinner and, no, they couldn't go to Pizza Pete's.

"But I want pizza."

"You can have pizza here. Or spaghetti," she told him, which reminded her to grab a handful of wet-wipes from the glove box to stuff into her purse. "You like spaghetti better, anyway."

Alex stifled a sigh as she watched her little boy scrunch his nose. The tiny golden freckles scattered over it seemed to merge as he considered her observation. Sometime in the last twenty-four hours, his baby-fine blond hair had managed to grow to below his eyebrows. He now needed a haircut as badly as he needed new tennies.

She supposed she should see if Brent wanted a haircut, too. The boy was beginning to look like a sheep dog.

Tyler's frown suddenly changed quality. She could practically see the mental gears shifting behind his dark brown eyes as he unbuckled his seat belt and opened his door.

"How fast will a Viper go?"

"A viper?" she repeated, doing a little mental shifting of her own. She had no idea how he'd gone from pizza to reptiles. "I don't know, honey. Is that the kind of snake that goes sideways?"

"It's not a snake." he informed her, as if she should have somehow known that. "It's a car."

"It is?"

"Yeah. And they go really fast. Does it go as fast as a Cobra?"

That, she knew, was definitely a car. Her next door neighbor's son-in-law drove one. Tyler loved that thing. Especially when its tires squealed.

"It sure sounds like it should." Checking her purse to make sure she had her pager, she looped the strap over her shoulder while Tyler scrambled out. She truly had no idea how his mind worked. The challenge was simply to keep up with him.

"Can we get a video with a Viper in it?" Tyler hollered, running around the back of the car.

Absently straightening the skirt of her sleeveless shift as she stood, Alex patiently told her forty-pound bundle of energy she didn't know if they made Viper videos, then tucked the back of Tyler's favorite T-shirt—a blue one sporting a green lizard—into the waistband of his cargo pants before she reached for his hand.

He was still talking as they crossed the street, informing

her now that Tom, their cat, could watch the video with him, which somehow reminded him that he'd forgotten to feed his gerbil. With the low sun slanting its warm rays against her face and her precious, precocious little boy chattering away beside her, she should have been enjoying the moment.

Instead, she was trying to figure out what it was about Chase Harrington that disturbed her most. The way she'd seemed to absorb his agitation or the fact that she couldn't seem to get him out of her mind.

The afternoon had been blessedly uneventful—if she discounted the fact that she'd discovered a new leak in her washing machine. After she'd finished rounds, she'd picked up Tyler at the hospital day-care center and headed for home. The guest room now had fresh sheets, the washing of which had revealed the leak, there was milk in her refrigerator and she and Tyler were on their way to a relatively quiet, uninterrupted dinner with her two closest friends and their families. There was no reason for her to be thinking of Chase now. She wouldn't have to deal with him again until tomorrow.

Grasping that thought, she pushed open Granetti's brass-trimmed door. The homey Irish-Italian pub-cum-restaurant was a comfortable, neighborhood sort of place that felt like a home away from home. On this particular evening, the atmosphere was even more welcoming.

Under the lattice-and-faux-grape-leaf-covered-ceiling and the Guinness beers signs on the back wall, a wide swath of black paper shouted *Happy XXXII, Alex* in bilious green. Neon-pink balloons hovered over the chairs.

Below the banner, tables had been pushed into a long line to accommodate the thirty-odd people who greeted her with a deafening "Surprise!" when she walked in holding Tyler's hand.

"Wow! It's a party, Mom!"

Stunned, Alex let his hand slide from hers. Before she could blink, her wide-eyed little boy had darted for the dark-haired preschooler dashing toward him. When he reached Griffin, his "very best" friend, they slugged each other and grinned.

"It's about time you caught up with us. I hate it when you're younger." Kelly Hall wrapped Alex in a quick hug. Her honey-blond hair was plaited in its usual French braid and her hazel eyes were laughing. "Happy belated birthday."

"We'd planned to do this yesterday, but you got called in." Ronni Powers-Malone, Ryan Malone's new wife and a good friend, moved in with a hug of her own. "Hi, Alex. Happy Birthday."

"I can't believe this." Feeling her smile spread, Alex hugged her friends back and took in the banner once more. "I feel like I'm a superbowl."

"The Roman numerals were the guys' idea. Ronni and I would have preferred to give you a quiet dinner with a gorgeous male at Le Petit Cinq," Kelly confided. "But we knew you were on call and it wouldn't be worth the arm-twisting to get you to go if you'd just get called away anyhow. It was either this or Pizza Pete's."

Petite and pregnant, pediatrician Ronni tugged her toward the tables. "We figured this was better, since it was closer to the hospital."

"And they have garlic-cheese bread. Ronni's been craving it," Kelly explained. "We're also fresh out of gorgeous males. We got the last of 'em."

"The lady has impeccable taste." The hug this time came with the scent of aftershave. Tanner Malone, Kelly's dark-haired, impressively built fiancé flashed a hint of his dynamite smile. "Hey there, Alex."

"Hey yourself, Tanner." Beyond them, the music of laughter and conversation underscored the strains of an Irish ballad. Wonderful aromas scented the air. "Where's the baby?"

Alex fully expected Tanner to tease her, to express some sort of feigned exasperation over having fought his way through the crowd to get to her only to have her ask about his child. Instead, looking unusually subdued, he simply murmured, "She's over there with Ryan and the nurses."

Despite his oddly reticent manner, pride lit his eyes as he nodded toward the people collectively cooing over his adorable infant daughter. Alex and Tanner had a lot in common. He'd been a single parent himself, until Kelly had rescued him, and he was intimately familiar with trying to manage parental responsibility and a demanding career. He owned the construction company building the hospital's new wing.

The thought of asking him if he could recommend anyone to fix her washing-machine leak was cancelled by the greetings of her colleagues from the clinic and the hospital as she was coaxed farther into the room. Ryan motioned to her from the knot of women cooing over the newest addition to the Malone clan, then pointed down to indicate that Tyler was with him and his kids and gave her an okay sign to let her know she didn't have to worry about him.

A little overwhelmed by what her friends had done for her, and what wonderful friends she had, she waved back. Anyone looking at Ryan and Tanner could tell they were related. Both brothers had thick, dark hair, and the same chiseled jaw. But their eyes were what truly gave them away. Rimmed with dark lashes, they were the bluest shade of blue Alex had ever seen. A woman didn't forget a man with eyes like that.

Rather like she couldn't forget the patient in room three-fifty-four.

"Whatever it is you're frowning about, forget it for now," Ronni insisted, handing her a frosty glass of iced tea. She clicked her own glass of the same against the rim. "I've seen enough long faces today."

"Me, too." Kelly lifted her wine before glancing sympathetically toward her fiancé. The concern in her expression was too apparent to hide, though her attempt was commendable. "This is a party."

If there was anything Alex could spot, it was strain. Now that the shock of surprise had worn off, she could see it clearly in her friends' faces.

"What's going on?" she asked, her glance bouncing between the petite redhead and the tall blonde. "I thought Tanner seemed a little quiet tonight. Is everything all right?"

Kelly and Ronni exchanged a glance. As if reaching some tacit agreement, they shifted closer, locking the circle so their voices wouldn't carry.

"Do you remember that phone call Ryan received during our engagement party?" Kelly asked Alex, her voice low. "From the man who said he was their brother, Andrew Malone?"

"Of course I do. We were talking about who had the most unique engagement surprise, remember? You two with that phone call, or Ryan and Ronni with that huge anonymous cashier's check for the new wing."

"We never have figured out where that came from," Ronni muttered. "But that was a good thing. This turned out awful. They were supposed to meet him last night," she said, in a near-whisper. "But he never showed up. You can't believe how disappointed Ryan is."

"Tanner, too. He's trying to hide it, but I know it's eating at him. On the way over, he said he wished the guy had never called in the first place. If he lost his nerve, the least he could have done was phone. As it is,'' Kelly continued, sounding as protective as she did irritated, ''neither one of them heard from him until this morning. Then, he just left messages on their answering machines that he'd been delayed and said he'd be in touch later.''

Alex's brow pinched as she watched both women look toward the men again, but she wanted to dismiss the thought that flashed in her brain almost as quickly as it formed. It had to be pure coincidence that Tanner's eyes were so nearly the same blue as her patient's. And it had to be coincidence that the rather stubborn line of his jaw had been carved at that same hard angle. Even if the world didn't know that Chase Harrington was...well, Chase Harrington, he wasn't built anything like Tanner. The younger Malone had the muscular physique of a man accustomed to physical labor. Chase was a little taller, according to his chart, anyway, and he had the lean, hard body of a runner. His hair wasn't black like Tanner's, either. It was more a rich, deep sable. If he looked like anyone, it was...Ryan.

''I don't remember,'' Alex prefaced, not sure she'd ever known the answer to what she was about to ask. ''Where was this brother from?''

''Seattle,'' they both said an instant before the clink of a spoon on a water glass had everyone quieting for a toast.

Alex tried to let it go.

She couldn't.

For the next hour, while her friends and associates mingled and laughed and passed platters of pasta and eggplant parmesan, the suspicion that had lodged in her mind nagged with the relentlessness of a toothache.

She could overlook the physical similarities. There were a lot of men with dark, to-die-for looks and wickedly beau-

tiful azure eyes who weren't related to the Malones. She'd
bet half the black Irish in Ireland fell into that category.
But Chase had missed a meeting last night, too. One that
had been so important to him that he'd come out of anesthesia wanting nothing other than to call the people he was
supposed to see.

I need them to know I didn't stand them up.

If it hadn't been her own party, she'd have excused herself the moment she recalled the almost desperate undertones in her patient's voice. Ryan and Tanner were her
friends and if there was any chance that Chase Harrington
was the man they'd been waiting for, she needed to do what
she could to let them know their brother hadn't simply decided not to show. But her friends had gone to a lot of
trouble for her, so she made herself wait until the cake
they'd brought had been cut and everyone was busy visiting
again before she caved in and turned to Ronni.

"There's something I need to check with a patient. Will
you keep an eye on Tyler for me for a few minutes?"

Knowing Alex was on call, familiar herself with such
interruptions, her friend didn't even hesitate. "Sure. If you
get hung up, just let me know and we'll take him home
with us."

"I shouldn't be that long," Alex assured her, then
slipped out to run across the street to ask a few questions
of her patient.

At eight o'clock on a Saturday evening, the long corri-
dors of the hospital were almost eerily quiet. The business
of treatments and therapies and diagnostics that created
traffic jams of gurneys and wheelchairs and lab carts was
over for the day. Dinner trays had been cleared and sent in
their huge stainless-steel carts back to the hospital kitchen.

The only sounds were from the television sets in a couple

of the rooms and the muffled conversations of visitors bearing mylar Get Well balloons and tidy bouquets of flowers.

There were no visitors in Chase Harrington's room. No balloons. And bouquet was too plebeian a term for the half-dozen fabulous arrangements filling the widow ledge and the tray table belonging to the other, empty, bed.

The head of Chase's bed was raised higher than it had been that morning. He lay back against the pillow with his head turned from the door, his braced leg extended and his uninjured one bent at the knee to make a tent of his blankets. With a business card in his hand, he tapped a slow beat against the raised siderail while he stared out the window at the construction lights glowing in the dark.

When he didn't notice her in the doorway, she glanced at the florist's card on the arrangement nearest the door.

The exotic creation of red ginger, bird of paradise and anthurium was sent ''with best wishes for a speedy recovery'' from the board of Claussen Aerodynamics.

''We just closed a deal,'' he said, talking to her reflection in the window. ''I'm sure they were relieved all the i's were dotted before I wound up here.''

''Maybe they just mean what the card says. That they hope you're better soon.''

He turned toward her, his level expression telling her he didn't believe that for half a second. The sentiment was business. An obligation. Nothing more.

''It's a beautiful arrangement, anyway,'' she told him.

''It's a write-off. They all are.''

His cynicism was unmistakable. So was his displeasure with whatever it was he'd been thinking about as he gave the business card an impatient flip onto the document-covered tray-table beside his bed. She'd never seen him upright, let alone moving under his own steam. But the image of a tornado chained in place sprang to mind as she quietly closed the door. She had no trouble picturing him pacing as he worked, his mind racing, his beautifully honed body rarely still. All that leashed energy and power bent on conquering…everything.

She couldn't help wondering if he regarded women as conquests, too.

She immediately banished the thought, along with the hint of warning that came with it. His sex life was none of her business. It was entirely possible that he would regard any part of his personal life as none of her business, too. But if she was right about who he was, there was far more going on with him than she had suspected, and the reasons for his agitation could be far more profound than she'd thought.

The soft fabric of her dress whispered faintly as she moved toward the glow of the reading light cocooning the bed. She hadn't had time to consider how truly unsettling it would be for a person to face siblings he'd never met. Or to ponder the circumstance that had allowed such a relationship to go unknown for so long.

As she'd hurried through the hospital, she'd been more aware of the faint stirrings of guilt. She'd always prided herself on paying attention to her patients so she wouldn't miss something that could impair their progress. With Chase, she'd simply adopted every one else's opinion of him as a difficult man and ignored the first stirrings of sympathy she'd felt for him.

"I see you got what you wanted. Are you working now?"

A large packing box sat in the green plastic visitor's chair by his bed. Its contents, a state-of-the-art fax machine, occupied the bedside table that had been positioned within easy reach. Someone had unplugged the phone for the other bed and run the fax line to it.

He'd gotten what he was after, but he still didn't look very happy.

With a subdued, "No," he pushed the tray-table aside, watching her as she stopped beside his bed. "I'm finished."

"Your color's improved," she noted, mildly surprised. Judging from the amount of well-marked paper stacked on the tray-table, he'd been at it for hours. He should have looked exhausted. "How's the new medication working?"

"Better."

"Good," she murmured, more aware than she wanted to be of his intense blue eyes. She nodded toward the night-blacked window, as much to get his focus off her as to ease into her reason for being there.

"I see our new wing had your attention. The construction was delayed for a while because of an embezzlement problem with the foundation funding it, but everything's back on schedule now. Our administrator…Ryan Malone…" she said cautiously, watching to see if he reacted to the name, "managed to pull more funding together.

"We're all anxious for the space," she continued, when all he did was blandly glance back at her. "If the new wing were finished, we might have been able to accommodate the request you made for a larger room. I'm sorry, but we don't have VIP suites here at Memorial."

Despite bruises that were working their way from dark cherry to concord grape, he truly did look better than when she'd last seen him. The dull glint of deep pain was gone from his eyes. But his edginess remained. It seemed to linger just beneath the surface, as carefully controlled as the man himself. Bridled as that tension was, it seemed to curl through her, knotting her nerves as his glance slid over the simple navy A-line skimming from her neck to midcalf.

There was no reason she should have felt exposed. He wasn't looking at her as if he were mentally disrobing her.

As his glance lingered on her taut and slender biceps, then moved to where she toyed with the single pearl hanging just below her throat, he was studying her in a way that was almost clinical.

"You don't strike me as the type who makes idle conversation, Doctor." His dark head dipped toward the closed door. "And I can't imagine we'd need privacy if all you came to tell me is that my request for a larger room has been denied. Why don't you just tell me what's bothering you so much that you left your party to talk to me?"

Alex didn't fluster easily. Remaining cool under fire was as much a form of self-preservation as a professional necessity. But this man had a definite knack for knocking her off balance. She suspected he knew it, too.

"How did you know where I was?"

"I imagine everyone within earshot of the nurses' station knows. I could hear them trying to decide who got to be at the restaurant when you arrived and who had to go over later and bring back cake." His glance slid to where her ringless fingers grasped her necklace. "They were also speculating about whether or not you'd have a date. As of a few minutes ago, word was that you didn't."

"It's nice to know the hospital grapevine is so accurate."

"It's an interesting distraction," he admitted, sounding as if he'd used it to keep himself from crawling the walls. "So, if you didn't have a date, who's this Tyler who was with you?"

"My son," she replied, and watched the dark slash of Chase's eyebrows merge.

"You have a son? I thought they were talking about some guy."

"He is a guy. He's just a little one."

That wasn't what he meant. And she knew it. It was just impossible to know what other thoughts flashed through his mind. There was no denying that her having a child had given him pause. The hesitation itself was enough to nudge her defenses. There were some men who tended to shy from women with such an encumbrance. There were others who regarded children as nothing but burdens that cost money and delayed goals.

She had no idea how this man felt. She just knew that Tyler had nothing to do with why she was there—and that Chase Harrington had an uncanny knack for bumping old bruises.

He'd even managed to do it when he was out cold.

"How did you know something's bothering me?" she asked, disquieted by that, too.

Sheets rustled as he crossed his arms, his fathomless eyes intent on her face as he considered her. A moment later, the quality of that consideration underwent a subtle shift when he nodded toward her hand. It was curled and resting below the base of her throat.

"Other than the reasons I just gave you, you've probably rubbed a full millimeter off that pearl since you walked in here. I wouldn't say you look nervous. In your line of work, you've had to deliver too much bad news to start out by hedging. You're too professional for that. But you're not comfortable with whatever's on your mind, either," he told her, sizing her up as she suspected he did his allies. Or his adversaries. "I don't have the feeling you're here because you're my doctor, either."

Unaware of what she'd been doing until he mentioned it, she slowly released her grandma Larson's pearl. It was disconcerting to be read so easily. Here, on her turf, she was usually the one making the analysis, judging, weighing. She was the one people looked to for answers. Her professional role was the one area of her life where she felt reasonably competent. It was everything else that threw her.

Yet, there was no denying the man's powers of observation, or disputing his conclusions. Most of them, anyway.

"You're good," she conceded, wishing she didn't feel that there was more he'd noticed, but discreetly failed to mention. "And you're right. I'm not here because of your treatment. But I'm not uncomfortable with what I want to talk to you about. I'm just not sure how to address it."

"Under the circumstances, why don't we just try the direct approach?"

He offered the suggestion mildly, encouraging her with a hint of a smile that threatened to be devastating if he ever put his heart into it. He hadn't reacted to Ryan's name at all, but she had the feeling he chose to reveal only what he wanted others to see. Since the tactic gave him an extraordinary advantage, she had no doubt he used it shamelessly.

"In that case," she quietly began, "I need to talk to you about the meeting you missed Friday night. It's possible that I misjudged its importance."

He didn't even blink. But he didn't move, either. "What about it?"

"By any chance was it personal rather than business? If it was," she said, before that formidable will of his could snap his guard more firmly into place, "and if it's about what I think it is, maybe I can help."

"Just what do you think it's about?"

"Your brothers. I think you were going to meet them."

For a moment, the only sounds in the room were the hum of the air system and the steady, rhythmic click of the IV pump beside his bed. She didn't doubt that he was a master of control. She'd seen him battle to stay conscious when anyone else would have given up. She'd seen him pinch back frustration to keep from lashing out when pain would have had anyone else raging. But his defenses had been strained by the physical toll on his body and he simply hadn't been prepared for her to hit in such a vulnerable place. Only seconds passed before he replied, but those silent seconds had already given her her answer.

He knew that, too.

Confusion and disbelief melded with a host of sensations he truly did not want to deal with. "How could you possibly have known that?"

"Ryan and Tanner were at my party." Her voice seemed to soften. "I was talking with Ryan's wife and Tanner's fiancée when their meeting with their brother came up. When I learned that the brother was coming from Seattle, it was just a matter of putting two and two together. Even if the coincidence about the meeting hadn't been there," she said, her glance slipping from his face to his rangy body, "there are a few similarities between the three of you. Once you get past the bruises, it's not that hard to tell you're related."

His glance cut warily toward the closed door. "Where are they now?"

"At the restaurant. You said that my being your doctor doesn't have anything to do with why I'm here. I *am* your doctor, though. That's why I can't say anything about this unless you say I can."

He was her patient. No matter how she felt about Ryan and Tanner, her patient had to come first. "I know how badly you wanted to get in touch with them." She was drawn by that need, too. Now that she understood why it had been there. "If you'd like, I can help."

Chase lifted his hand, threading his fingers through his hair. The gesture was new, recently acquired and absolutely no help in dispelling the agitation knotting every one of his already tender nerves. He hated that he couldn't move. He hated that he couldn't pace. More than anything, he hated the way his stomach jumped every time he thought about the moment he'd finally see the two men he'd never laid eyes on before.

His brothers.

Until a couple of months ago, he hadn't even known they'd existed. But he'd discovered a lot of things in the four months since he'd learned that the people he'd thought were his parents…weren't.

"You haven't said anything to anyone?"

"No one," she assured him, sounding as sincere as she looked.

"Then please don't. I still intend to meet them, but not in a bed, and not wearing this." Lifting his hand, trailing IV tubing with it, he plucked at the neck of his hospital gown. "I'll call them after I get out of here."

"They won't care if you're in a wheelchair or flat on your back on a gurney. And they certainly won't care what you're wearing." All she'd have to do was make one phone call and Ryan and Tanner would be there in a heartbeat.

The set of Chase's jaw turned defensive.

"I'll care. I've already left messages that I'd been detained," he said, dead certain she was going to argue with him. She had the same look that she'd had when she'd told him he was acting like a wounded bear. Stubborn and sympathetic. Only now it was confusion rather than exasperation that diluted the latter. "I'll call them when I'm better."

Alex opened her mouth, only to close it again. Her first thought was that he was just being his usual headstrong self and wanted the meeting to take place on his terms. Yet, seeing his brow furrow with strain as he reached to knead a spot above his brace, it didn't seem to be ego or pride prodding him. When she'd explained the seriousness of his injury, how it was possible that, given the worst scenario, he could lose his leg—or his life—he'd scarcely blinked.

What she saw in him now, was the anxiety she would have expected then.

That made no sense at all to her. But she'd seen enough fear in patients to recognize it all too easily. She just couldn't imagine him being afraid of anything. Unless, she thought, caught short by the idea, he was afraid that if his brothers saw him now, they would accept him only out of pity. Or, maybe, he was afraid they wouldn't accept him if he appeared weak. Not that they were likely to think such a thing with his reputation, she thought—then remembered that his brothers had no idea who he was. They'd been expecting Andrew Malone. Not Chase Harrington.

Conscious of how his jaw tightened when he leaned back, the feeling she'd had when she'd left him in recovery washed over her again. She remembered how he'd struck her then as being so very alone. Only now she had a strange sense that being alone wasn't his choice. It was simply the only way he knew how to be.

"I won't do anything you don't want me to do," she agreed, shaking off the disturbing thought. "But there is something I can do, if it will help. I can't release you any sooner, but I can get you out of this room. For a while, anyway."

His glance shifted to her, curious and intent.

"I'm sure it won't do for you to meet in Ryan's office. That's his turf," she added, letting him know she had a few observational powers of her own. "But I can find you an empty meeting room. You'll have to be in a wheelchair, and you'll still be hooked up to an IV," she cautioned, "but your nurse can help you into your street clothes."

She tipped her head, trying to think of what she'd overlooked. Trying mostly to ignore the way her stomach fluttered when his attention lingered on her mouth before settling on her eyes. "I can set up the meeting for you myself."

He didn't even try to hide his skepticism. It narrowed his gaze, seeped into his voice. "Why do you want to help me with this?"

"Because you're my patient," she told him, unable to imagine why he looked so suspicious. "And your brothers are my friends. I think you should know they want to meet you as badly as you want to meet them. And I know you do," she informed him easily. "You wouldn't have come this far if you didn't."

"I'd rather wait until I'm on my feet before I met them. It would just be…easier. I don't have any clothes right now, anyway. They cut off what I was wearing in Emergency and I have no idea what happened to my travel bag."

The words rang more of excuse than reason. He had to know that.

"It's your call," she conceded. "Just let me know if you change your mind. If you like, I can give you a number where I can always be reached."

Looking as if he were complying only because it was easier than not, he nudged the business card on the tray-table toward her. It had landed face down, so she wrote her pager number on the back and dropped his pen beside it.

"For what it's worth," she said, because the knowledge might make it easier for him, "all that matters to them is that you're family."

He looked at her as if he hadn't a clue what difference that should make. He didn't ask, either. When ten seconds ticked by and he hadn't said a word, she stepped back from the bed. She had no problem helping people when they really needed or wanted it. The one thing she'd learned not to do was step in where she wasn't welcome. She'd done what she could for Ryan and Tanner. And for Chase. But Chase clearly preferred to handle the matter on his own.

The only thing he'd asked of her was why she would want to help him in the first place. He'd looked at her as if she had some angle; as if he couldn't believe she wanted to help him simply because he needed it.

"I should get back."

"Yeah. You probably should."

There were people waiting for her. Telling him she'd see him tomorrow, telling herself there truly was nothing more she could do, she turned away.

She was halfway across the room when she heard him murmur, "By the way, I understand it was yesterday, but happy birthday."

He watched her pause by the door. Surprise, then a smile moved over her face. That smile was as gentle as a spring rain and just as inviting.

"Thanks," she replied, and slipped out before he could admit just how much he wished she'd stayed.

She must have thought he wanted his privacy. The door closed behind her, leaving him isolated with the thoughts that had him feeling as if he wanted to crawl out of his skin.

He hated the thoughts churning inside him, hated the sense of uncertainty that came with them. It hadn't been so bad when he could numb himself with the anesthetic of work. As long as he was pushing himself mentally or physically, he was fine. When he wanted to avoid the very sort of thoughts plaguing him now, he simply switched into a higher gear, demanding more of himself and, by extension, everyone around him. He'd even managed to escape for a few hours that day, hassling with the fax and working on his contracts. Now, grounded, and with his contracts finished, he had no idea how to escape.

She'd said there were similarities. That meant there were traits he and his brothers shared, things that somehow identified them as being, at least in some ways, the same.

He couldn't begin to imagine what they had in common.

He already felt sorely disadvantaged where Ryan and Tanner were concerned. In the last few minutes the feeling had compounded itself. He knew from his detective's report that his brothers had dealings with each other because of the work Tanner was doing for the hospital. He knew, too, that they spent time together apart from their jobs, that they were close.

He had no idea what that sort of bond was like. He had no idea, either, how a person went about establishing one. He'd learned long ago to insulate himself from the need for the approval of others. And he'd told himself a dozen times that he didn't really care what Ryan and Tanner thought of him. Yet, even as he'd assured himself over and over that he was coming to meet them only out of curiosity, he had wondered if they would let him in.

You're family.

He could still hear his doctor's voice, the quiet encouragement in it. Obviously family meant something to her—and to his brothers—that he wasn't familiar with. He wasn't sure what compassion looked like, either, but there were times he could have sworn that was what he saw in her face. The thought that anyone could understand what churned inside him was impossible to comprehend. He barely understood it himself.

The thought that she wanted to help him because he was the brother of her friends was a strange feeling, too. When people offered him their assistance, it was usually because they were angling to get a piece of him. Or because they wanted something in return. His money. His influence.

He'd never had anyone offer help just because they were thinking of him.

He picked up the business card and stared at her hurried scrawl. She hadn't written her name, just numbers that were surprisingly legible. They were for her cell phone, he imagined. Or her pager.

He turned over the small white rectangle. The name *Ryan Malone* stared back at him. One of the nurses had brought the card to him that afternoon, along with another bag of the yellow fluid that constantly dripped into his vein. She'd told him in an obscenely cheery voice that the hospital administrator knew he didn't want to be disturbed, but that Mr. Malone wanted him to know that if he needed anything, he wasn't to hesitate to call him or his assistant.

Had Chase just been some regular guy off the street, he sincerely doubted that the administrator would have bothered having his card dropped off. Ryan Malone had offered his services because he was Chase Harrington. He would have done the same had he learned that a politician or celebrity occupied one of his hospital's beds. Accommodations were made for those it could be useful to know. It was simply good business.

It was something he'd have done himself had the situation been reversed.

He actually found a small measure of comfort in that. But it wasn't anywhere near enough to take the edge off the apprehension he simply couldn't seem to shake. It was almost like the adrenalized anxiety he felt when he was climbing and rock or ice unexpectedly gave way. Or when a storm swept in from nowhere and threatened to capsize his boat. But there he could at least rely on his experience to get him out of whatever had gone wrong. Here, he felt as if he were in a freefall and no one had told him how to open the parachute.

He'd never felt so unprepared for anything in his life. He'd never before faced a meeting where he knew so little about the key players. But as he turned the card over once more, vaguely aware of the panic calming when his glance settled on the numbers again, he knew he now had access to someone who apparently knew them well. And her scent, something clean and light and far more provocative than the mother of a young son should probably wear, still lingered in his mind.

Chapter Four

Alex smoothed Tyler's hair and kissed his warm little cheek. He lay curled on his side, sound asleep, one arm hooked around a bedraggled purple dinosaur and his fist grasping the satin edge of his blanket. The rest of his stuffed menagerie guarded him from their appointed positions along the bright blue bookcase headboard.

He'd crashed and burned within seconds of his head hitting the pillow. He hadn't even asked for a story.

A soft smile touched Alex's mouth as she ran her fingers lightly over his forehead. The softness of his skin still amazed her, the incredible downiness of it. She remembered when he'd been an infant, thinking how it had felt as soft as air. Back then, she thought, wondering at how much he'd grown, everything about him had seemed so impossibly fragile.

He'd terrified her.

She'd been twenty-eight years old, a promising, some

even said gifted, surgical resident with an above-average knowledge of the human body and its gestational processes. And six pounds, twelve ounces of sweet-smelling, mewling baby had left her feeling totally incompetent.

She slowly pulled back, tucking the covers around him. Tyler was no longer that helpless, frighteningly dependent baby. But there were times when she desperately missed the infant she'd hardly had time to hold, the toddler who'd taken his first steps without her. She hadn't really even known him then.

His first word had been *Nana*.

She'd had to spend his first birthday in surgery.

She turned off his light with a quiet click. Picking up a truck she'd stepped over earlier, she set in on the dresser before pulling his door partially closed. She didn't want to go where her thoughts seemed to be leading her. Those years were behind them now. She and Tyler had struggled through the last of her residency with the help of her parents and they were doing just fine.

If she was feeling a little melancholy about having missed his infancy, it was probably because she was missing Wendy and her baby. The pregnant teenager had lived with them only for a few months, and Wendy had stayed for just two more weeks after she'd delivered before moving in with a relative, but Alex had bonded with them both.

It was just baby-withdrawal, Alex assured herself, and headed down the hall in her oversized sleep shirt, stretching her neck to relieve the tension tightening it.

She and Tyler had been home for half an hour, long enough for her to supervise the feeding of the gerbil, the fish and the cat and get Tyler through the getting-ready-for-bed routine. All she needed to do now was get coffee ready for the morning, turn off the lights in the rest of the house, and shake the restive feeling haunting her so she could go to bed herself.

Thomas, their wiry ten-pound ex-alley cat trotted by her, his long tail waving like a regal banner, replete on Nine Lives, and disappeared through Tyler's door. In another ten seconds, he'd be curled up in a mottled gray ball at the foot of Tyler's bed.

Everyone was where they were supposed to be. Tucked in. Bedded down. Safe. Secure.

The house suddenly seemed far too quiet.

It didn't feel empty, exactly. Not with all the hearts beating in it. Still, there seemed to be a vague, almost lonely feel to the place as she moved about her little kitchen with its Big Bird cookie jar and the crayon art on the refrigerator.

Alex reminded herself again of Wendy and the baby. She was just going through an adjustment period. She'd suffered the same loose-ended sensation after the female doctor from India who'd stayed with them last year had returned home. She just didn't want to believe the hollow feeling had anything to do with the funny tug she'd felt when she'd watched Ryan and Ronni walk off hand in hand tonight.

Or when she'd seen Tanner drape his arm around Kelly as they'd left the restaurant.

She didn't want to believe it had anything to do with the fact that, except for a quick platonic hug, she hadn't had a man's arms around her in over four years.

And she definitely didn't want to believe it was there because she couldn't shake the loneliness she'd sensed in Chase when she'd left him tonight.

That kind of empathy she could do without.

Warning herself that she'd never get to sleep if she started thinking about him, she flipped off the kitchen light—and heard her pager go off.

A groan escaped a second before she bumped her forehead against the doorjamb.

Knowing better than to acknowledge how tired she should be, she padded barefoot to where she'd dropped her purse on the credenza in the hall and unclipped the little black nuisance from the strap.

She recognized the hospital prefix on the telephone number displayed on the digital readout, but the rest of the numbers were unfamiliar. The call wasn't from the emergency room or the nurses' station on the med-surg floor. Unless one of the other floors had paged the wrong doctor, she could think of only one other person who'd be calling her now.

Picking up the phone from the end table by the sofa, she punched in the numbers.

A male voice, smoky and rich, answered on the first ring.

"That didn't take long. It's Chase. Are you still at the restaurant?"

It was difficult to ignore the familiarity in the way he identified himself, or the sensual slide of that deep voice over her nerves. "I left there a while ago," she replied, trying to overlook the latter, anyway.

"I didn't think you'd be leaving so early. I don't suppose you're anywhere near the hospital, are you?"

"Actually, I'm home. But your timing is fine," she assured him, not wanting to discourage his reason for calling. "Did you change your mind about letting me set up that meeting?"

He hesitated. "I don't know yet." The faint rush of an indrawn breath filtered over the line. "I wanted to talk to you first. About my brothers," he explained, a wealth of unease slipping into his tone. "You said they're friends of yours. I'm hoping you can tell me something about them."

Alex could almost see him propped in his bed, his jaw

working, his grip on the phone tighter than he wanted it to be.

She had no idea how he'd found his brothers, or what circumstances had led to him being separated from them. All she knew of the Malone brothers' background was that their parents had died when they were very young. But this wasn't about her curiosity. It was about her patient. And he was doing something she never would have expected of him. He was asking for her help.

With the cordless phone pressed to her ear, she rounded the end table and sank to her teal-blue sofa. In front of her, the big brass trunk that served as a coffee table was stacked with paint color-chip samples, unread gardening magazines and the children's library books she'd intended to return last Thursday. The pretty pottery bowl she'd bought at an outdoor art fair to display flowers or lacquered fruit held Matchbox cars and a stress-reduction tape.

Propping her bare feet on the edge of the trunk, she raised her knees to block her view of the entire lot.

"What do you want to know?"

"Anything you're willing to tell me."

"Do you know anything about them at all?"

"I know where they went to school and what they do for a living. And that Ryan was widowed and remarried not long ago. But that's the sort of thing any investigator can turn up," he told her, revealing how he'd come by what information he had. "That's not what I'm looking for from you. You said you figured out who I was because there are…similarities."

He wanted to know what he might share with his siblings, what it was that identified them as belonging to each other. Those were the things an investigator wouldn't be able to uncover. They were the traits that someone who wanted to fit in would want to know. "There are. I take it you haven't seen any pictures."

"Nothing recent. Only a newspaper photo of Ryan in an article about that funding problem you mentioned. A profile shot. I couldn't tell much."

An image of Chase's own chiseled profile formed in her mind; the hard cheekbones, the noble nose, that firm, sensual mouth.

She cleared her throat. "Actually," she said, tugging her shirt toward her bare knees, "you all have dark hair and the same color of eyes. And you and Ryan have similar...bone structure," she decided to call it, since telling him they had that same lean, hungry look lacked the professional edge she needed to keep with this man.

"Anything else?"

"Well...there's your personalities..."

"What about them?"

Considering, she slipped the hem of her sleepshirt through her fingers. "How honest do you want me to be?"

"I'm not sure I trust the sound of that."

"You're my patient. I don't want to offend you," she admitted, holding back a smile at the pure male caution that had entered his tone.

"Meaning you wouldn't mind offending me if I wasn't?"

Her fingers stilled, her heart giving an odd little bump at the unexpected hint of teasing in his tone. The man had a voice as intoxicating as hundred-year-old brandy. Smooth, seductive and guaranteed to make a woman slip right out of her inhibitions. There was just something a tad ironic about talking to a man with a voice like that while wearing comfortable cotton that said Save the Chocolate and sitting propped between a Monet-print pillow and a large Nerf ball.

"Meaning just what I said," she murmured, thinking he'd probably never seen a woman in anything other than imported silk.

"For what it's worth, I don't offend easily."

She didn't imagine that he did. Under normal circumstances, that shell of his was probably steel-belted and double-ply.

"Let's just say that you and Tanner both share a certain...cynicism." He was actually light years beyond Tanner on that score. "And Ryan can be charming, but he can be just as stubborn as you can. Don't get me wrong. I think the world of your brothers. They're enormously generous, caring people. But you asked for similarities—"

"And you gave me what I asked for."

Which, as she considered it, probably hadn't been a very good idea. She'd just told him she found him cynical and stubborn. All she'd left out was controlling, disturbing and impossible to forget.

"Tell me," he said, generously letting her off the hook. "Do you have family?"

"Pardon?"

"Do you have family?" he repeated mildly. "Parents? Brothers? Sisters?"

"I'm an only child. And I have both my mom and my dad."

"They're your natural parents?"

She hesitated, but even as she did, she began to suspect what Chase was doing. "Yes," she said quietly. "They are."

But the people who had raised Chase hadn't been his. She just didn't know if he was trying to see if she could relate to him. Or trying to prove that she couldn't.

"What about you?" she asked, wanting to know where she stood. "Any siblings?"

"Not until two months ago."

That was when the investigator had turned them up, he told her. It had actually been four months since he'd learned he was adopted, but it had taken that long for the man he'd hired to find out who his birth parents were and discover that there had been more than one child of the deceased Andrew and Cecilia Malone.

Chase said nothing about his adoptive parents. As Alex listened, it became apparent from the deliberate omission that he was either protecting them or trying not to think about them at all. She wasn't sure why, but she suspected it was more of the latter. Because of that, she didn't ask how he had discovered what had been kept from him for so long. She focused only on how long it had taken him to work up the courage to contact his brothers. And that he seemed to be trying hard to come to grips with the fact that they even existed.

"I'm not going to pretend I know what it's like to be in the position you're in right now," she admitted quietly. "I can't tell you what it's like to have siblings. And I don't know how I'd feel if I discovered my parents weren't really my mom and dad. They're wonderful people, but I imagine I'd feel a sense of betrayal at having something like that kept from me."

"Yeah," he mumbled, as if pondering what she'd said. "Betrayed works."

She wished she were with him. But this wasn't about some physical problem she could help him deal with, and the need she felt to touch him, just to reassure him, didn't feel professional at all. With only the phone to connect them she didn't have to worry about how strong that need felt just then. Her only thought was that he needed to know he had the right to feel as uncertain and uneasy as he did.

"I really can't appreciate what you're facing right now,"

she reiterated, "but I do understand what it's like to have something I thought was real jerked out from under me. The only thing you can do is take it one day at a time and start building from there. There might be rewards in this that you can't even imagine. You didn't ask for advice," she conceded. "But I am your doctor, and I know it's not doing you any good lying there worrying about what it's going to be like to meet your brothers. They're just as anxious about meeting you as you are about meeting them," she assured him, thinking of how much easier it was for Ryan and Tanner than it was for Chase. They had each other. In this, Chase was truly alone.

Except for her.

She had the feeling he knew that, too. He probably didn't like it, either. She could almost see him plowing his fingers through his hair. The hiss of air on the other end of the phone seemed to tell her he'd done just that.

"You shouldn't make abrupt moves," she murmured.

There was another moment's silence before she heard him mutter, "I'm figuring that out."

Sheets rustled. "This puts you in an awkward position, doesn't it?" Chase asked.

His words were more acknowledgement than question, something that surprised her, since she hadn't thought he would have considered how she'd be affected at all.

"Yes," she admitted, careful to keep accusation from her tone. "It does. It's hard to know something that could put their minds at ease and not be able to tell them about it. But that's my problem. You have enough to deal with."

From somewhere above her came the creak of the house settling in for the night and the rattle of pipes as the ancient hot-water heater kicked on. From the telephone, all she heard was a faint tapping. The sound was restless, edgy, like a pen or card being tapped against a table.

"If you can find me an office and get me some clothes, then go ahead and set it up."

She dropped the hem of her shirt as she sat straighter. "They're going to want to know why I'm involved. That means I'll have to tell them who you are and what happened."

The tapping stopped. "Go ahead." Resignation shadowed his tone. "Let's just do it before Ryan decides to pay me a visit."

Chase didn't get a chance to ask what his brothers' reaction to her news had been. When Dr. Alexandra Larson breezed into his room at one o'clock the next afternoon carrying his brown leather travel bag and his briefcase, she slowed down only long enough for him to get the basics. She told him she'd been at the towing lot picking up his bag, which had still been in the back seat of the wrecked rental car, when she'd been paged to surgery. Since she was on her way to OR at that very moment, she'd hurriedly explained that Ryan and Tanner were meeting him in the boardroom on the second floor at two-thirty, that she was leaving instructions with his nurse to take him there and that she'd check with him later when she did her rounds.

She didn't even stick around long enough to let him say thank-you.

He couldn't believe she'd gone to so much trouble for him.

He couldn't believe, either, how badly he'd wanted to grab her hand to stop her from leaving when she'd slowed down long enough to curl her fingers over his arm, steal his breath with her scent, and tell him she was sure everything would be fine.

The fact that he'd felt the need to reach for her for moral support should have disturbed him. He never allowed himself to need anyone on that level. But he was sure the circumstance was temporary. Only a fool would refuse to use a compass in uncharted waters. Once the familiar shoreline came into view, he could rely on his own navigational skills.

Right now, though, he really didn't think he'd mind if she showed up again. His brothers would be walking through the open conference-room door any minute.

The long polished mahogany conference table reflected the light pouring through the long banks of windows. Just inside the doorway, off to the side, a comfortable arrangement of deep burgundy chairs and a sofa flanked a large square coffee table sporting a model of the newly expanded hospital. From the materials on the table, it appeared that a dedication was being planned for the first of September.

The orderly who'd brought him in had turned his wheelchair to face the door and moved one of the telephones to within Chase's reach. Now, shaved and showered—something that had required far more assistance than he'd liked—and wearing an open-collared dress shirt and slacks, Chase sat with his bandaged leg jutting out and brushed a speck of lint from his charcoal-gray worsteds.

His tailor would sob like a baby if he saw what the nurse had done to his good Armani trousers. To get them on over the external fixation device—EFD in medical shorthand— she'd had to slit the side seam darn near to his hip. Chase didn't care. His khakis had been too wrinkled to wear and there was no way he'd meet his brothers without pants.

The heavy beat of double footsteps caused his insides to pitch. But all anyone saw when he raised his head at the movement in the doorway was the same ruthless control he usually exerted over himself.

Two men, both big, both imposing, formed a united front

as they came to a halt just inside the door. Two pairs of eyes as blue as his own fixed on his face.

They didn't have to identify themselves for him to know who they were. Chase's guarded glance moved from the tall, polished man in the impeccably fitted navy blazer and tan slacks to the more muscular, more skeptical-looking one in the denims and a chambray shirt. Neither man seemed able to look from him as they searched for the similarities even Chase himself could see. Every morning, he shaved around the same cleft Ryan had in his chin and the same squared angle of Tanner's jaw.

Ryan was first to move. Approaching with easy, athletic grace, he extended his hand.

Chase offered his own.

Their hands connected, their grips firm and suddenly, a little unwilling to let go.

"I'm—"

"Ryan," Chase supplied, conscious of an odd knot under his breastbone as the pressure of his hand increased.

"Your brother," Ryan expanded, his deep voice more raw than he'd probably intended. His glance swept the bruises, the leg he'd scarcely seemed to notice. But when he opened his mouth, masculine reserve frayed. Muttering a choked-sounding oath, he bent—and hugged him.

Chase felt his chest burn. Before he could think, he found himself hugging him back. His throat tightened. Swallowing hard, he bit back the unfamiliar sensations and looked up to see Tanner walking toward him.

Looking as awkward as Chase felt himself, Tanner gripped his hand when Ryan stepped back and started to pop him on the shoulder. Seeing the dangling IV line, he caught himself, sparing Chase the more typical display of male affection. Apparently, he didn't want to hurt him any more than he already had been.

One look at the EFD and he'd blanched.

"Man, you're a mess."

Chase couldn't dispute the observation. The mirror hadn't been kind. "Yeah," he agreed, watching the man's jaw work. "But you should see the truck."

A ghost of a smile flickered in Tanner's eyes. "I don't know about the truck, but Alex said it really creamed your car. She's amazed you came out of it as well as you did."

"Alex?"

"Dr. Larson," Ryan supplied. "She called on her way back from the towing lot this morning to tell us why you hadn't shown up Friday night. I can't believe you were here all this time. I had no idea you were... I mean... Well, I just had no idea," he repeated and cut himself off because it didn't seem to matter who he was now that he knew Chase was his brother.

"I don't know what to call you," Ryan continued, his smile coming more easily as he lowered himself to the chair beside him. Tanner took a chair, too. The arm of one anyway. He didn't look comfortable enough to settle into it. "When you called, you identified yourself as Andrew Malone."

Chase felt his reserve lock into place. "That's the name on my original birth certificate. I thought if you knew of me, that's the name you'd recognize."

He watched Ryan lift his chin in acknowledgement. Chase had known there was a possibility that his brothers would have recognized his legal name—the name he'd grown up with—but he hadn't wanted them to be influenced by that part of who he was. He'd wanted them to agree to meet him because they were related. That was all. And they had.

He couldn't begin to admit how much that meant to him.

"Let's just stick with Chase," he remarked, not knowing

how to think of himself as anyone other than who he'd always thought he was.

"It would be confusing calling you Andrew, anyway," Tanner agreed. "That's our nephew's name."

"Our nephew?"

"Ryan's oldest boy."

"I have another, boy, too," Ryan told him. "Griffin's four. And my little girl, Lisbeth, is six. Tanner has a daughter, Lia. And my wife's pregnant." He grinned, though it looked as if he tried not to. "That's our family."

Chase pulled a breath, catching himself when his expanding ribs reminded him of the bruises there. He hadn't known about Tanner's child, but he had known of Ryan's kids. Somewhere in the report from the PI there was a list of their names and ages. He'd just never thought of them as being part of the deal. If he had nieces and nephews, that made him an uncle.

He wasn't sure why he thought of it just then, but his doctor had a child, too. Alex, he now knew she was called, though the name seemed awfully hard for someone whose skin looked so soft it fairly begged to be touched.

"So…Chase," Ryan began, then blew a breath himself. "I don't even know where to start."

Tanner did. "How did you find us?"

"I hired an investigator," Chase admitted frankly. "My father…the man I thought was my father," he corrected, ignoring the host of conflicted feelings that came with mention of the man, "died four months ago. I learned that I'd been adopted at the reading of his will."

Walter Harrington acknowledges that Chase Randall Harrington is his adopted son and that he desires that Chase Randall Harrington receive nothing from this trust or his estate.

He still remembered the stunned disbelief that had

washed over him in the moments following the attorney's reading of those words. The money hadn't mattered. He had ten times the holdings Walter had accumulated. But he still lived with the odd, empty sensation that had opened inside him when he'd walked out of the study with his mother begging him not to be upset with her for not mentioning the "detail." The only thing that helped alleviate it was the sense of relief Chase felt finally knowing why he'd never been able to win the man's approval. He'd never been "blood." He'd never been the man's son at all.

"The man I hired was able to get information on the two of you. Your education and business involvements," he continued, wanting to move past what had started his investigation to admit that he had, in effect, checked out the two men who'd just glanced uncomfortably at each other. "He said you were in foster care when you were kids. Sometimes together. Sometimes not. What he hadn't been able to find out—"

"They kept us together when they could," Ryan explained.

"Except for the dozen or so times they split us up," Tanner muttered.

"Sorry," Ryan said, apologizing for the interruption. "What was it he couldn't find out?"

"He couldn't find out what happened to my…our," Chase corrected, totally unaccustomed to thinking in the plural, "…parents. He said you were three and four years old when the state took custody. I was told I was six months old when I was adopted."

Tanner looked to Ryan, not so much deferring to him as sparing himself the recitation. The trace of bitterness in his tone moments ago had been unmistakable. And understandable, considering what such a childhood must have been like.

Ryan was actually the tougher read. He was undoubtedly as familiar as Chase himself with the boardroom negotiating tactics that allowed information to be exchanged without betraying whatever was going on inside him. Listening to him as he began to tell of the car accident that had taken their parents' lives, Chase figured Ryan was either guarding himself the same way he did, or Ryan really had no reservations about accepting him.

Just because he was family.

Chase had absolutely no concept of acceptance on that level.

"We were told they were on their way home from San Francisco and hit a patch of black ice in one of the passes," Ryan was saying. "Apparently our grandmother had been seriously ill so they'd left us with friends and gone to see her."

There had been no other family willing to take them on. Their mother had been an only child and her parents had been frail and elderly even back then. Their father's mom had died years before that, their dad had long been estranged from his father and his only brother was a bachelor college professor who had no interest in taking on one kid, let alone three of them. The brother had signed off on them so they could be adopted, but only Chase actually had been. Tanner and Ryan had grown up in foster care.

It was absurd for him to feel guilty. But as Chase looked from Tanner's remote expression to Ryan's thoughtful one, guilt was what he felt. His brothers had been two little kids who'd had no one but each other, living in a system that kept pulling them apart and putting them back together again. While they were being bounced around, he was being raised by nannies. Until he was seven years old anyway. Then, his grooming had started and he'd been shipped off to the private schools that had been his home away from home until he'd escaped to college.

Watching the two brothers exchange another glance, he realized it wasn't guilt he felt after all. It was envy. These two men might not have grown up with material wealth, but even when they'd been apart, each had known the other was there. They'd had...a bond.

Chase had no idea how it would feel to have that sort of connection to another person. He'd never felt connected to anyone in his life.

"How long are you going to be here?" Tanner finally asked.

"My doctor won't let me go for another few days."

"I mean in Honeygrove."

"I...don't know." Fully appreciating his brother's reticence, he decided to let him know he had doubts of his own. "I had no idea what to expect when I got here. I'd left the weekend open, but I also had a reservation for a flight out yesterday morning."

For a moment, Tanner said nothing else. He just stared at him, weighing, judging until, finally, he gave a tight nod that seemed to say that was fair enough.

"I would like a tour of that wing over there sometime, though," Chase mentioned to them both. "I've been staring at it for two days now. I know you're building it," he added to Tanner, already impressed with the scope and scale of the multi-million-dollar project "And it's your hospital," he said to Ryan. "So, which one of you would I talk to about that?"

Ryan and Tanner both looked at the IV bag hanging on the pole above the wheelchair.

"We'd better check with Alex," Ryan said. "If she clears it, we'll get you a hard hat and we'll both take you."

"She's in surgery." Chase glanced at his watch. "At

least that's where she was going when I last saw her. Why don't we just tell the nurse where we're headed?''

''Sure,'' Tanner agreed, looking as if he wouldn't mind showing his little brother what he was justifiably proud of. ''It's not like we're taking him off the property.''

Ryan didn't look so sure. Chase thought he understood Ryan's hesitation, too. Taking a patient into a construction area opened up all manner of potential liability. But when Ryan frowned at Tanner, that didn't seem to be what he was thinking about at all.

''Alex said we're not supposed to tire him out,'' he reminded his brother, just before he turned his concern to Chase. ''You're sure you're up to it now? We could do this anytime.''

''Ryan,'' Tanner muttered, ''you're sounding like a big brother.''

''I *am* the big brother,'' Ryan muttered back. ''I don't want to set him back. You're Alex's patient,'' the tall, sophisticated-looking man said to Chase, sounding as if he wanted them all to be aware of that as he planted his hands on his thighs to push himself upright. ''But you're our brother. If you're up to it, we'll call the floor and tell them where you'll be in case they need to bring you another bag of whatever that is. Alex probably won't mind.''

Chapter Five

"They're *where?*"

"Somewhere in the basement of the new wing," the slightly flustered Kay replied from behind the nurses' station counter. "I told Mr. Malone that you hadn't authorized Mr. Harrington to go anywhere except the boardroom, but he said Mr. Harrington wanted to see the new wing, and he was sure you wouldn't mind. It's not as if I could argue with him. I mean, after all, Mr. Malone *is* the administrator and it's not my place to question him. But I've never lost track of a patient before. Not that he's really lost," she hurriedly defended, fanning herself with a file. "I mean, he's over there somewhere and Mr. Malone did give me his pager number so we were able to track them down and give Mr. Harrington his four-o'clock pain med.

"But, really, Doctor," she huffed. "I'm short staffed as it is today and his nurse shouldn't have to run all over creation to take care of a patient nosing around a construction zone. Just because he wanted to see our new wing doesn't mean he had to. That man's behavior breaks every rule in the book. And now he's inconveniencing you. Do you want me to send an orderly to bring him back?''

It was as clear as a test tube that Kay held Chase responsible for the present disruption. It seemed she also expected Alex to share her indignation over the affront to hospital routine. After all, when a busy doctor showed up on the floor to check on a patient, she had a perfect right to expect to find the patient there. Somewhere.

Unfortunately for Kay's sense of propriety, Alex wasn't concerned about the rules or about this particular patient's tendency to make his own policy. She was concerned about Chase. She knew how he pushed himself, and how he tended to ignore pain. She also suspected he fought fatigue with the same tenacity, and his body needed rest to heal. But the last thing she wanted to do was interrupt the three men if they were bonding over boilers and conduits or whatever it was about the innards of a building that men seemed to find so fascinating.

Trying not to concern herself with how their reunion was going, assuming it was going well since they'd been together for hours, she told the indignant woman that Ryan Malone regarded Mr. Harrington as a special patient and that they'd just have to work around rules while he was there.

Kay greeted that news with thin-lipped disapproval—which had also been her reaction when she'd learned Chase was having a private audience with the hospital administrator. She already thought the man was getting far too much preferential treatment.

Seeing that Alex wasn't going to give her the understanding she wanted, the nurse handed over the charts Alex needed for her rounds. From behind her, the unit secretary, whose frizzy blond hair was tamed with a huge butterfly clip, added her two-cents' worth.

"Yolanda thinks they're meeting because Mr. Malone wants to prime him for a donation for the new wing. Or maybe it was Alison who said that. She's his nurse today, right? Anyway," she continued, dismissing the need to properly identify the source with a wave of her arterial red nails. "The man *is* filthy rich. It makes perfect sense."

"Our administrator is hardly a vulture," Kay admonished. "I can't imagine he'd do that while a person is a patient here." Apparently seeing the potential advantage to the hospital, she relented ever so slightly. "He'd wait until he was discharged."

"But it would make sense to start priming him now, wouldn't it?"

Figuring the rumor as good a cover as any until the men wanted their relationship made public, Alex tuned the women out, along with the ringing of the phone and the hurried steps of soft-soled shoes scurrying back and forth behind her. She flipped through the first chart, anxious to get on with her rounds. "Do we have test results back on Mrs. Tillman?"

Kay took the hint. Dropping the subject, she turned to the computer to scroll up the results Alex wanted. Alex figured it would take at least an hour to round on her patients. Then, after she changed out of her scrubs, she'd have to stop by Children's Hospital to check on the little girl whose ankle she'd just pieced back together before the child was transferred. Memorial didn't have any pediatric beds. Not until the new wing opened, anyway.

Thinking that surely Tanner and Ryan would have Chase back on the floor by the time she was ready to leave, she headed in to greet a shyly smiling Brent. But when the Malones still hadn't returned their brother to the floor by the time she had checked everyone but Chase, she decided the men had played enough. She needed to check her last patient, and, according to his harried nurse, it was time for a new bag of antibiotics.

Asking Kay to find out where they were, Alex whipped her stethoscope around the neck of her lab coat and grabbed Chase's chart to study in the med room while Alison, a wiry young nurse with a head of stick-straight brown hair and a quick smile, prepared the antibiotic cocktail Alex would hook up herself. As she leaned against the counter, she checked the vitals that had been taken just before he'd left the unit. Chase's blood pressure had been a little high, but that didn't surprise her—considering where he'd been about to go at the time. Everything else—pulse, temperature and respirations—were more suited to someone about to run a marathon than a person who couldn't even walk at the moment.

Two minutes later, a ten-inch bag of IV solution in hand, she walked through the unit's open double doors to see Tanner and Ryan flanking Chase in the elevator lobby forty feet ahead.

They must have decided to return when Kay had called to get their location. Deep in conversation, not one of them seemed to notice her as she came to a halt by the wall.

She couldn't hear a word they said, but both of the tall, dark-haired Malones gave their equally compelling brother a pat on the shoulder. Seeming a little reluctant, they stepped back at the soft ping of an arriving elevator. After waiting for an elderly couple to emerge from it, they disappeared inside.

The couple, obviously visitors, stood studying the directory on the wall while Chase wheeled himself around and headed for the unit alone.

It was only then that he noticed her watching him.

Even from that distance she could see him look from the collar of her lab coat to the blue paper booties below the hem of her surgical scrubs. She was dead certain that by the time his attention returned to her face, he would know she wasn't pleased.

Moments ago, her only thoughts had been of how relieved he must be to have the anxiety of the meeting behind him. Considering the time the men had spent together and the ease of their smiles, Chase's included, the worst moments were long over. But the need she'd felt to ask how he felt about his brothers was cancelled by disbelief. And exasperation. With all of them.

She couldn't believe Ryan and Tanner had left him to get back to his room on his own. Besides the fact that she'd specifically told Ryan that Chase would tire easily, Chase obviously wasn't in any shape to be maneuvering a wheelchair. Every time he moved his elbows back to push forward on the wheels' metal rings, fresh pain tightened his cleanly shaven jaw.

She was already moving toward him, unable to bear watching the senseless effort.

He didn't even possess the good sense to stop.

"Why didn't you let Ryan or Tanner bring you back to your room?" she demanded as they drew closer.

"Because it wasn't necessary." A muscle in his jaw jerked as he gave another shove on the rings. "I've got it," he muttered, seeing her move past him. "It's not that far."

Ignoring his claim, she stepped behind the green and silver chair. "I'd always heard pride was painful. I'd just never seen the concept in action before. Hold this." The bag of pale gold solution landed in his lap with a soft plop. "And move your other hand," she ordered, seeing that he'd only given up his grip on one of the rings when he'd caught the bag.

She considered it a sign of fatigue that he didn't argue. The instant his hand cleared the wheel, she shoved him forward herself. "You weren't pushing yourself around down there this whole time, were you?"

"Most of it."

The admission came without a shred of apology or defense. As she stared daggers at the back of his meticulously cut hair, all she heard was pure, unadulterated challenge.

She was about to tell him that her four-year-old had more sense than the three men combined when she saw Kay striding toward them. Disapproval resounded with every squeaking step.

"His nurse is with another patient, Doctor." With an annoyed glance at the patient who was now requiring his physician to act as an orderly, the perturbed nurse inserted herself behind the wheelchair. "I'll change that IV and get him into bed."

"I'm not getting into bed." Chase's tone went as flat as a specimen slide. "This chair is fine."

"Your doctor has been waiting to examine you." Admonishment coated the clipped words. "You need to be in a gown and in your bed."

"I'm not getting in one of those—"

"Mr. Harrington—"

"It's all right, Kay."

Alex shook her head as Kay's mouth fell open to further her protest. There were procedures and protocols to follow. Under other circumstances, Alex would have bowed to those formalities. But as the trio maneuvered around an empty gurney and turned into Chase's room, she was far more concerned with the tension radiating from Chase's broad shoulders than with Kay's sense of decorum.

"If you'll take him over by the bed and hang the IV,"

she asked, bending to that bit of protocol, "that's all I'll need for now."

"If you're sure."

"I'm sure." Avoiding the blue eyes narrowed on her face, she took the bag from Chase and handed it over. "I need to speak with Mr. Harrington alone."

It was clear that Kay thought Alex was about to give their troublesome patient a piece of her mind. Satisfaction fairly glowed in the woman's otherwise militant expression. Given that sort of motivation, it only took her a minute to get everything connected, check the position of the needle in Chase's arm, and reset the pump.

"I'll see that you're not disturbed," the nurse promised moments later, and closed the wide door behind her.

In the sudden silence, the quiet click of the pump sounded like the ominous tick of a time bomb.

Alex stood at the foot of Chase's neatly made bed, two feet from where he sat refusing to break that silence himself.

The white shirt he wore was open at the collar, rolled to his elbows and bore an embroidered white CRH on the pocket. The foot planted firmly on the footrest was shod in soft, and undoubtedly expensive, black leather. His gray slacks were cuffed, sharply creased and, considering the device pinning his leg, recently altered.

She'd thought him formidable before. Dressed with such casual elegance, his dark hair combed back from his face and his blue eyes lasering hers, the man was downright dangerous.

"Open your shirt for me."

His dark eyebrows merged into a single, disgruntled slash, but he said nothing. Watching her step toward him as she warmed the bell of her stethoscope in her palm, he moved his hand to the front of his shirt. His fingers slipped down the placket, flicking open buttons, the motions almost defiant.

She felt a little defiant herself. Deliberately ignoring his beautifully formed pectoral muscles when he pulled the shirt open, she bent forward and placed the bell beneath his flat male nipple. "Breathe," she ordered.

His chest expanded. As it did, the scent of warm male and aftershave registered deep in her consciousness, testing her concentration on the sounds she was listening for. Lifting the smooth fabric of his shirt with the back of her hand, she moved the bell to the other side. "Again."

Chase did as he was told, pulling a breath that brought her impossibly fresh scent deep into his lungs and played utter havoc with the nerves at the base of his spine. Or maybe it was the feel of her small hand on his shoulder as she focused on the heavy beat of his heart that had his body going taut as a trip wire.

She straightened, green fabric rustling, and gently nudged his shoulder forward. "Hurt?"

"Not much."

He thought he heard her mutter "liar" just before she moved the stethoscope down the back of his shirt and pressed the bell to the left of his spine.

The thought of how her hand would feel caressing his skin had him breathing in before she had to ask.

Twenty long seconds later, she hooked the earpieces around her neck. "Your lungs are clear. Look up."

He'd only been able to imagine how her hands would feel roaming his back. He knew for a fact that they felt as soft as satin when she slipped them up the sides of his neck and worked her fingers along the undersides of his jaws.

She did the same thing under his arms, her examination quick, efficient and totally impersonal.

"Your lymph glands feel normal and I'm not seeing any

signs of infection so far," she said, after she'd carefully lifted the bandage on his leg and checked the surgical wound. "You still have to finish the antibiotics, but I want to stay on top of your white count to make sure."

He hesitated. "You have to draw more blood?"

Alex didn't expect the faintly squeamish look that washed over Chase's stoically set face, or the edge of consternation that entered his voice. He thought nothing of pushing himself to his physical limits. Yet, the thought of getting stuck with a needle turned him as gray as ash.

"They won't take much," she assured him, too irritated to be sympathetic.

Her exam finished, she crossed her arms over her lab coat. "Now," she said, torn between wanting details of the meeting and wanting to throttle him, "I'm assuming everything went well with your brothers?"

There was something about her tone he didn't trust. The chill in it, probably.

"It went fine."

"You'll be seeing them again?"

"Tomorrow."

"Do you have any more hospital tours planned?"

"That's what we're finishing up. Attila told Ryan you were annoyed because you had to wait for your patient, so we cut it short."

"I never said I was annoyed."

"You think you had to?" His glance narrowed on her face, his expression one of pure disbelief. "The temperature is about twelve degrees in here," he informed her, though he sounded more curious than disturbed by the fact.

"If I'm concerned," she calmly stressed, preferring that to the more personal reactions he invariably evoked, "it's not because I had to wait. It's because of what you were doing. You didn't break your shoulder, but the muscles there are strained and bruised. You need that shoulder to heal so you can support your weight on crutches. It's not going to heal if you keep irritating the tissues.''

''It doesn't hurt that much.''

''That's because your medication is masking the discomfort. Pain is your body's warning system. It's what tells you something is wrong. Even with the medication it was hurting you to push yourself in that chair. I could see it.''

''You've never heard of no pain, no gain?''

''What works for you in a gym doesn't apply here.'' Despite her best efforts to avoid it, exasperation leaked through. ''I know you're accustomed to pushing yourself. And it probably goes against every fiber of your being to have to slow down. But you have to listen to your body. You also need to let go of that pride and let people help. If you go with your brothers again, you have to let one of them drive that thing for you.''

''I don't think so.''

''Fine. I'll tell them myself.''

''I'll put the tour off for a couple of days.''

''Your shoulder won't be healed enough.''

For a moment, Chase said nothing. He just sat with his elbows on the arms of the wheelchair, one hand resting loosely against his trouser-covered thigh. The thumb of his other hand was hooked under his chin, his curled fingers pressed to his top lip as he considered her.

If the odd light in his eyes was any indication, he was pushing her on purpose.

The thought that she amused him somehow had her starting for the door. ''I'm trying to help you. If you're not going to take me seriously—''

She was even with the side of his chair when he dropped his hand and curled fingers around her wrist. The rest of her words promptly stalled in her throat. Beneath his thumb, her pulse leapt. That betraying beat coincided with the slam of her heart against her ribs.

"I take you very seriously," he said, his glance boring into hers. "But you seem to think I'm operating with some overblown sense of pride. I'll be the first to admit there's nothing wrong with my ego, but you aren't seeing this from my perspective at all. I only rely on other people for information and whatever it is I've paid them to do. I'm not used to being dependent. The idea of not being able to get around on my own terrifies me. Okay?"

The fear didn't surprise her. What did was that he would admit it.

It seemed to surprise him, too. Defensiveness shifted over his carved features, hardening the line of his jaw. She doubted he ever revealed his vulnerabilities to anyone, much less allowed himself to acknowledge that he had them.

The fact that he had to let her see them didn't sit well at all.

The pressure on her wrist increased as he tugged her down. "Do you understand?" he demanded, his face inches from hers.

The heat of his hand seared into her skin. She could almost feel it course from where he held the fragile bones of her wrist to the quickening low in her belly. But it was the way he watched her mouth that made her heart feel as if it might pound its way out of her chest. He was looking at her as if he were sorely tempted to yank her closer and work out a few of his frustrations by discovering exactly how she would feel, how she would taste.

He wasn't the first male patient to reach for her. He was just the first to short-circuit the protective mechanism that would already have had her moving back. Every time she breathed, she drew his breath inside her. Every shallow, erratic breath that managed to escape her lungs filled him in turn.

His eyes darkened on hers.

"I understand," she whispered and told herself to move.

Chase let go first. When he did, it was clear from the displeasure shadowing his face that he hadn't been pleased with what he'd done.

Scrambling to collect her thoughts, Alex stepped back and crossed her arms over the nerves fluttering low in her stomach. She wasn't too pleased, either, but she needed to focus, to remember what they'd been talking about.

Dependence, she reminded herself, willing her heart rate to slow. He'd just told her he didn't rely on anyone unless he had to.

She told herself to remember that.

"You won't be dependent for long if you'll just give yourself a chance to get better." She tightened her hold on herself and took another step back. "There are things we can do to help you help yourself. Exercises and therapy," she elaborated, seeking the distance her job required.

She scanned his face, forcing herself to overlook the tension in it and focus on the fatigue. "Do you still want to stay in that chair?"

She was no longer annoyed. Wariness now shadowed her eyes. Seeing it, irritated with himself for having let his frustration get the better of him, Chase slowly shook his head. He didn't believe for a moment that she was offering to help him to the bed herself. She wasn't likely to get any closer to him than she absolutely had to right now.

"No," he murmured, figuring it wouldn't hurt to let her know he didn't want her that close, either. He was already thinking about her in ways that would make a stripper blush. If he were to get near enough to her to know how those lithe curves felt against his body, his frustration level would shoot right through the roof. "You can send Attila back in."

"Do you have any questions before I leave?"

She probably didn't even realize how relieved she looked when he told her he didn't. She didn't even bother to frown at his name for the nurse. She told him only that she'd send someone right in, and turned for the door.

He'd just heard her open it when his conscience made him stop her.

"What you did this morning," he began, "tracking down my bags and setting everything up, I mean. I know you didn't do it for me. You did it for Ryan and Tanner. But I appreciate it." He couldn't have faced that meeting today without her help.

With his back to her, he'd turned his head slightly as he'd spoken. He couldn't really see her. But he could feel her hesitation.

Alex stood with her hand on the edge of the door. Ahead of her stood the current bane of Chase's existence. Kay had practically been camped on the other side of the door.

"I'm glad it worked out," was all she could say before the woman pushed the door wide and cocked a curious eyebrow at her.

"You can help him into bed now," she told the nosy nurse. "He'll need ice and heat for his shoulder. Alternate those for ten minutes each for the next hour and keep him off crutches. I'm ordering physical therapy for his shoulder in addition to his leg. I'll be at Children's, then I'm going home."

Before Kay could say a word, Alex was moving away at her usual no-nonsense pace. With her insides churning, it felt more as if she were running.

It shouldn't have bothered her. She shouldn't let it matter that every time she got within six feet of him, she found herself getting upset, irritated or edgy. It shouldn't have mattered, either, that Chase so firmly believed people did things for him for reasons other than because they cared about him. He certainly wasn't concerned about it. The man deliberately sought emotional distance, so he was getting exactly what he wanted. But the admission had disarmed her. It was almost as if he'd pushed her away, only to pull her back again. And that bothered her, too.

The good news was that he wouldn't be around forever. The bad news was that he'd set himself back by pushing himself in that wheelchair. She hadn't cared to mention just how far back his progress had slipped, though. She was through arguing with him for the day. Right now, she wasn't even going to think about him anymore.

The tingling on her wrist mocked the assertion. But she wouldn't let herself consider the thoughts that had scrambled her mind when he'd pulled her down in front of him. If she did, she'd have to admit that the thought of being in his arms and meeting that hard, sensual mouth held far too much appeal.

She would also have to admit that she wouldn't have stopped him.

It was because Alex wanted to avoid any further arguments with Chase that she had Mike Reiker, a very Nordic-looking young man from the hospital's physical therapy department, with her when she broke the news to Chase the next day that he'd set himself back at least a week.

She was in a hurry because she had a patient in ICU that she was worried about, but Chase also needed to know he would need help at home after he was discharged. So she told him that Mike would assist him in coordinating home health care in Seattle, unless he had a friend he'd rather have stay with him.

Chase was well aware that he had no one to blame but himself for the delay in his recovery. She would have reminded him of that, too, had he given her any grief about his estimated recovery time. But he didn't challenge her with the other man present. He never challenged her when there was anyone else around. Not verbally, anyway.

"I'm not asking anyone to stay with me," he informed her, his tone even, his eyes fixed on her face. "And I'm not hiring a nurse. Just get me on crutches and I'll be fine."

"If you don't have help at home," Mike pointed out, oblivious to the faint tension snaking between patient and doctor, "it could be longer before you're released. We'd want to keep you until we know you can take care of yourself on your own."

"I'm not hiring anyone," he repeated in that same very civil but inflexible tone.

The flat refusal clearly puzzled Mike. After all, it wasn't as if Chase couldn't afford the help. "But, sir, you'd be able to leave sooner. I don't understand—"

"Dr. Larson does."

Chase held her glance, the certainty in his eyes melding with something that almost looked like defense. He'd left no doubt in her mind about how he felt about requiring that sort of assistance. And she remembered all too well how she'd come by that understanding. But this wasn't about what had happened when his frustration and fear had collided with her annoyance. It was about him not wanting to explain how he felt to anyone else.

Even if she hadn't been his doctor, she wouldn't have shared that information. For reasons she didn't have time to consider just then, it felt too personal, as if she would be betraying an even deeper trust.

"If that's the way he wants it," she said to the younger man, "we just won't let him go until you think he's ready."

She excused herself then, warning Mike not to let him push himself too hard, and headed for the door.

She could feel Chase's quiet scrutiny on her back in the moments before she turned into the hall to head for ICU. She had a patient rejecting an implant who would have to be taken back to surgery, a perfectly legitimate reason to leave the therapist to explain Chase's treatment to him. Yet, he had her feeling as if she were running from him again.

The problem was his unnerving ability to see straight through her defenses. The way he'd arched his eyebrow at her when she'd first walked in with Mike made it perfectly clear he knew she'd brought the strapping therapist along as a buffer.

Had she not been in the process of shifting mental gears, she might have been even more disturbed than she already was by how he was getting to her. But with a critical patient demanding her attention, her only thought about Chase was that the next time she saw him, she'd make sure she was alone. She might be drawn to him, and he might have worked past a couple of her rustier defenses, but she didn't need to prove it to him.

She didn't get the chance to make her point.

When she walked into his room the next morning, Chase was on the telephone, talking to his lawyer about the meeting taking place in Chicago at that very moment. He sent her an apologetic look, placed his hand over the mouthpiece and asked if she could please, just this once, check whatever she needed to check on him while he finished his conversation.

"It's a conference call," he explained.

Understanding perfectly how difficult it could be to get the requisite parties lined up for such a call, she gave a shrug, checked his shoulder and his leg and left him discussing stock options and bonus tie-ins.

The next day, he had his secretary there. The moment Alex walked in, Gwen Montgomery rose from the chair where she'd been going over lists on a legal pad. The woman introduced herself because Chase was, again, on the phone and immediately started to leave so Alex could examine her patient.

The slender, middle-aged woman seemed to epitomize the perfect executive assistant. She looked as professional as she did efficient. Her suit was tailored, her slightly graying dark hair was skimmed back in a sophisticated knot and she positively reeked organizational ability. Judging from the size of the rocks on her finger, she was also very married.

"There's no need for you to go anywhere," Alex told her, wishing she could pull off that polished look. "I'm just going to check his leg. He doesn't even need to get off the phone," she said, shaking her head at Chase when he held up one finger to indicate he'd cut his call short if she wanted him to. "We're getting this down to a system."

There really was no need to interrupt him. She could tell him his leg was looking good simply by giving him a smile. Which she did—and felt her pulse jump when his glance held hers long enough to stall her breath before he smiled back.

It didn't matter that the smile looked tired. Not just then, anyway. Her only thought was that the man didn't play fair. He didn't even have to touch her to jerk around with her heart rate.

Conscious of the other woman's presence, she glanced toward Gwen. Chase's secretary wasn't paying any attention to them at all. She was back in her chair with her lists.

Alex was gone a few moments later, leaving him to his calls and his secretary and telling herself it would do no good at all to remind the man that he needed rest. He'd just argue with her and that was what she was intent on avoiding.

She was pretty much convinced he was trying to avoid it, too, by the time she met Ronni and Kelly for lunch the next day.

"I'm sure there are details that Tanner left out. I mean, he was far more interested in the kind of construction Chase had used on his corporate tower than in where he'd been all his life. You should have seen him." Kelly's hazel eyes smiled as she leaned forward to be heard over the lunchtime buzz of conversation at Granetti's. "He was going on and on about some sort of plastic laminate Chase's contractor used to insulate something or other and all I wanted to know is what he thought of the man."

"What did he think?" Alex asked mildly.

"When I finally pinned him down, he said he seemed like a regular guy. In guyspeak, that's a compliment. Overall, I think he's adopted a wait-and-see attitude. Tanner's pretty reserved when it comes to really accepting people." She lifted her teacup. "He did say he thought the people who adopted Chase were a pair of 'real jewels,' though. So I think he's got a little sympathy going for him there."

"Ryan said pretty much the same thing. About the Harringtons," Ronni clarified. She'd pushed her chicken Caesar aside and sat with her arms crossed on the table, her fingers loosely wrapped below her elbows to keep from reaching for the basket of garlic-cheese bread. Two pieces were all she'd allowed herself. "It didn't sound as if Chase wanted to talk about his own life, though. He was more interested in what had happened to their natural parents and in the two of them. Apparently, he hadn't known he was adopted until Mr. Harrington died and the lawyer was reading the will."

"It was in the will?" Alex asked.

Ronni shook her head, red curls bouncing. "Ryan didn't say. I don't know how it came up. But can you imagine how that had to feel?"

"Or how about this?" Kelly asked, remembering something else. "Tanner said Chase asked his mother…his adoptive mother, I mean…why he hadn't been told before that he was adopted. Apparently, she said his adoptive father got him for her with the understanding that Chase never be told because he didn't want Chase's relatives showing up someday expecting financial help. I guess he figured that when he died it didn't matter anymore."

Alex nearly choked on her coffee. "Got him for her?"

"That makes it sound as if he was a toy or something," Ronni muttered.

"I'm still hung up on the part where the Harringtons obviously knew about his brothers. He had family they deliberately kept from him." Kelly shook her head in disbelief. "Tanner said Chase was really low-key about all of this, but it was pretty obvious he and the Harringtons had been estranged for a while before the old goat croaked."

Alex frowned into her coffee. She couldn't begin to imagine how Chase must have felt to have heard what he had. But she could clearly recall how unimpressed he'd looked when she'd told him that the only thing that mattered to his brothers was that he was family. It was easy to see now why the word had left him so cold.

"Have you met him yet?" the pregnant pediatrician asked, handing a passing waiter the basket of bread to get it out of her reach.

Kelly shook her head. "You?"

"Not yet. Ryan thinks it might be easier if we wait until he's discharged. He said if it were him, he'd want to feel better than Chase looks before springing a whole new family on him. What about you?'' she asked Alex. ''You're his doctor. What do you think of him?''

Alex gained a moment by leaning back to let the waitress take the remains of her salad. ''He's my patient,'' was all she was willing to say.

''We know that.'' Ronni's tone was as bland as the milk in her glass. ''We're not asking for anything confidential.''

''Which you could tell us anyway,'' Kelly informed her. ''He's our brother-in-law. That makes him family.''

''He's not immediate family.''

''Then how about a little professional courtesy?''

Ronni leaned closer, her voice dropping. ''She's avoiding the question.''

''No kidding.''

They were right.

They wanted to know how she felt about Chase. The problem was that she didn't want to *feel* about him at all.

''Let's just say that as a patient, he's…difficult,'' she allowed, since that was hardly a secret. ''He pushes himself too hard and his personality isn't well suited to taking orders.''

Ronni eyed her evenly. ''So we know what you think of him as a patient, but that's not what we're asking. What do you think of him as a man?''

''I try not to think of him that way.''

''Because he's a patient?'' Kelly inquired with deceptive innocence. ''Or because he happens to be an incredibly perfect specimen of Malone masculinity and he's getting under your skin?''

Alex's brow furrowed. ''I thought you said you hadn't met him.''

''I haven't.'' Smiling at her friend's unguarded response, Kelly lifted her shoulder in a shrug. ''But I've seen pictures. And every female in the hospital under the age of fifty is talking about him.'' The smile turned knowing. ''So what's going on?''

''Not a thing.'' Not a thing Alex could describe rationally, anyway. ''I'll admit he's gorgeous. And he's not as big a jerk as I first thought he was,'' Alex conceded. ''He's a complicated man, with a lot going on in his life right now. But that doesn't mean I care about him except as a patient. Or as Ryan and Tanner's brother.

''Even if he were interested in me, which I don't really think he is,'' she had to point out, because he'd seemed more cautious around her than anything else, ''he's not someone I'd want to get involved with. He'll be gone in a few days, anyway.''

Neither Kelly nor Ronni said a word. They just looked at each other as if to say the woman was protesting far too much, and glanced back at her.

''He's not going anywhere for at least three months,'' Ronni nonchalantly advised. ''Ryan leased the Pembroke estate for him.''

''He's staying at the Pembroke estate?''

''It's just sitting there empty since that little weasel, Axel Pembroke, absconded with the foundation funds. The foundation owns it anyway and they were more than happy to have someone like Chase Harrington lease it for a few thousand dollars a month. They've cleaned out all of Axel's personal stuff and changed the locks, but Ryan said the furniture's all still there. And the stuff in the kitchen.''

''I understand it has art,'' Kelly mused.

Ronni nodded. ''True. But I hear they've already sold the most valuable pieces and a couple of huge televisions.''

''Excuse me?'' Alex muttered as her friends veered off track. Glancing at her watch, she grimaced. Her afternoon appointments started in five minutes. Fortunately, the clinic was only three minutes away. ''What I meant was, he's staying in Honeygrove?''

Since it was her turn to buy, Ronni had snagged the check. Taking her credit card from her wallet, she looked at Alex in confusion. ''I thought you knew that. He said you told him he'd have to have a few months of therapy and since he has to do it somewhere, he might as well do it here.'' She dropped a platinum card on the bill. ''He's interested in the old Taylor Building across the street, too. I guess he could see it from his window and got curious about it. It's been empty for a year. He's looking into tearing it down and putting new medical offices in there.''

Chase hadn't said a word to her about his plans. But, then, there hadn't been any opportunity for discussion, either. He'd said he wasn't leaving Honeygrove until he'd accomplished what he'd come to do, but he'd connected with his brothers now, and she'd assumed he'd want to go back to Seattle as soon as he could. If he wanted to stay in Honeygrove, that was certainly his prerogative. The hospital's physical therapy department was excellent.

Focusing on the practicalities was what Alex would have done with any patient. And with any other patient, that was all the thought she would have given the matter as she gathered her purse a few minutes later and she and her friends left the crowded little restaurant. But Chase wasn't any other patient. And now that he was going to be around for a while, she didn't know if the knot in her stomach was one of anxiety or anticipation.

She wasn't going to worry about it. She had an afternoon of appointments, and after she picked up Tyler and Brent, who was staying with her now, she had to feed them, see to baths and whatever else they required before she sat down with the two charts she needed to review for surgeries in the morning. If she had time, she also had a tape of a new pediatric femoral reduction procedure she wanted to watch and a mountain of laundry to attack.

She fell asleep ten minutes into the tape and only finished half the laundry. Because she really needed the white load, she threw it into the washer on her way out the utility-room door the next morning. After adding soap while she verbally hurried Tyler along, she helped Brent secure his arm in his navy-blue canvas sling, then hustled them both into the garage and the car.

The fog of sleep had lifted while she'd stood under the shower listening to the ancient pipes rattle and her mind had been on fast forward ever since. She never assumed that her schedule for the day would hold, but she liked to pretend she had at least some control over her life by starting out the day with a plan.

Today, she would drop Tyler off first. Then Brent. Her latest houseguest had a long day of therapy ahead of him. But the sessions would be broken up by spending time in the therapy center's lounge and visiting with the friends he'd made on the med-surg floor.

Assuming her arthroplasty and her arthroscopy went well, she would then join Tyler for a quick lunch, see the four appointments she had in her office that afternoon, round on her patients in the hospital and be home with the boys in time to feed them something reasonably nutritious by seven. She still had the tape she wanted to watch, so she'd try it again after the boys went to bed.

She'd forgotten to feed the cat.

The thought of Tom meowing his little heart out in front of the pantry door had her turning around four blocks from her house. The delay only cost her five minutes. Next to nothing in the overall course of her day. But as she left the driveway for the second time that morning, the car's CD player booming Shania Twain instead of Disney since it was Brent's turn to pick the music, she couldn't help thinking that anyone who'd known her five years ago wouldn't believe what they were seeing now.

Before she'd become pregnant with Tyler, her world had been ordered, focused and almost boringly predictable. She'd known where she was going, what she wanted and when she was going to get it. She'd loved living that way. Her life had centered around medicine, an occasional trip to a museum or a symphony, and Dr. Matt Bowden. She'd been one of those rare people who was actually content with everything. Except the hideous hours and pressures of residency. But she'd known that wouldn't last forever. She'd just focused on the dream she and Matt had shared, until she'd become pregnant and Matt had pulled the plug on all their plans.

But that was ancient history. And her life had evolved in a totally different direction.

Out of sheer necessity, she'd developed a knack for rolling with the punches, and she didn't think much about what might have been. Her life was full. She had Tyler. And if she didn't always deal as well with chaos as people thought she did, that was her business. She was fine in a crisis. She could handle disruption. It was usually afterward, when she was alone at night, that she sometimes wondered how she'd made it through the day—and where she was going from there.

As she approached Chase's room at five o'clock that afternoon, she couldn't help thinking about the curve life had thrown him and wondering if maybe he didn't feel a little like that, too.

Chapter Six

The ring of the telephone at the nurses' station blended with the conversation of a doctor and nurse in the hall behind her when Alex stopped in the doorway of Chase's room. Beyond the dozen plants that had joined the lush tropical arrangement that had first caught her attention, she could see him on the telephone. Again.

He was speaking in low, certain tones as he tossed a notepad into the open briefcase on the narrow table bisecting his bed. A small calculator occupied the beige surface, along with a yellow legal tablet and a partially opened map.

She needed to talk to him about his decision to stay in Honeygrove. Apparently he needed to talk to her, too. The instant he caught her eye, he hesitated, his expression changing almost imperceptibly. Without breaking his visual hold, he murmured to his caller that he had to go.

"Is Gwen on a break?" she asked, since she'd halfway expected to find his secretary there.

''She's running errands for me.''

With one hand in the pocket of the open lab coat covering her knee-skimming gray jersey dress, another fingering the single pearl at her throat, Alex moved into the room. The late-afternoon light slanted through the narrow window blinds, glinting off his pen when he tossed that aside, too.

''Do you even know how to relax?'' she asked, frowning at the documents in the fax machine's receiving tray.

''Probably not.'' Totally at ease with the admission, he ran a glance the length of her legs and skimmed to where she fingered the pearl resting just above her breasts. ''But you shouldn't have any problem relating to that.''

Realizing what she was doing, she dropped the pearl and shoved her hand into her pocket. ''I shouldn't?''

''You're the one with the medical practice, a four-year-old, a menagerie and a rotating door on your guest room. All I'm doing is trying to keep from climbing the walls.''

There was still a certain caution about him, the same watchfulness that made her feel as if he were guarding what he said and did around her. It was just less noticeable with that droll glint in his eyes. ''It's not a menagerie,'' she informed him, determinedly matching his ease. ''It's only a cat, two goldfish and a gerbil.''

''Tanner said it was a rescued lab rat.''

Confusion caused her to hesitate. ''Why were you and Tanner talking about something like that?'' Their resident rodent wasn't a rat. Tanner just said it looked like one.

The glint in those intense blue eyes disappeared. Looking as if he wasn't sure just how much he should admit, or how much he wanted her to know, Chase watched her continue to the foot of his bed. ''I asked him about you. Ryan, too,'' he finally decided to say. ''I make it a point to know everything I can about the people around me.''

Dismissing the admission with a shrug, his gaze narrowed on her face. "From what I understand, the only time you slow down is to collapse. Considering that, you have no room to criticize how I choose to spend my time."

He wasn't challenging her. He sounded as if he were merely stating a fact he knew she couldn't dispute in order to answer the first question she'd asked.

"Our circumstances are hardly the same." Reaching into her pocket at the electronic beep of her pager, she glanced down at the number she was to call. Not recognizing it as one that required immediate attention, she ignored the page along with the validity of Chase's assertion. "I'm not the one who needs rest."

He might have argued that one with her. Sparring with Alex Larson had been the brightest spot of the past six days and he truly wouldn't have minded the diversion now. But ever since he'd made the mistake of touching her, they'd avoided disagreement as diligently as they would a stroll through a minefield.

Knowing she was leery of him, all he considered as she turned to his unbandaged leg was that he was growing more intrigued with her by the day.

He'd taken it for granted that she was divorced. But Ryan had said she'd never been married. His brother hadn't known who her child's father was, though, or the circumstances that had led to her raising a child alone. It hadn't occurred to Chase that she was doing so much on her own. From everything he'd heard, it seemed, too, that she was always willing to take on more.

Or, maybe, he thought, studying the graceful curve of her neck, it wasn't a willingness so much as it was a need.

There was a restlessness about her. He recognized it because he felt it himself. Fought it relentlessly. Even when she looked tired, something inside her wouldn't let her stay completely still.

At that very moment, absorbed in her assessment, that inner agitation showed. He doubted anyone else would notice. The hand inside the pocket of her lab coat was moving almost imperceptibly. He'd bet every share of stock he owned that she was worrying something between her fingers.

"There was something neither Ryan nor Tanner could tell me."

"What was that?" she asked, absent-mindedly withdrawing her hand to flick a piece of thread into the trash sack taped to his nightstand.

"Why you became a doctor. And why you chose orthopedics? I figured I should know since I'll be under your care for a few more months."

If she suspected any other reason for his interest, there was nothing in her expression to betray it. She didn't even look surprised that he was staying. "I wondered when you were going to mention that."

"Sounds like you've been talking to my brothers, too."

"Ronni and Kelly."

"It seems we have our own personal grapevine."

"Seems so," she agreed, mirroring his faint smile.

"So, why orthopedics? What made you choose that over everything else?"

"It fascinated me," she said, suddenly looking as relaxed as he'd seen her in days. "I remember sitting down with an encyclopedia when I was a girl, trying to figure out how a bird I'd found was put together so I could set its wing. My dad helped me. A lot," she added, her mouth curving. "But when the bird actually healed and flew away, I decided I wanted to be able to do that for people, too."

"Put them together when they were broken?"

"Something like that."

"How old were you?"

"Twelve."

The memory was more than just a story she related to satisfy the curious. Chase was sure of that. There was a softness about her smile, and a light in her lovely brown eyes that spoke of something he rarely ever saw. He was seeing affection, he realized. The kind of feeling a child has for a parent she respects.

He couldn't imagine the man who'd raised him doing anything like her father had done. Walter Harrington would have regarded a request such as hers as totally frivolous and demanded to know why he was pestering him with something so insignificant.

The thought should have chafed more than it did. Focused on the healing warmth of her smile, he realized he wasn't really thinking of what had been. He was wondering more what life would be like for a child with a father like hers. He knew nothing of children, but his brothers had them. They were crazy about their kids, too. Maybe even patient the way her father had been.

She tipped her head, the smile lingering. "What made you change your mind about staying?"

"I'd never made up my mind," he corrected, as her pager went off again. "One of the perks of doing what I do for a living is that I can do it from just about anywhere." He nodded toward the window. "There's some property out there that could use developing. And Ryan can use some help pulling together the rest of the funding for that wing. I have a few friends who might see a pediatric wing as a good cause. Especially since it's tax deductible."

He didn't have to stay in Honeygrove to supply that kind of help. He could make those calls from anywhere. She knew he knew it, too.

"I imagine you could also use some time to get to know your brothers."

She wasn't sure what it was, the way he held her glance or the way it finally faltered, but she knew his brothers were the main reason he wanted to stay. He just didn't want to admit they mattered that much.

She also suspected that he didn't want to hear how generous it was of him to offer to help.

"So how does it look down there?" he asked, pointedly changing the subject.

He'd nodded toward the railroad track of stitches crossing his lower thigh. Another set of sutures angled upward beyond the pins holding bone in place. It was the sort of injury that hurt to look at. Especially with the barbaric-looking device holding him together.

"A lot better than I would have expected it to at this stage. You've surprised me," she admitted graciously. "It usually doesn't look this good for another week."

"I could have told you nothing slows me down for very long."

"You haven't had to. I've been getting that message."

"Dr. Larson?" A pretty young nurse's aide with a high, sunny-blond ponytail poked her head around the doorway. "I'm sorry to interrupt, but your office has been trying to page you to call your neighbor. When you didn't answer they told her to try here."

"My neighbor?"

"Mrs. Mason. She's on the phone at the desk."

The Masons had the married son with the Cobra sports car that Tyler was always talking about. Alex knew them well enough to wave to them and to pick up their newspaper when they went away on weekends, but she couldn't imagine why Gladys would be calling her at the hospital.

"Would you please ask her what she wants?"

"She already said." The aide's round face screwed up in an expression reminiscent of Tyler faced with a plate of broccoli. "I know it sounds weird, but she said there's water coming out of your garage and running down the street."

"It's no wonder you don't know how to relax," Chase muttered.

Giving Chase a droll glance that had him arching his eyebrow, she turned on her heel and headed out to take the call. She knew perfectly well how to relax. Give her thirty minutes in a hot bath and she'd be pure putty. She just hadn't had the chance to truly unwind lately. And this particular week was just more hectic than most because she had Brent to get up and moving in the mornings.

Overlooking the fact that she *always* had others she needed to worry about in her life, she took the call that confirmed there was, indeed, water flowing from her garage. But as far as Alex was concerned, there were crises and there were crises.

In the overall scheme of things, a little water hardly constituted a catastrophe. The interruption was an inconvenience, to be sure, but she figured that if water was coming from the garage, the water heater must have broken or cracked or whatever it was old water heaters did. She'd just go home and turn off the water, and tonight she could mop it up from the garage and call Tanner about where she should buy a replacement and who she could hire to install it. As long as she had a plumber there, he could fix her drippy washing machine too. She'd been meaning all week to get it fixed, anyway.

Ten minutes later, she hit the automatic garage-door opener as she pulled into the drive and felt minor annoyance turn to something that felt suspiciously like dread. The water heater sat a few feet from the door leading into the house. But the water wasn't coming from it. It was leaking from beneath the door which led straight into the utility room.

The pipe leading to the washing machine had burst. Probably not long after she'd left for work.

It wasn't just a little water, either. And it wasn't only in the utility room and garage. The door from the utility room to the kitchen was open and water had flowed freely into the dining room. The living room. The hall. The bedrooms.

It had soaked every square inch of carpeting, been drawn a foot up the walls, into the drapes, and had seeped into furniture and closets.

As she stood in her stocking feet on her warping hardwood floor, trying to coax down the cat clinging to the top of the fridge, her only thought was she didn't dare let herself think beyond what immediately needed to be done.

She needed to call her insurance person. She had to finish rounds, dictate chart notes, pick up the kids, come back and pack up whatever clothes and things they'd need for the next…what. Week?

She remembered telling Tyler they'd go to the video store on the way home to rent something about fast cars, since that was his latest thing, but that had just dropped to the bottom of the list.

Guilt joined the knot of other less-definable sensations twisting her stomach. She hated disappointing her little boy. But as she left a message on her insurance agent's voicemail, and another at Ronni's office to please call as soon as she could, her priority was finding them a place to spend the night. She could leave the goldfish and gerbil for now, but the cat would have to go with them.

By six o'clock Alex had made arrangements with Ronni for her and her brood to stay in their guest house for the night. The tiny house was far too small to contain an active pre-schooler, the Larson pets, Alex and a teenage boy, so

Ronni had offered to put Brent up in the main house that evening.

The imposition was huge, but tomorrow, Alex would come up with something else. One day at a time. It was how she'd lived her life for the past five years.

She was thinking more in terms of one hour at a time when Ryan called her at her office just as she hung up from checking on the patient in ICU who had her far more worried than she'd let on to his family.

"Of course you're welcome to use the guest house, Alex," he said, after he'd told her that his wife had just told him what had happened. "But I have a solution that'll be a lot less hassle for you.

"I just left Chase," he hurried on. A riffling sound filtered through the line, making it sound as if he were gathering up papers. "The house he's renting is huge, and since you're not discharging him for a few more days, you can stay there. That will give you time to make more long-term arrangements while your house is being repaired and you won't have to farm out the boy. I'm running late, so I've got go, but you can pick up the key from Chase."

"Ryan. Wait a minute." Her mind raced as she toed around under her desk for her shoe. "It's very nice of you to—"

"Hey, it's nothing," he interrupted, obviously thinking she was thanking him. Which she was. Or would. Or had planned to do, right along with declining the arrangement. "Good luck."

The phrase served as a sentiment and a goodbye. Before she could do much more than draw a breath, he'd hung up.

That breath leaked out like a slowly deflating tire as she reached across her neat oak desk with its mauve blotter and replaced the receiver. It wasn't at all unusual for Ryan Malone to do what he'd just done. He was known for taking charge and taking over, a trait that tended to get the job done with a minimum of fuss since his diplomatic skills were usually excellent. At the moment, however, his solution for her and her charges simply left her feeling railroaded.

She couldn't accept the arrangement. She wouldn't even consider it. Since Ryan wasn't available, she'd just have to deliver a polite refusal to Chase after she rounded on her last patient.

Having found her shoe, she slipped it on, and snagged her jacket from the brass coat tree by an overstuffed peach tweed guest chair. It didn't make a lot of sense that Ryan's call should have left her feeling more agitated than anything else that had gone wrong in the past two hours, but it did. Probably, she figured, because his well-intentioned effort to help had just added one more thing for her to do in a day that was already pushing its quota.

Occupied with that thought, she slipped on her jacket and promptly grimaced when the sleeve dragged over the cat scratches stinging the inside of her arm.

Tom hadn't gone willingly into his carrier. He hated the thing. Not that Alex could blame him. The only time he was ever in it was when she took him to the vet, an experience he hardly relished. But he'd fought even more than usual today. She swore that every time she'd tried to stuff him through the door, he'd stiffened and spread every appendage he had so he wouldn't fit through it.

He was in the carrier now. She'd set it between a tall potted palm and her bookcase because she thought he'd feel more secure in the cozy spot, and he was looking pathetically through the wire window on the molded plastic box. If he was trying to make her feel bad, he was succeeding. But at least he wasn't pacing and meowing anymore. That had been harder to watch.

It had come too close to reminding her of how Chase had to feel—except the image that had come to mind when she'd thought of him was more of a panther pacing his cage.

The fact that Chase kept slipping to the forefront of her thoughts when there was so much else on her mind wasn't a good sign at all.

"I really appreciate the offer. It's very generous of you," she said to the man silently watching her from his raised bed. "But I can't stay there."

The overhead lights caught hints of silver in Chase's dark hair. She barely noticed the bruising or the Steri-strips on the gash high on the ridge of his cheekbone. She was far more conscious of the unnerving habit he had of seeing right through her.

"I'm not being generous. I'm being practical. You need a place to stay and there's a perfectly good house sitting there empty. And it's not that you can't," he blandly informed her. "It's that you don't want to."

Having clarified their positions, he eyed her with the same cool aplomb he undoubtedly employed at the negotiating table. "Why not?"

She hadn't expected him to force her hand. When he'd set aside the newspaper he'd been reading when she'd walked in, she'd thought for sure he would shrug off her refusal. After all, her little problem shouldn't matter to him one way or another.

"For one thing," she returned, latching onto the first argument that came to mind, "you're my patient. It wouldn't be professional."

"So I'm your patient. I'm also the brother of friends of yours. There's nothing unprofessional about you staying out there. No more so than having a patient live with you.

Which you already do,'' he pointed out, clearly referring to Brent.

She stood even with his knees, a foot from the edge of the mattress and the white thermal blanket spilling over it. His tone was utterly reasonable, his argument logical. It was the knowing look in his expression that kept her arms crossed over her lab coat to keep her hands away from the pearl.

''I won't even be there,'' he murmured, making it clear he knew exactly what lay at the heart of her objection.

She was about to tell him she realized that when he turned away to pick up something from the tray-table on the opposite side of the bed. Eyeing her tightly crossed arms when he turned back, he reached toward her and slipped his fingers around her exposed wrist. As he did, his knuckles brushed the soft undercurve of her breast.

Soft flesh yielded to hard bone. At the intimate contact, his glance jerked to hers, something electric charging the air and jolting inward where he touched. Her breath hitched. An instant later, the line of his jaw tightened along with his grip on her wrist and he tugged her toward him.

''Let go,'' he muttered, and pulled her hand free.

Alex winced as the motion rubbed the scratches.

Whatever he'd been about to do was forgotten. His dark eyebrows shot together as he eased her hand over and pushed up the cuff of her jacket.

Three needle-fine crimson lines slashed the pale skin of her forearm and wrist.

''What did you do?''

''I didn't do anything. Tom just didn't want to go for a ride.''

''Tom?''

''The cat.''

"That's original," he muttered. "Did you put anything on this?"

"Of course...not," she concluded lamely. "I will. I just haven't had time."

She'd thought he'd let go. Instead, with her hand resting in his, he touched his finger to the edge of a particularly angry-looking welt. There was incredible strength in that long elegant hand, but it was the gentleness that caught her breath in her lungs. His touch was light, more sensation than actual contact.

Her pulse scrambling, she saw his scowl intensify. It was almost as if he were imagining how the small injury would sting as he paralleled the scratch across the fine blue veins inside her wrist.

When he reached the heartbeat echoed there, she realized that he'd held her frozen with nothing more than a touch.

She couldn't begin to imagine what sort of mastery he'd have over her if he ever pulled her into his arms.

"The way I see it," he said, his voice sounding a little rougher than it had moments ago, "you helped me with Ryan and Tanner, so I owe you one." His eyes steady on hers, he dropped a key in her palm and folded her fingers over it. "I don't like owing people. Now we're even.

"Don't," he warned, the instant she opened her mouth. "You can't come up with a single reason that's going to convince me you won't be wasting time by not moving in there."

There was no denying that the man expected to get his way. He was accustomed to it, after all, and she'd seen little evidence to prove that he didn't get pretty much what he wanted, whether it was good for him or not. She'd caved in a time or two herself.

Having fought hard to pull her life out of the tailspin it had once been in, she envied the control that came to him so easily. But she had more than just herself to consider. And she couldn't fault his logic no matter how hard she tried.

With the boys and the cat waiting to be picked up, and with them and a gerbil to feed and clothes to gather, she had no business worrying about the crazy things he did to her heart rate.

As if he knew her concession was coming, he picked up a slip of paper from the tray-table.

"You'll need this. It's the security code," he said, handing her the folded white square. "There isn't a garage-door opener. I guess Pembroke took off with it and the estate hasn't bought a replacement yet. I'll be using a limo service to get back and forth to therapy, so I told them not to bother on my account. Just leave your car in the driveway." He settled back against the pillow. "Do you know how to get there?"

"I know it's on the west side." That was the part of town with the views. "But I don't have the address."

"Thirty-six Ridge Commons. There's a map in my briefcase if you need one. Gwen will be in and out," he continued, moving on to wrap up details now that the agreement had been reached. "She's set up the office for me and put my clothes in the master bedroom. Take any of the other rooms you want."

"Is she staying there?"

"She's in a hotel, but she's going back to Seattle in a couple of days. I'll fly her down when I need her back here."

Slipping the things Chase had given her into her pocket, Alex felt the tug of a frown. "Why aren't you doing that? Staying in a hotel, I mean? I understand the new hotel on the river has a couple of beautiful suites. You'd have room and maid service right there."

"Not enough space. I can handle a hotel for a week, but not for three months. I'd feel like I was in a cage."

The picture of the panther flashed through her mind. Dark, predatory. All that leashed energy restlessly prowling the perimeter of his confines.

The image disturbed her, but so did Chase's plans. "Your therapist said you still aren't planning to have any-one help you when you leave here. I know how strongly you felt about dependence," she hurried on before they could get into that discussion again. "But it would be better if there was someone around. You'll have a housekeeper, won't you?"

"I'll be the only one living there. I told you, I'll be fine. And I will. We're talking about what you need right now," he flatly reminded her. "Not me."

"What I need doesn't matter." Her knee-jerk response had her folding her arms again, the posture hinting faintly at exasperation. "I can understand why you don't want a nurse, Chase. And I'm not pushing that idea. I just can't picture you in a kitchen or with a dust rag. Especially on crutches. Do you have a religious objection against hired help?"

"I do fine in a kitchen. In fact," he said, her hesitation at that claim pleasing him enormously, "I make a shrimp linguine that will bring you to your knees. I've just never liked the idea of having hired strangers living in my house. I've never even seen the woman who takes care of my place in Seattle. She cleans and she leaves. Gwen found her for me. She should be able to find someone like that here."

The vision Alex had of him with an entire staff gave way to the realization that he lived completely alone. Something about that caused more air to leak from his overinflated public image of arrogant demanding tycoon. He could be demanding all right. But he wasn't a man who expected to be waited on. People just expected him to expect it.

What she hadn't anticipated was that he could cook.

"Excuse me, Doctor."

The same blond nurse's aide who'd advised Alex of her flood leaned around the edge of the doorway. "Sorry to interrupt," she said, including Chase in her dazzling white smile. "But Child Care needs to know if they should give Tyler dinner or if you're picking him up."

Chase watched Alex's attention snap to her watch. The expression was fleeting, so quick he wouldn't have caught it had he not been studying her so closely. Her eyes closed for a instant, the energy sagging from her. Yet, even as she drew the breath that straightened her slender shoulders, she was smiling easily at the woman waiting for her reply.

"Please tell them I'm on my way," she said, her betraying reaction to the duties pulling at her completely masked. "I'll be there in five minutes."

"No rest for the wicked?"

His quiet comment drew her glance back to his. He'd hoped to catch a fragment of that smile. There was a quiet softness about it that he found far more appealing than the cheerleader quality of the young blond's. What he caught instead was a hint of the weariness he wondered if Alex ever admitted. "Something like that."

"You'd better go."

She gave him a nod, took a step back.

"And don't think about it," he warned, certain she was still wrestling with the idea of staying at the house he'd leased. He'd never had to ask anyone to take anything from him before, much less argue them into it. People were usually angling to get a piece of him. But something about this woman told him she could accept help for everyone but herself.

What I need doesn't matter.

"The decision's been made," Chase said.

Yeah, Alex thought, by you and your brother. But all she did was give him a look that let him know she was acting under duress and offered a quiet, "Thank you."

If Alex had been able to come up with a better solution, she would have. But she couldn't on such short notice. There was no way, either, that any solution of hers would have landed her where she found herself at nine o'clock that evening.

The Pembroke house was huge.

It was also very…white.

Inside. Outside. Ceilings, walls, floors and furniture.

"Awesome," Brent murmured, standing in the hall and gaping at the enormous crystal chandelier hanging from the center of the octagonal living room that looked a football field away.

"It looks like ice," Tyler concluded, except he was staring at the gleaming white marble floor that did, indeed, look slick enough to skate on.

"Don't touch a thing," she ordered the two boys and set the cat, still in his carrier, on the tail of the cream marble P inlaid in the entry floor. "And stay here. I'll be right back."

She headed for the wide hallway on the left, flipping on lights and found an office, library and four bedrooms, the largest of which was half the size of her house and obviously the master. Sweeping back through the entry, encouraged to find that the boys had only moved to the edge of the white carpet that spread like a snowfield through the living and dining rooms, she told them to back up and gave herself a whirlwind tour of the opposite wing.

That end of the house contained an enormous brass,

glass and white kitchen, and two small suites obviously intended for children. Or, possibly, the servants. The bedrooms with their individual bathrooms were also done in shades of beige, a color more compatible with young males.

Those rooms were where she ushered the boys before shutting the tall, arched glass-paned doors that closed off the kitchen from the dining room and the skating rink of an entryway and she declared everything but the kitchen wing off-limits.

She'd become fairly adept over the past few years at schlepping the various items a child required whenever he traveled more than a block. Though her energy was beginning to wane, afraid to slow down and discover just how low her reserves were getting, she left Brent in charge of Tyler while she dragged in their bags, the gerbil and the little bowl of goldfish and made up the beds with the bedding she'd brought from the house because she hadn't been sure what she'd find available.

By ten-thirty the boys were asleep, and she was in the bathroom dragging a cotton sleepshirt over her head and fighting a totally insane urge to cry.

She was just tired. The day had been impossibly long. And tomorrow would be even longer.

Self-defense had her cutting off the thought before she could even begin to mentally list all she had to do. Pressing her index finger and thumb to her eyes, she drew a long, steadying breath.

She wouldn't think about tomorrow. Not now. Right now, she told herself, pushing her fingers up to massage the tension in her forehead, she needed to concentrate on something that didn't threaten to overwhelm her. She needed to focus on a serene place, somewhere quiet, safe, free of demands.

She usually imagined her fantasy bath.

All she could see was a chiseled face with blue eyes that seemed to see straight to her soul.

All she could think about was Chase and how those eyes had darkened when his hand brushed her breast, and the incredible gentleness of his touch when he'd traced the marks on her arm.

So much for serene, she thought, and reached for the washcloth she'd had to borrow from Chase's room. She didn't want the attraction she felt to him. All it did was taunt her with needs she'd finally managed to bury. She wanted someone to share with, to rely on. Someone who cared enough about their relationship not to bolt because things weren't going his way.

Chase shared with her, but it was more out of necessity and frustration than any desire to be close. He didn't want to rely on anyone, much less need someone to be there for him. And as for having his way, that wasn't even worth thinking about.

If she could just feel about him the way she felt about his brothers, she'd be fine.

The electronic warble of the telephone filtered in from the kitchen. Fighting the urge to sigh, she wiped her hands on a towel she'd also had to borrow and slipped into the kitchen. She'd already given her service the phone number. She was sure Ryan had it too.

Desperately hoping it wasn't the service, she headed for the portable phone housed below a row of glass-doored cabinets. An acre of white granite counters reflected the stove light she'd left on and caught the glint of brass pots hanging above the wide center island.

"Dr. Larson," she answered.

"Did I wake you?"

"No. No," she repeated, conscious of the way Chase's

deep voice rumbled through her. "Why aren't you sleeping?"

"Because I'm not tired. Listen, can you find the office my secretary set up and see if there's a file marked ZyTek in there? I need it in the morning."

Touching her fingers to her forehead, she began rubbing again. "Do you want me to look now?"

Finding the file was hardly an imposition. It was just a short walk down a long hall and she could take him with her since the phone was portable. What bothered her was that even at this hour, he wasn't ready to wind down for the day and let himself rest.

"I don't want to interrupt whatever you're doing. Just bring it whenever you get to the hospital." He paused, making her aware of the steady hum of the refrigerator. "How's the house?"

She thought he'd been about to say good-night. Since he hadn't, she dropped her hand and leaned against the counter.

"It's…big," she told him, thinking he was just after another opinion since he hadn't seen it himself. "I don't know what Ryan or your secretary told you about it, but if it's space you're after, you've got it."

"I meant for you. How is it for you and the kids?"

She hadn't expected the question. Or the concern in his voice. She wanted to believe she'd only imagined it. Feeling the way she did, tired, a little needy, that concern was far too seductive.

"Alex?"

The way he said her name, nearly stripped her defenses.

"It's perfect. Really," she assured him because the odd tightening in her chest had robbed her first words of strength. "I really appreciate—"

"That's not what I want. I just wanted to make sure you

got in all right. And to make sure you have everything you need there. If you don't, let me know. I'll call Gwen and she'll get it for you.''

The thought of calling the secretary he'd imported from Seattle to bring the towels she'd forgotten in Honeygrove almost made her laugh.

The sound that escaped her throat sounded more like a sob.

"Hey," he murmured. "Are you all right?"

The honeyed tones of his voice washed over her, the soothing sounds drawing the tension from her shoulders, coaxing her eyes to close. He couldn't see her, but she shook her head at his question and threaded her fingers through her hair once more.

She wasn't all right. When he'd folded the key into her palm and told her they were even, his message couldn't have been any clearer had he written it in Magic Marker on the surgical schedule board. He wanted no personal obligations. He wanted no strings. She'd reminded herself of that not three minutes ago. Yet, he was pulling her to him, anyway.

"I'm fine," she said. She'd survived far worse days. It was fatigue. And maybe a little mental overload. Nothing she couldn't handle with a few hours' sleep.

The length of Chase's pause seemed to question her conclusion. "Get some rest, Alex."

Chapter Seven

"Did you have any trouble finding it?" Chase asked, setting aside the ZyTec file Alex had just handed him.

"There were only three files on the desk and it was right on top. Is there anything else you need from there?"

His glance skimmed over the earth-tone casual slacks and white T-shirt she wore to settle once more on her face. Her short, silky hair was swept back from her delicate features, making her dark eyes look huge and drawing his eyes to the peach tint glossing her lush mouth. The slight fullness of her bottom lip was what usually drew his attention, along with those languorous eyes and just about everything else about her. This morning, he was more conscious of the faint shadows beneath her lower lashes.

"Thanks. This was it," he told her, though he hadn't really needed the file at all. He was feeling a little guilty about that, too. It was Saturday and she'd come to the hospital just for him. When he'd called last night, he hadn't thought about her schedule. He'd just wanted an excuse to see if she was all right. He wasn't quite sure why it had felt so necessary to make sure she was okay. But it had. And he always went with his instincts.

"What's your insurance company doing about your house?"

She dropped the chart she'd also brought onto the bed. He knew she didn't have to check him over. The doctor on call from the clinic would have done it. But he'd overheard Alex telling his nurse moments ago, that she'd check him over herself, since she was there anyway. Then, she'd be on her way to the mall for the haircuts and shoes she hadn't managed last weekend.

"I dropped a key off with my agent so a crew could start pumping out water," she told him, her tone lacking the deep-seated fatigue he'd heard on the phone. Slipping her hand under his knee, she gently lifted upward. "My agent said the adjuster will be there sometime Monday morning, but I'll be in surgery, so I don't know when I'll talk to him."

Easing his knee back down, she glanced toward him. "On a scale of one to ten with ten the worst, how much did that hurt?"

Since he hadn't been thinking about his leg, he paused. "Maybe a three," he decided. "Did the water get up into the walls?"

"And the drapes and the furniture."

"Those are easy to clean or replace. It's the structural damage you have to worry about. How high up were the water marks?"

"I don't know for sure. It could have been a couple of inches. It could have been a foot." A sigh slipped into her voice. "I just remember seeing a darker border along the kitchen and living-room walls."

The fact that she didn't remember surprised him. The woman was normally observant to a fault. Her mind was trained to soak in details, sort the important from the extraneous and react accordingly. Either she hadn't thought this particular detail mattered, or the enormity of the problem had been too much to deal with all at once and she had blocked everything but what she'd needed to deal with just then.

Strongly suspecting the latter, he leaned forward to let her slip his gown from his bruised shoulder. Her hands were gentle, her touch clinical.

She might as well have slipped that small, soft palm over his chest and down his stomach.

"What kind of floors do you have?" he asked, ruthlessly ignoring the way his body stirred. "Not hardwood, I hope."

"Only the entry and kitchen. But it looked okay. The rest is carpeted."

"There's probably wood under that. I have a hotel in San Francisco that had some pretty extensive water damage. It's not necessarily what you can see that you have to worry about."

She shot him a level glance. "I don't think I really wanted to know that. Lift your arm for me," she instructed, shoving her own concerns aside to concentrate on him. "I want to see how your range of motion is coming along. And don't go beyond where it starts to hurt," she warned him, as if she knew he'd do exactly that.

She cupped her hand on his shoulder to feel the motion of the joint muscles beneath as he did as she asked. When Mike-the-therapist did that, Chase was aware of a dull ache and the pull of hard muscle and bone. With Alex, he was far more conscious of the heat of her palm and the sensation of muscles relaxing, of somehow being soothed. Calmed.

In a way, it was almost as if he were being healed, a thought he once would have dismissed as both naive and improbable. The feeling had nothing to do with anything mystical. It wasn't even because she was a physician and healing was her job. It was just…her.

"Good," she murmured. Genuine pleasure at his progress warmed her eyes. Sliding his gown up his arm, she pulled the back ties together so he could sit back against the raised mattress and pillow. "Mike had said you were doing really well. You can try crutches today."

"I'd planned on it."

The smile in her eyes turned to forbearance, but she said nothing as she glanced toward the IV pump she'd ordered disconnected. Her examination finished, she was checking her bases, making sure she hadn't forgotten anything before she moved on.

He knew her time was at a premium. He also suspected that she'd been operating at her present pace for so long she didn't even know how to slow down. Having spent years caught up in that same sort of constant motion, he was coming to recognize more of himself in her every day.

What he didn't recognize was the intense awareness she provoked in him. The physical attraction he could understand. There was nothing complicated about sex. It was his awareness of what was going on inside her—and the fact that he cared about it—that was so unfamiliar.

Beneath the soft cotton of her shirt, her shoulders seemed to have sagged with the weight of her thoughts. Yet, she immediately did what he'd seen her do a dozen times before. In the space of seconds, she'd drawn a breath that straightened the steel in her spine. Only now, the expression he'd once taken for calm composure looked more like resignation.

"Why don't you give me your insurance agent's phone

number?'' he suggested, a troublesome empathy tugging at him. He couldn't imagine what made her push herself the way she did. She had family, friends, a career she truly seemed to love. Yet, she was running from something. Or hiding. The signs were too uncomfortably familiar. ''I can deal with him and the adjuster for you.''

The surprise Alex felt at Chase's offer showed clearly in her face. She would have given up a rib not to have to deal with the hassle of playing phone tag with Mr. Chester-please-call-me-Chet Skinner and whoever the insurance company sent to handle the claim. But the problem was hers.

''I appreciate the offer, but it's my fault the place flooded. I'll take care of the mess. Besides,'' she added, getting to the root of her refusal, ''you've done enough by letting us stay in your house. You don't need to do something like that.''

A frown entered his voice. ''How do you figure it's your fault?''

''I'd been meaning to call a plumber and I didn't.''

''Because you didn't have time,'' he concluded flatly.

''Because I didn't take the time,'' she clarified, thinking he ought to appreciate the difference. He was the one into semantics, after all.

She had fallen asleep thinking about the concern she'd heard in his voice last night. It had been her first conscious thought when she'd awakened that morning. Though she was a little afraid to believe it, it almost sounded as if he were concerned about her now. Or she might have thought so if he hadn't been scowling at her.

''Why would you want to deal with it, anyway?''

''Because it makes sense. You don't have time to take care of it and I do.''

It was hard to argue with a person when he sounded so reasonable. It was even harder when he was right.

"You wouldn't refuse if Ryan or Tanner made the offer, would you?"

He posed the question mildly, but she didn't doubt for a moment that he knew exactly how loaded it was. If she told him she wouldn't, she'd be admitting she was refusing because of him and she'd be walking on quicksand if they headed there. If she said she would refuse, he'd want to know why and she wasn't sure she could answer that without sinking herself, either.

He had her nailed anyway.

"I didn't think I was the only one who had trouble accepting help," he finally said, his voice as flat as a slab. "You don't like to do it, either, do you?"

There was accusation in his words. What threw her was the understanding there, too.

The understanding lured her. The accusation required defense.

"Sometimes it's just easier not to rely on other people too much."

"I know I have a problem with that," he admitted, since he knew she was already well aware of it. "But why do you?"

His eyes held hers, the quiet intensity of them drawing her in, drawing her closer even though she never moved from where she stood beside his bed.

"Does it have anything to do with your son's father?"

His perception startled her. "What do you know about Matt?"

"Absolutely nothing. Except that you didn't marry him."

He spoke as if it had been her choice. But that wasn't how it had been at all. She'd adored Matt—until she'd realized that the only thing they'd truly had in common was their love of medicine. "It was the other way around. He didn't marry me."

"Why not?"

The question was so simple, so blunt, so…Chase.

"Because I got pregnant and a baby wasn't in the plan."

"The plan?"

It was more of a grand scheme actually. Alex didn't usually talk about the direction she'd once thought her life would take, but that was more because she'd grown beyond that time than because there was any pain in the recollection. At least, there wasn't any now.

"Matt and I were going to get married and open a clinic with two of our friends when I finished my residency," she explained, her voice low and matter-of-fact. "It takes an enormous amount of planning and money to open your own practice, and when I got pregnant, Matt wouldn't even hear of me keeping the baby."

"He didn't like kids?"

"That wasn't it. We'd planned for them later." After the clinic was up and running. After they'd built their home, toured Europe. "A child just then would have been a drain on our time and our money. He had no intention of delaying or jeopardizing his investment."

He'd pleaded with her for a solid week to think about what she was doing to their project, to them. He reminded her of how hard they were working and of the life they would have. She tried to tell him they could still have it. They'd just have to adjust a little, focus more on their work and family than the big house and big vacations. He wouldn't listen. He'd dreamed all his life of doing exactly what he had mapped out for himself, and he'd finally told her they were through if she didn't get an abortion. The clinic would proceed on schedule, with or without her.

She'd told him it would have to proceed without.

She didn't mention to Chase how devastated she'd been. How she'd walked around in a numb fog for weeks feeling as if her heart had been cut out of her chest. Matt had insisted that he loved her, but he insisted, too, that she was the one ruining their chance to be together. She'd been so stunned by his rationale that she hadn't even bothered to point out that she hadn't gotten pregnant on her own.

What she did tell Chase was that she didn't remember exactly when she'd realized how completely different she and Matt really were. So much about that long, interminable year was a blur. All she remembered was knowing she needed to protect the tiny being growing inside her— and that she'd tried hard to be adult about their breakup because her residency had depended on it.

The intention was honorable. The execution had lacked a lot. Matt had been the chief surgical resident. Her boss. With her presence a constant reminder of the child he didn't want, their professional relationship deteriorated as rapidly as a patient removed from life support.

"So what did you do?" He tried to picture her pregnant, dealing with the stresses of her occupation, the circumstances. He could barely get past the pregnant part.

"I quit my residency in my seventh month. A surgeon who felt I had promise helped me get on at another hospital and I finished my training there after Tyler was born. My parents watched him for me. That feels like a lifetime ago," she murmured.

He imagined it did. But what impressed him even beyond the way she'd moved on, was what she had just revealed about who she truly was. She'd given up a way of life that could have been so much easier in order to keep her son. He'd never known any woman who didn't think of herself first.

"So that was when you started building over. When you left the guy."

Puzzled, Alex glanced up, dropping the edge of the sheet she hadn't realized she'd been toying with. A breath later, comprehension moved through her eyes as she remembered the conversation they'd had the first time he'd called her. "I suppose that was the defining moment."

Just as the moment that had changed everything for Chase had been at the reading of a will.

She didn't need to say the words to know that was where his thoughts had headed. And he didn't need to say anything for her to know that building over was what Chase was trying to do. He'd reached his own turning point—and found a new family waiting for him. The relationships he formed now could well define the rest of his life.

"Oh, hi, Dr. Larson. I didn't know you were still here."

At the sound of the nurse's voice, Chase's brow furrowed and Alex stepped back from the bed.

"Mr. Harrington wanted to go to the solarium." The scrub-clad woman pushed a wheelchair ahead of her, her smile bouncing between Alex and the man who suddenly looked a little edgier than he had moments ago. "I'll just leave this here and come back for him later. I forgot to bring a robe, anyway."

"You can take him now." Matching the woman's expression, Alex picked up the file from the rumpled bedding. "We just finished."

"Except for that insurance matter," Chase reminded her as the nurse headed back out for the robe.

"Except for that," she echoed.

Chase had implied that Matt was somehow responsible for her need to do things on her own. In a way, she supposed, he was. Not that it mattered. The need wasn't even that big a deal. She'd just had to accept so much help from her parents that she felt compelled now to prove, to herself anyway, that she was capable of handling her life. Most of it anyway. But she was more concerned with Chase's restlessness than any need to set him straight on that score.

She already knew he was trying to stay busy to keep from going stir-crazy. He'd told her as much himself. If helping her would help occupy his time, his taking over the task would benefit them both.

"If you wouldn't mind," she finally said. "I'd appreciate it."

She wouldn't be at the hospital tomorrow. But she'd just told him she would call him with her agent's phone number and give the man permission to deal with him when the nurse walked back in. Moments later, she was on her way down the hall, waving to Tanner who was headed for his brother's room and trying not to think about why she would miss seeing Chase tomorrow.

Alex knew that the solarium at the end of the hall had become a refuge of sorts for Chase the past few days. His nurses had told her that when the walls started closing in on him, he'd gather up whatever he was working on and ask for a wheelchair so he could escape the confines of his room. Not once had anyone seen him pushing that chair himself, which told Alex just how desperately he wanted to get out of the hospital. He wasn't going to risk another setback by doing something he shouldn't.

His determination paid off. By Monday, he'd made it to the open and airy room at the end of the hall under his own steam. On crutches.

Alex hadn't seen him on them herself. When she walked into the solarium, smiling at the nurse escorting an elderly patient out of it, Chase was sitting at one of the two game tables by the windows overlooking the park. He was still wearing the clothes he'd worn for his workout in therapy: hospital-issue green T-shirt and jogging shorts. His injured leg was propped up on a chair, and a copy of the *London Financial Times* lay on the table in front of him.

The only other people in the room occupied two of the institutional, green plastic chairs near the wall of donated books and magazines. The middle-aged couple appeared to be visitors, relatives of the elderly woman who'd just left, Alex assumed from the gist of their furtive discussion. It sounded as if they were about to break the news that she was going to a nursing home.

Blocking out their tense conversation, Alex walked around the game table as Chase looked up, and lowered herself to the chair across from him. Her glance promptly slid to the crutches propped against a large potted ficus.

"You don't have to remind me to take it easy," he told her before she could say a word. "But just for the record, I'm getting around fine."

"That's what I hear." Forcing herself not to think of how his progress affected her, she laced her fingers together on the checkerboard laminated into the tabletop. Except for the quick sandwich she'd grabbed at lunch, she'd been in surgeries all day. It felt good to sit. "I just talked with Mike. He can't believe the progress you've made." Her mouth curved. "I have some good news for you."

She thought she would finally see him smile. Instead, amazingly, something like apology knitted his brow. The expression didn't look comfortable on him at all.

"I wish I could say the same for you."

An instant ago, she'd been thinking of how his formidable will had hastened his progress. Now, she was aware of nothing but a bated sort of dread. "You talked to the adjuster?"

"Actually, I've talked to him a couple of times today."

He leaned forward, mirroring her position by spreading his elbows on the table and linking his fingers six inches from hers. "I've always believed in saving the good news for last. Let's talk about you first. How do you want this—straightforward or sugarcoated?"

She swallowed. She didn't feel particularly brave at the moment, but it never hurt to pretend. "Straightforward."

He seemed to question her choice. Or, maybe, he was trying to figure out how she was going to react if he gave her what she asked for and plotting his strategy accordingly. The man took risks, but he wasn't reckless. Risks could be calculated, and she doubted he made a move without knowing what the next was going to be.

He'd probably figured out by now that she pretty much just took things as they came.

"It will be a month before you can move back in."

She sagged forward, staring. She couldn't possibly have heard correctly. "A month?"

"That's everyone's best estimate. The adjuster's, mine and Tanner's," he said, looking much as she suspected she did when delivering bad news to a patient. There was sympathy in his eyes, along with an unyielding sort of certainty that said the diagnosis wasn't going to change no matter how badly the patient wanted it to.

She'd figured it would take a week. Ten days, tops.

"After I talked to the adjuster the first time, I asked Tanner to run by and check it out. He feels the carpet is too old to be worth drying, stretching and reinstalling, so I'm talking to the adjuster about replacing it all. You've lost some books. Your furniture is salvageable. The problem is the walls and floors."

He'd warned her. Two days ago, he'd told her it wasn't the things she could see that she had to worry about. Feeling totally unprepared anyway, she listened with her eyes trained on the dark hair on his sinewy forearms while he explained exactly what the problems were.

He talked about water being pumped out and blowers brought in to dry out the hardwood floors. He talked about the underflooring where the carpet had been, the need to dry that, too, and the need to replace sections that had become so waterlogged they'd already buckled. But when he got to the part about drywall having to be cut out and support timbers dried, her numbing mind began to focus more on the low, confident, competent tones of his voice than on what he was actually saying.

There was strength in his voice. Assuredness. She kept listening, absorbing the deep soothing tones, letting them wash over her. She'd yet to look from where his arms rested across from hers. There was strength there, too. The kind that could make a woman feel protected if he were to wrap her in them. The kind that made her want very badly to know how being protected would feel.

It occurred to her that he was saying something about scheduling a painter after the new drywall was in when she looked up and saw how carefully he was watching her.

Given the course of her thoughts, being close enough for him to read them added an element she simply couldn't deal with right now.

"A month," she murmured. She focused on his hands, his long fingers so close to hers. She wished he'd reach over. Just touch her and tell her it wasn't as long as it sounded. Even though it was, and he wouldn't.

With a little shrug that seemed to say, "Oh, well," she drew her hands back and rose from the chair. "I really didn't think it would take that long."

"I didn't think you did." He steepled his fingers, watching her as he leaned back. "But you don't want them to rush through the job. You'd just have problems later."

"No. Of course, I don't. But if it's going to be that long, I guess I'd better look for an apartment tomorrow instead of trying to make shorter-term arrangements. Make that to-night," she amended, her smile holding more defeat than bravado. "There's no medical reason to keep you here any longer. I came to tell you I'll discharge you in the morn-ing…if you feel comfortable enough with the crutches."

The news should have pleased him. She'd been so sure that it would. But his expression didn't change. He didn't seem to react at all. He just sat with his eyes steady on hers.

"I'm comfortable," he finally said—just before his jaw locked.

His reaction wasn't what she'd anticipated at all. Patients were invariably eager to leave, especially patients who were accustomed to activity. Most especially those who'd fought the confinement in the first place.

Thrown by his response, struggling with a sudden need to regroup, she turned to the window. Two blocks of grass, evergreens and flowering dogwood stretched in front of her.

It was no wonder Chase spent time here.

For a moment, she did nothing but stare down at that peaceful spot, breathing in and out and telling herself ev-erything would be fine if she just took it one thing at a time. Right now, she should focus on her patient. Not her-self.

It was impossible, though, to figure out what was going on in Chase's mind. So she concentrated on the fact that finding an apartment might actually be simpler than finding a place for just a week or so. She would need someplace furnished, that took pets and wouldn't insist on a lease. She'd pick up a newspaper after she finished her rounds. Make calls while she fed the boys. If it wasn't too late. And, in the morning she'd make sure everything at his house was as she'd found it before she left for her eight o'clock arthroscopy.

A knot had formed in her throat.

Empty. With a dozen things demanding to be done, she couldn't imagine why she felt so…empty.

The couple was leaving. She could hear their movement behind her, the scrape of their chairs and their lowered voices as they walked past Chase to get to the door. The door thudded softly when it closed.

"Hey."

Chase's voice drew her, the quiet sound of it bringing her head up.

With her arms crossed like bands beneath her breasts, she turned around.

Looking straight ahead, all she could see was a solid wall of chest and shoulders and the crutches braced under his arms. Her glance jerked up, past the tuft of dark hair peeking above the band of his shirt, the hard line of his jaw, the sensual cut of his mouth.

He was big. Solid. And close enough for her to touch. Close enough for him to touch her, though something about him said the thought had already occurred to him, and he'd thought better of it.

It seemed that they could talk. They could share little pieces of themselves. But whether it was because of where they were or what they'd be admitting, there was an invisible line beyond that odd friendship that neither seemed willing to cross.

"You don't need to worry about any of this, Alex. I said I'd take care of it and I will. How long is that boy staying with you?"

The question seemed to throw her. Confusion swept her face, making her look even more vulnerable than she had in the moments before she'd turned away. It was that vul-

nerability that had brought him to his feet, that had made
him want to put his hand on her shoulder and soothe her
the way she'd often soothed him.

Not trusting that need, he kept his hands curled around
the grips of his crutches and reminded himself that he still
owed her. He might care about her. But, ultimately, this
was about payback. That was all.

"I'll have him for another week. Why?"

"When's your next day off?"

She shook her head as she thought, the light from the
window touching hints of fire to the rich auburn depths of
her hair. "Not until Saturday."

"Wait until then to look for a place."

"You don't want me to discharge you?"

"I didn't say that. I don't want to stay here a minute
longer than I have to. But you and the kids can stay where
you are. It's only for a few days," he pointed out, as if to
make the idea easier for them both. "I have a basic idea
of what the place is like, and you said yourself it has plenty
of room. Just leave me the key so I can get in," he asked,
refusing to let her balk. "Ryan said he'd take me to the
house anytime I'm ready. What time are you letting me
go?"

Doubt shadowed her eyes. It lingered there, letting him
know she questioned the wisdom of his solution. But it was
practical. And the thought of not having to deal with the
situation now seemed to replace some of her misgivings
with relief. "I'm rounding in the morning after surgery.
Probably around noon."

It was actually closer to one o'clock when Alex finished
examining Chase, reviewing the X-rays she'd ordered taken
of his leg, and released him to his big brother. Ryan assured
her that he'd make sure her patient got in and settled and

that he wouldn't overdo, but Ryan was also the person who'd taken her patient into a construction site in a wheelchair two days after major surgery, so she had about as much faith in him as she did in Chase. Especially when she heard them making plans to swing by an electronics store for a television, since the house no longer had one, before Ryan took Chase to his temporary home.

Ryan was saying something about dinner with Tanner and their families at Pizza Pete's when she gave them the same quelling look she used on Tyler when he did exactly what she'd just told him not to. But the threat of taking a time-out would be totally lost on grown men, so she ignored the way her heart smiled when Chase arched his eyebrow back at her and left to tend those who took her advice a little more seriously.

The man was free for the first time in nearly two weeks. With his brother as an accomplice, she doubted he'd even be home when she and the boys got to the house. She knew all about the Malones' pizza nights. Ever since Ryan's first wife had died, he and his children had met up with Tanner on a regular basis for a couple hours of family bonding. Their little circle had expanded as their lives had changed. It was only natural that they would want their newly discovered brother with them.

"He's really going to be here?"

Brent's voice cracked at the end of the sentence. Too awed by the prospect of meeting the man to care, he added another "Really?" as he walked backward through the kitchen doorway.

"Really. But you probably won't meet him until tomorrow." Setting the bag of groceries she carried down on the island, Alex smiled at the enthusiasm in the boy's gray eyes. Brent had opened up considerably in the week he'd been with her, his shyness rarely apparent at all.

"How about putting the milk in the fridge for me?" she asked as Tyler darted past her. "Did your therapy go well today?"

"I guess." His shoulders lifted in a laconic shrug, giving her as much as she suspected any teenager did when asked about his day. "I see him working his leg on the weight machine sometimes. In therapy I mean. He sure is big."

Yeah, she thought. He is that.

"Tyler?" she called, wanting to know what her little whirlwind had been in such a rush about. "What are you doing?"

"I'm gonna feed Tom," he hollered from around the corner.

"Can you manage the cat food?"

"Yeah, 'cept he's not here."

"I'm sure he is, honey. It's a big room," she said, referring to the utility room they'd left the cat to prowl around in all day. "Look up on the windowsills. Or, maybe he's behind the washer and the dryer. Don't even think about crawling on top to check," she warned. "I'll be there in a minute."

Draping the navy jacket that matched her sleeveless sheath over the back of a chair in the breakfast bay, she stepped out of her heels and headed for the sink.

"Dinner in fifteen minutes," she told Brent, who was ripping into a bag of chips. Smiling sweetly, she traded him for a bag of carrots. "I know you're starving, but I told your parents I'd take care of you."

"I hate rabbit food."

"Dip it in this." Tipping her head from side to side to relieve the tension in her neck, she dug a bottle of raspberry vinaigrette dressing from the sack. "But wash up first."

A martyr couldn't have looked more persecuted. Tucking the bag of carrots under his left arm with his left hand, he wrinkled his nose at the dressing she handed him and stuck it in the fridge. His right hand curved against his stomach, held there by the blue sling covering half of his white-and-purple Diamondbacks T-shirt. He still didn't have much of a grip in that hand, but he'd come up with some pretty inventive ways to help himself.

Sometimes.

"There isn't any soap."

"It's right here."

Popping the top on a container of liquid soap she took from the sack, she set in on the sink in front of him and turned to see what Tyler was up to.

Her little boy was right behind her, his cornsilk hair brushing his pale eyebrows and the hem of his black T-shirt nearly hitting the hem of his baggy shorts.

"Tom's not there," he pronounced, his button nose wrinkled with worry.

"You didn't climb up on the washer, did you?"

"Unh-uh. I got on the counter and looked over. But he's not there."

Pinching the bridge of her nose, Alex drew a deep breath. "Okay," she said, calmly. He hadn't disobeyed her. She hadn't said a word about the counter. "I closed him in there this morning." She was sure she had. "Tom can't open doors."

"I let him out."

The sound of that deep voice had three pairs of eyes darting past the long wall of cabinets and granite counters. Chase stood framed by the open glass doors in the tall archway, his crutches planted on the marble floor and his glance moving guardedly over the boys before settling on her.

"Gwen was showing me around the place." With his injured leg bent back at the knee, he swung the crutches forward. A white polo shirt stretched over his broad shoulders. Loose khaki cargo shorts covered most of the EFD, and he wore his boaters without socks.

"He shot out when I opened the door. Don't worry about it," he said, when Alex closed her eyes and the little boy's widened, "he's around here somewhere. Gwen made sure he didn't get outside when she left."

Chase's glance slid over the children. The smaller one had taken a step closer to his mom and stood with one arm looped around her thigh and his neck cranked back, looking up at the bruises and the healing cut on his face. The teenager simply stared, his Adam's apple bobbing as he swallowed. His recent-looking buzz cut was a couple of shades darker than the little boy's longer hair and he was a shade taller than Alex. He also had a long way to go before he caught up to the size elevens on his feet.

"Hi," Chase said to him, since somebody needed to speak. He'd seen the kid in the therapy department before. He just hadn't realized he was the one Alex had taken in. "How's it going?"

"I've gotta wash up," Brent said, his voice cracking. The tips of his ears turned pink. Looking as if he couldn't believe what he'd just said, the rest of his face colored, too.

"'Scuze me," the boy muttered and bumped into the counter when he turned around, turned redder yet, and disappeared around the corner.

An unfamiliar twinge of sympathy tugged at Chase's chest. It had been years, but he could remember feeling that same awkwardness with his body, that same humiliation when he'd open his mouth wanting to impress and ended up looking foolish instead. Walter Harrington had always looked at him as if he couldn't believe how inept he was when it happened, which invariably was whenever the man was around.

Hating the thought, he closed it away. He needed to do what Alex had done and open himself to the idea of building on what fate had allowed him to discover. Since he was the uncle of a four-year-old he'd yet to meet, he let his glance fall to the three feet of towheaded innocence clinging to his mom.

A teenager he could relate to. He had no idea what went on in the minds of people as small as Alex's son. The child's attention had moved from the bruises to stare in morbid fascination at the gashes and insertion points for the EFD.

"How come you're hurt?"

"He was in a car accident, Tyler," Alex murmured.

"What kind of car?"

"Ah…a Jaguar," Chase replied, having to think for a second to remember what he'd rented. The kid's focus had changed with the speed of light.

The boy's eyes went bright. "Does it go fast?"

"I imagine it did."

"Can I see it?"

"Tyler," Alex said, her expression apologetic. "Let's not bug Mr. Harrington. You've already seen his car. It's the wrecked one we got the luggage from at the towing lot."

"For the man who gave you a headache?"

"Yes," she muttered, cupping his little chin and bending forward to see his face. "Now be quiet."

Chase bit back a smile. "You want to go find your cat?" he asked, torn between wanting to talk to Alex and wondering what else she'd said that she didn't want him to hear.

The little chatterbox tipped his head back farther. "Can I, Mom?"

"I'll do it. I don't want you getting into anything back there."

"I'll keep my hands in my pockets," he promised, showing her by pulling up his shirt and stuffing them into place. "Just like at the store. 'Cept when I have to crawl under something. Okay?"

Alex hesitated. Tyler wandering through expensively furnished and unfamiliar rooms probably couldn't cause any more damage than a cat who may or may not remember where she'd put his litterbox. "Stay out of Mr. Harrington's office and his room."

"How do I know which ones they are?"

"He's okay," Chase assured her, frowning a little as she tipped her head to stretch the muscles in her neck. He'd seen her do the same thing when she'd first come into the kitchen. She'd been working at those same muscles yesterday. "Just don't touch the computer. All right?"

Inquisitive gray eyes blinked up at him. "You have a computer? Do you have games?"

"The cat, Tyler. You can look for the cat," his mother patiently reminded him. "And take off your shoes. I don't want you wearing shoes on that carpet."

"How come?" he asked, dropping to his bottom and tugging off his new tennies.

"Because it's white. And keep your hands in your pockets."

"'Cept when I crawl."

"Except when you crawl," she agreed, bending to gather his shoes as he rolled to a sprinter's stance and bolted for the archway.

"No running!"

He skated to a stop, arms out to balance himself. Coming to a halt, he huffed out a breath, dutifully stuffed his hands out of sight and trudged off in search of the missing feline.

"If he's not back in three minutes, I'll go play search party."

Talking more to herself than to Chase, she dropped Tyler's shoes by hers, thinking she'd put them all away later, and headed back to the sink.

"They're…interesting," he observed. "Are little kids all that…?"

"Literal?" she offered, turning to see him staring after Tyler. "Curious? Energetic?"

"Yeah."

"Pretty much." The man looked confused. He also looked a little wary. She just wasn't sure if it was because he was obviously unfamiliar with small children or because he was reconsidering the idea of having one around.

"I thought you were with your brothers," she said, taking his focus from her son.

"What made you think that?"

"I heard you and Ryan talking when I left. It's pizza night."

Looking very much at ease in the expanse of high-ceilinged room, he leaned against the counter and picked up the blue-and-yellow box of macaroni and cheese. "I'm under doctor's orders to take it easy," he replied, cavalierly using her for an excuse to avoid the little gathering. "I told him that maybe I'd go next time." He held up the box. "You're eating this?"

"The boys wanted it." Having filled a brass pot with water, she carried it to the commercial-sized stove. "There's also salad and chicken. Can I get you anything?" she asked, searching out the right knob.

"I'm fine. I just wanted to talk to you for a minute." After a quick frown at the box, he set it back down. "Do you have to go anywhere, or are you in for the evening?"

"I'm in." And she would bless him forever for not having to start the apartment hunt tonight. "Why?"

"There's wine over there if you want some." He nodded to the glass door of the built-in wine cooler under the counter. "I had Gwen raid my cellar for a few bottles. There's a pretty decent Riesling there, and a nice chardonnay if you want something drier. I'd let the reds settle for a few days, though. She just brought them this afternoon."

Alex stopped dead in her tracks six feet from him. He had the same look about him that he'd had yesterday when he'd told her it would be a month before she could have her house back. He was trying to soften a blow. She was sure of it. He just wanted to numb her before he hit her with whatever it was. "Did you talk to the adjuster again?"

"I did. But that has nothing to do with why I offered you wine." His voice gentled. "You just look like you could stand to unwind a little."

Relief that nothing else had gone wrong almost canceled the odd twinge she felt at his thoughtfulness. Almost. The emptiness she felt was still there, clouded for the moment by demands. But it was getting harder all the time to keep that hollow feeling at bay.

He wasn't making it any easier.

Realizing she'd already stood there longer than she should have, she covered the growing ache with a little laugh.

"Heavenly as that sounds, I'll have to pass. I have children to feed and a case to review."

"Do I hafta take a bath tonight, Mom?"

"And a bath to supervise," she added at Tyler's disgruntled question when he walked back in carrying the scruffy ball of wiggling, variegated gray fur. "Wine relaxes me too much. I'd be putty and wouldn't get a thing done. Where was he, Tyler?"

"Under the bed in the room with the big TV. Can we go watch it? We don't got one." He looked hopeful, the exact opposite of how distressed he'd been when he'd first discovered the gaping hole in the family-room wall behind them where the cable line dangled.

"We don't have one," she corrected gently. "Remember what I told you in the car? That we have one end of the house and Mr. Harrington has the other? The TV's on his end."

"But he's on our end now," the child pointed out ever so reasonably.

Rather than try to explain why the man taking in their discussion didn't have to stick to her plan, she took Tyler by the shoulders and turned him around. "Close the door over there before you put Tom down so he doesn't get out again. Then, go get Brent so he can set the table while you wash up."

Giving him a gentle nudge, she looked up at the man curiously watching her son. "What did the adjuster say?" she asked, since that seemed to be why he was sticking around.

She took a bag of mixed lettuce and a box of croutons from the sack and, leaving them on the island, headed for the big refrigerator. Opening the door to get the bottle of dressing Brent had shoved in there, she felt her shoulders drop.

Chase's secretary, Gwen, had stocked the fridge. She'd stocked his wine. The woman had probably filled the pantry, too.

She wanted a Gwen of her own.

"You're going to have to pick out new carpeting," Chase said as she returned to the sack for the precooked chicken breasts she'd heat in the microwave. "I have the names of a couple of stores for you."

Picking up the box of croutons, he opened it for her and set it beside the lettuce. "They won't lay it for a while, but it wouldn't be a bad idea to choose what you want sooner rather than later in case they don't have enough of what you want in stock."

"I'll go Saturday, while I'm apartment hunting."

"Why don't I have them send someone out with samples instead? Give me a time and I'll have them bring them to your office or meet you here." He leaned a little more heavily on his crutches. "It's more efficient," he insisted, wincing slightly.

Alex had nothing against efficiency. At the moment, she didn't even have an objection to his tendency to counter her. The dull gloss of discomfort was visible in his eyes. She had no idea what all he'd done that afternoon. She just knew it had been far more than he should. Now, he was pushing himself because of her.

"Does your leg just ache, or is it throbbing?" She was sure it was doing one or the other. It was just a matter of which. "You've had it down too long," she concluded, when his silence indicated that it hurt more than he wanted her to know. "Go sit down and prop it up and I'll get you an ice pack. Have you eaten?"

"Yes. And you have enough to do. I'll take care of it."

"Brent says he's not hungry."

Wearily pushing her fingers through her hair, Alex pulled her glance from the determination carved in Chase's expression. "Of course he's hungry," she said, looking at Tyler, though she was really talking to herself. "Five minutes ago, he was starving."

"It's because of me." Maneuvering on his crutches, Chase started opening drawers in the island. "I'll get a bag of ice and get out of here."

"I'll get the ice and bring it to you."

"I said I'd do it," he muttered, snagging her arm when she moved beside him to take up the search for a zip-top bag to put the ice in. "You don't have to take care of me while you're here."

His fingers had closed completely around her biceps. Beneath his hand, she could feel his heat seeping through her bare skin, causing her breath to thin, her heart to hitch.

"And you don't have to take care of my house," she told him, amazed she could sound so calm with her insides jumping. "So let me help you and we'll consider ourselves even."

He said nothing about having his own words used against him. She didn't think he even considered that she might be feeling a little obligated herself. He just held her there with his deep, clear blue eyes darkening on hers before his gaze dropped to her mouth and the air left her lungs.

The instant her lips parted to draw a breath, his features went taut.

"Get the ice." He offered the concession quietly as his hand fell away. "But Tyler can bring it to me."

Hearing his name, the little boy stuck his head between them and looked up. "Then can I watch your TV?"

"Not tonight," Chase told him, saving Alex the trouble. "I'm kind of tired, so I'm going to bed, and you have to eat and take a bath."

He wasn't as tired as he could have been. He'd slept after Gwen had gone and hadn't gotten up again until he'd seen Alex's car pull up the drive. It just seemed necessary to get a little distance between him and the woman whose skin felt like cool satin and whose scent reminded him of a hot night, cold champagne and long, slow sex.

With her kid standing right there, the thought should have died as soon as it formed. With the confusion surrounding her, it shouldn't even have formed in the first place. But it had. The instant he'd heard her breath alter at his touch. And the thought remained.

He wanted her in his bed. He just didn't want her thinking he expected anything from her because she was staying under his roof.

Chapter Eight

"Brent wants a Triple Bacon Cheese Deluxe and Tyler wants a Kiddie Meal," she told Chase when she called him from the Burger Barn's drive-through at six-thirty the next evening. "If you haven't eaten, I'd be happy to bring you something, too. Not necessarily from here." She doubted that a man who stocked vintage wine, made killer linguine and regarded boxed macaroni and cheese with abject skepticism would go for something so plebeian. "I can bring you Chinese food, Italian from Granetti's or there's a Greek place on the way."

Chase's only response was a heavy pause.

Alex hadn't seen him that morning. She didn't know if he'd even been up when she and the boys had left a little after 7:00 a.m. After the way he'd distanced himself last night, it was pretty clear that he intended for them to keep more or less to themselves. Still, there were practicalities to consider. It made no sense to her that he should fend for himself when she had to come up with a meal anyway.

"Alex," she heard him say, ever so patiently. "You don't have to do this. But make it easy on yourself. Bring me whatever you're having. I should be finished by the time you get here."

She assumed he was working on the fund-raising. Or, possibly, on one of the projects in the files in his office. Or, maybe it was on the property he was trying to acquire.

She hadn't considered that he'd be playing handyman.

The boys had already raced through the entry, past the ten-foot potted palms that had to be Gwen's latest handiwork and were in the kitchen when she walked in and dropped purse, sacks and her briefcase on the center island. Brent was just behind her, looking a little uncertain about going any farther. She doubted Tyler had even slowed down. She could see him across the back of the large beige sectional, standing next to Chase who leaned on his crutches in front of a wall of niches and the fireplace. The niche that had held nothing but the cable connection now contained a rather large television. On the floor around them were clear plastic packets of operating instructions, pieces of white molded foam and the empty packing box.

"He got us a television, Mom!"

She would have explained it wasn't for them. Since Chase would be there for a few months, he obviously wanted the place to feel like a home. The sort of home he was apparently accustomed to anyway. But Chase had just glanced over his shoulder, catching her eye long enough for her to glimpse the tension in his chiseled features and the words died in her throat.

Her first thought was that he'd been irritated by her little boy's interruption. But it didn't appear to be impatience shadowing his face. Before she could take a step to move

Tyler away from him, he'd turned his attention back to her excited son and calmly ask him if he knew how to operate the remote control.

Nodding vigorously, Tyler assured him that he did. He said he didn't know what made the channels change, though.

"Electronic signals," she heard Chase explain. "They come out here." He patiently pointed to the front of the black plastic rectangle he handed Tyler. "And they're picked up here." Looking as tall and solid as an oak, he motioned to a tiny grill in the television.

"But I can't see anything," Tyler said, squinting at the end of the remote.

"That's because the signals are invisible. It's kind of like a voice. A person opens his mouth and you can hear what he says, but you can't see sound waves traveling to your ear."

"Oh, yeah." Nodding as if he'd known that all along, Tyler looked up at the man looking down at him. Dimples deepened with his grin.

Alex saw Chase smile back. There was a hint of amusement in that otherwise strained smile, but what struck her most was how it relieved her. Whatever was wrong, it didn't appear to have anything to do with their presence.

"How did you get that in there?" she asked carefully, hoping he hadn't actually wrestled the set into place himself.

"The guy who delivered it unpacked it for me." Lean muscle shifted beneath his black T-shirt as he left Tyler searching out cartoons and moved toward her. "I needed something to do with my hands, so I told him I'd wire it myself."

The tension she'd first noticed had been carefully

banked, but it was still there. It lurked like a coiled snake beneath his impassive facade as he drew closer.

She wanted to know what was wrong. But she couldn't ask. Even if the boys hadn't been right there, she wasn't sure anymore where to draw the line with her concerns about him. They were just two people helping each other out. Two people who weren't quite friends, and because the doctor-patient roles had somehow blurred, weren't quite anything else, either.

"I thought maybe Gwen had done it," she admitted, turning her attention from his marginally faded bruises. "I'm beginning to think she's superwoman."

A huge basket of fruit, so perfect it looked plastic, occupied the center of the sparkling white surface of the center island. Since focusing on anything else felt safer than focusing on him, she ran a finger lightly over the curve of a perfectly ripe pear. "She's obviously been here again."

"Actually, I needed her at the office in Seattle. She went back yesterday." An edge entered his voice. "That's from my mother."

That edge made her draw her hand away. It also made it hard to know what to say, though her first thought was that a fruit basket seemed an odd thing for a mom to send—unless she'd done it to make sure he ate healthily, in which case it didn't seem odd at all.

"So what's for dinner?" he muttered, saving her from having to say a word.

"Can I eat in my room?" Brent mumbled from behind them.

There was a wealth of self-consciousness in the quiet question.

Turning to see the teenager studying the neon-green laces on his black athletic shoes, Alex forced a smile he didn't even see.

"How about helping me instead?" she asked. She knew exactly what his problem was. It was standing next to her. Six-feet-plus of dark-haired intimidation that towered god-like in the young boy's eyes. "Since we're tossing nutrition to the wind tonight, we might as well blow all the rules and you can watch television while you eat. You can get the milk for me."

A pained looked crossed Brent's thin face. Having to eat in front of a man he could barely speak to was apparently cruel and unusual punishment.

"Why don't you let us do this?" Chase suggested.

Brent's head jerked up. Alex simply looked puzzled.

"Go get comfortable," Chase said to her, giving her a look that asked her to let him take over. "We've got this covered out here."

"Sir?"

"The name's Chase. You're Brent, right?"

"Yes, sir."

"I saw you working your arm with the free weights in therapy this morning. How much are you lifting?"

"Five…" Brent cut himself off when his voice took an embarrassing upward pitch. "Five pounds." He cleared his throat. "I know that's not much."

Five pounds for a boy who'd had no use of his arm at all was a huge accomplishment. The part of Alex that felt protective toward all her patients wanted to remind Brent of that. He worked so hard. But Chase had deliberately ignored the boy's attempt to minimize, much as he was now ignoring her.

"What are you aiming for?" she heard him ask as she picked up her purse and briefcase and, still listening, hesitantly moved toward the hallway by the breakfast bay.

Shoes squeaked against the floor as Brent shuffled his big feet. "Fifty."

"That's what Dr. Larson wants you to do?"

She was aware of Brent's uneasy glance slicing toward her.

"She just wants me to get to twenty-five."

"Good man," Chase claimed, sounding as if he might be smiling. "Always set your goals higher than what people expect. When you reach 'em, it baffles the heck out of people who thought you couldn't do it and makes everyone else think you're an expert.

"I'm a long way from where I want to be with the weights, too," he confided, paper crackling as he opened one of the sacks and took out a french fry. "I had no idea how hard lifting a few measly pounds could be. Did you?"

Alex didn't hear Brent's reply. But she suspected Chase was doing more than simply distracting himself from whatever was eating at him. He'd deliberately overridden the introverted young man's timidity, praised him and shown him that he was just like him in some ways himself.

It took a man of considerable compassion to recognize what Brent had needed. Or a man who'd once needed the same understanding himself.

The thought that Chase, confident, dominant and powerful as he was, could once have been as unsure of himself as Brent simply refused to gel. He'd already cancelled the thought anyway. As she turned the corner into the room she was sharing with Tyler, she heard Chase call her little boy to come help them in the kitchen because they needed help getting glasses to the table.

The thought of a four-year-old carrying anything breakable across the unforgiving marble-tiled floors had her working the zipper of her dress back up and turning on her heel. She was back in the kitchen in seconds. But the phone rang just as she turned the corner.

Frowning at her, Chase snatched up the receiver.

"I'm just going to take care of the glasses," she defended, even as he said hello to the caller.

With his glance on the strip of bare skin visible between the six inches of zipper she hadn't managed to fasten, he murmured, "It's for you."

It was a colleague she'd been trying to hook up with all day about a patient. Needing to take the call, she tucked the phone to her shoulder and took care of the glasses. A minute later, listening to Tyler tell Chase that his mom said Vipers go fast, she smoothed her hand over her little boy's head and felt her heart snag when Chase moved behind her and tugged up her zipper.

Dr. Trevor MacAllister was chatting away in her ear about bone graft substitutes. With Chase's fingers brushing the back of her neck, the surgeon might as well have been talking about his dog. She hadn't a clue what the man had just said. But she'd no sooner gone still at the contact than Chase was asking Brent to bring the sacks and Tyler to get the napkins, and he'd moved away.

Requesting that Dr. MacAllister please repeat what he'd just said, she cast a glance toward Chase's back and forced herself to concentrate as she headed to her room and left the males to their meal.

By the time she was finished with her call, they were finished, too—and Chase had retreated to his half of the house.

He'd thought being with her would help. It usually did.

Tonight, it had taken less than thirty minutes to realize that being with them, and especially with her, only made it harder to avoid the thoughts he'd been trying to avoid ever since that damn fruit basket had arrived at nine o'clock that morning. It hadn't helped that he hadn't quite been able to keep his hands to himself, either.

Disgusted, Chase tossed aside the novel he'd been trying to read and carefully swung his injured leg over the side of the king-size bed. Grabbing his crutches from where he'd propped them against the antique Italian renaissance-style nightstand, he levered himself up, swearing at how clumsy he felt, and headed past the long dresser on the opposite wall.

His physical limitations were gnawing at him, too.

Opening the sliding glass door that led to the huge sweep of patio, he angled himself through and headed for the lounge chairs by the pool. The night was a little cool, but feeling the way he did, he needed to be where the walls didn't feel like they were closing in on him.

He was in totally unfamiliar territory. He was becoming more aware of that with every passing day. The world he knew began at six in the morning with a call to his broker and ended with a business dinner, or out at the refitters where his sailing sloop was being readied for a race he didn't care about anymore or, occasionally, in the company of an attractive woman who understood from the beginning that he wasn't interested in anything that so much as hinted at permanence.

He knew absolutely nothing about being part of a family.

He wanted to. He was trying to. But even though his brothers were including him, there was too much of their history he didn't share. There was too much about their lives that he simply couldn't relate to.

Alex had said to take it one day at a time.

He was thinking about making the thought his personal mantra when he eased himself into one of the cushioned chaises near the dark oval pool.

He was still thinking about it when he heard a door open. In the pale glow from the low security lights lining the wide arch of flagstone, he saw Alex's lithe graceful silhouette step from the shadows.

She hadn't turned on the patio lights. Like him, she seemed to prefer the dark. She paused for a moment, seeming more shadow than substance herself as she tipped her head back, then rolled it side-to-side. A few moments later, she crossed her arms over the sweats she'd changed into and walked slowly to the edge of the pool.

"It's not heated."

Alex whipped around, slapping her hand over her heart as if to keep it from jumping through her chest.

"Chase." His name came out with a rush of breath when she saw him stretched out on a lounge chair twenty feet away. "What are you doing out here?"

"Trying to do something my physical therapist told me I should do."

She hesitated, her hand sliding from her heart. "What's that?"

"Relax." The word came out harsher than he'd intended, as if it contained four letters instead of five. "If I thought you knew how to do it, I'd ask for a little advice."

He thought he saw her smile. He just couldn't tell for sure until she moved close enough for the low lights behind him to reach her face.

"I know how," she assured him. "I just can't picture you using my methods."

"And those are?"

"A long soak in a hot tub scented with sweet lavender and mandarin, though that never happens," she conceded with longing. "Or, reading a book to Tyler."

The image of her slipping naked into hot, scented water wasn't relaxing at all. "I tried reading. It didn't work."

It wasn't just reading, Alex thought. It was having her little boy snuggle into her, the motion of feathering his hair through her fingers while he listened to her voice and feeling his little body relax so trustingly against hers. It was smelling his sweet little-boy smell and hearing his breathing soften as he fell asleep, knowing he was safe and loved and the most important being in her life.

Since there was no way she could make him understand that, she let it go with, "It's not quite the same."

Any other time, Chase might have asked for other suggestions. But he was too aware of the softness that had stolen over her to seek any other diversion. He wondered if she even knew how often she touched her little boy, letting him know by that unguarded, nurturing contact that she cared. She listened to him, too, instead of brushing him off as some adults did when a small child was pestering them. The child clearly adored her.

He couldn't remember ever wanting to share anything with his adoptive mother. He couldn't remember her touching him, either, unless it was to straighten a collar or brush a speck of lint from his jacket or to nudge his back to remind him to stand up straight. Never would she have let him have a pet, much less three, and never would he have been allowed to wrap his arms around her the way Tyler had his mom last night. She would have been too afraid of having her dress wrinkled. When he'd been growing up in the museumlike home where nothing was to be touched, he was literally to be seen and not heard.

"Chase?" Caution stole through her voice. "Are you all right?"

No, he thought. He wasn't. He hadn't been since the moment he'd found out he wasn't who he'd thought he was.

"Yeah," he muttered, hating the feelings churning inside him. He was usually in better control than he'd been in lately. He never thought of his childhood. Until a few months ago, if he even felt a hint of the old resentments take hold, he would banish them as a foolish waste of energy and bury them under a mountain of work. Since the accident and meeting his brothers, escape had been impossible.

Seeing Alex with her little boy had made it harder still.

"Do you want to talk about it?"

"About what?"

"The fruit basket."

In the sheltering light she could see little beyond his sudden stillness—and his quick, dismissing shrug.

"What about it?"

His nonchalance didn't fool her. Just because she couldn't see the way his jaw tightened didn't mean she couldn't hear that tautness in his voice.

She'd known something was wrong from the moment she'd seen him tonight. He'd had that same preoccupation about him that he'd had the night she'd asked if he'd come to meet his brothers. She hadn't thought twice about offering to help him then. She shouldn't now.

"You didn't seem too pleased that your mother had sent it."

"I was just surprised to hear from her. I didn't realize she was back from her cruise."

"She just now heard about the accident?"

"I guess so," he murmured. "Gwen said she called the office after a friend asked her about me."

Another chaise paralleled the one Chase occupied. Between them sat a low, wrought-iron table, graced with a small azalea plant. Sitting down to face him, she reached for a blossom that had dropped to the table's glass surface and ran a smooth petal through her fingers. "She had to be relieved to know you're doing so well."

He skimmed a glance over her, watched the motions of her slender fingers.

"You know, Dr. Larson, you're surprisingly naive for someone as smart as you are."

She frowned across the three feet separating them. "I don't suppose you'd care to explain that."

"Don't you ever suspect ulterior motives?"

"Not about fruit baskets."

"Not everyone is like you, Alex," he muttered, remembering a similar attitude about flowers that had been sent by someone's secretary. "People do things because they want something or out of a sense of obligation. If she was relieved, it was because nothing was required of her."

Disbelief washed over Alex. "I don't believe that. About people, I mean. Or, your mother for that matter. There are plenty of people who think of others simply because they care," she defended, feeling attacked even though she supposed he'd somehow just paid her a compliment. "No matter what the circumstances, she wanted you enough to adopt you." His father may have "gotten him for her," but the woman had obviously wanted a child badly. "She raised you from a baby—"

"She wanted me like she wanted a new dress or a new car." His voice sliced sharp as a scalpel. "Like anything else, the novelty wears off."

Deliberately, forcibly, he sought to blunt that betraying edge. All he managed to do was lower his tone.

"My mother…the woman I thought was my…Elena," he grated, sounding as if he didn't even know how to think of the woman anymore, "is a collector. She's happiest when she's just acquired something that she can show off or brag about. Art. Jewelry. People. I doubt she's ever believed she had any value herself, so she surrounds herself with things she thinks will give her worth.

"As for her raising me, there's no way she can take credit for that. I was raised by hired help. I'd come home from school for vacations and they'd be gone somewhere else. It was just me and the staff. But that was a blessing,'' he insisted, the dull edge of pain darkening the silvery shadows of his face. ''The thing I'm not sure I'll ever get past is that they knew I had brothers.''

The bitter edge of anger tested the control in his voice. The Harringtons hadn't denied him those relationships because they'd wanted to protect him somehow. Walter had wanted to protect his own money. Elena had just been too possessive to share. But Alex knew that Chase's anger had been there long before he'd encountered that last bit of proof of their selfishness. He'd reined it in, denied or ignored it. But it had existed far longer than he'd wanted to acknowledge. Those dark emotions were eating at him, consuming him as surely as a malignancy left unchecked destroyed its host.

It had already nearly destroyed his ability to let people get close. He hadn't even wanted to admit how important it was to him that he meet his brothers. He hadn't wanted to admit that he was staying around because of them, either.

In a way, she couldn't blame him. He probably couldn't honestly tell when someone was genuinely concerned for him. He'd grown up surrounded by people paid to ''care'' for him.

She was his doctor. On certain levels he was paying for her care, too.

''I see now why you didn't want anyone helping you here.''

He pushed his fingers through his hair, the motion screaming with the agitation he ruthlessly banked. ''You shouldn't have come out. I can't believe the stuff I unload on you.''

She was sure he couldn't. He was a man who needed to be in control, who held himself in, guarded his heart and his thoughts so no one could get close enough to take advantage of him, to hurt him. He was a man who needed to have all the answers because not having them meant he was vulnerable somehow, and that sort of threat scared him to death.

"Maybe you just need to talk."

"You're my orthopedist, not my shrink."

She blinked twice, then looked down at the blossom she'd shredded.

She'd been listening as a friend.

Chase said nothing. He just watched her long enough to realize his disclaimer had stung and let his hand fall.

He'd never dropped his guard with anyone as much as he did with Alex. He'd said things to her that he'd never even admitted to himself until he heard himself growling them at her. He didn't know what it was about her that caused all those feelings to surface when they were together. Maybe it was because he couldn't get within six feet of her without wanting her, and that frustration fueled all the others.

Whatever caused it, he felt exposed and defensive. It was so much easier when people didn't know what mattered to him. It was so much easier when nothing had.

He hadn't intended to hurt her feelings.

Needing to make up for it, lousy at apologizing, he tried to change the subject completely.

"How about I take Brent with me to therapy?" he asked, disturbed by how uneasy she looked as she rose from the chaise. "He said his first session isn't until ten. If he goes with me, he won't have to wait around so long in the morning."

The same strained silence that had filled the air before he'd spoken rushed back to fill it again. The lilac-scented breeze stirred the leaves of the trees. The mating call of crickets melded with the distant bark of a dog. They were peaceful sounds. Calming sounds. Or, they should have been.

Alex was far more conscious of the tension radiating from Chase's long, lean body as he shifted on the chaise and eased his injured leg over the side.

"I'm sure he'd like that."

"I'll be out of there before his afternoon session, but I'll send the driver back for him when he's through so he doesn't have to wait until you're finished. He can hang out here and watch videos or something."

She knew what he was doing. She even appreciated his effort to smooth over his blunt rejection moments ago. The efforts just weren't working all that well. He still sounded as tense as he looked and when he reached for his crutches to pull himself upright, he knocked one from where they rested against the table and swore.

"Let me—"

"I can do this," he muttered, clearly hating the idea of not being able to simply stand up when he wanted to.

"You won't have any leverage," she muttered back. Ignoring his glare, she bent to retrieve what he'd dropped. He had a right to his anger. He had the right to let her know he didn't want her getting any closer than she already was. But he had no business doing something that could require her to go back into surgery tonight. "There aren't any arms on that thing to push yourself up with."

"I said I can do this."

"Possibly," she conceded, not caring that she was about to butt heads with his pride. "But you're not going to want to get halfway up and find you don't have your balance. If those pins hit these flagstones, there's a good possibility you'll add a couple more fractures to the ones you already have. That femur happens to be some of my best work and I don't want it screwed up.''

Crouched in front of him, annoyed with his stubbornness and nursing a hurt she didn't want to feel, she planted one crutch beyond his bent leg and the other beyond his extended one.

"Now," she said, trying to ignore the fact that she was right between his heavy thighs, "take these and I'll help you. Push up with your good leg and balance with the grips. I'll put my arms around your waist and pull you up."

He didn't budge. "You can't pull me up. I weigh twice what you do."

"You only weigh seventy-five pounds more," she gamely informed him. "And I can handle you just fine."

"Oh, yeah?"

"Yeah," she muttered, and made the mistake of looking up.

His eyes glittered hard on her face, but his voice went suddenly, deceptively soft. "Prove it."

The quiet statement hung in the suddenly still air. It shimmered like a gilt-edged gauntlet thrown down between them, part challenge, part warning. And it had nothing at all to do with helping him to his feet.

His eyes never moved from hers as he took the crutches and simply let them go.

The clatter would have raised the dead.

Alex wasn't sure she even heard it.

His hands were already moving over her shoulders. The warmth of his palms skimmed the curve of her neck when he slipped his fingers through her hair and cupped the back of her head.

"This is why I didn't want your help." His glance swept her face. "Tell me you haven't thought about this, Alex. Tell me, and I'll let you go."

She opened her mouth, trying to be rational. Rational was good. It was responsible. More than anything else, that was what she was. Responsible. At that moment, she just couldn't remember why it was so necessary.

He drew her closer, lowering his head.

"That's what I thought," he murmured, and closed his mouth over hers.

There was no demand. Just a gentle pressure that increased with the quick hitch of her breath. Or maybe it was his. She felt him draw her closer, the pressure increasing, until he parted her lips with his tongue.

A jolt of heat melded with the sweet, hot taste of him. His scent filled her, his strength drew her. She didn't encourage his touch so much as she allowed it. But what she allowed was utterly devastating.

She felt his warmth seeping inside her, melting her, beckoning her closer. Until that moment, she hadn't honestly realized how very cold she'd felt inside. It had been easier when she hadn't known. But he wasn't letting her regret that discovery. He kissed her slowly, deeply, drugging her with sensations she scarcely remembered. Or, maybe, had never known.

Craving more, she leaned toward him, flattening her hands on the hard wall of his chest and felt him sweep his arm down her back. That arm locked around her like a steel band, drawing her up, easing her forward to her knees. She could feel his heart hammering beneath her palms, sense the restraint tensing his hard body.

With her head bent back, his arm bracing her, he drew her closer, slipping his free hand over her ribs, up along the curve of her breast.

He heard her breath catch, felt the quick stiffening of her supple limbs. When she relaxed in his arms a moment later, a groan came from deep within his chest.

He'd expected heat, though maybe not the intensity of it. He wanted to feel her. All of her. He wanted to lean back, drag her with him and feel her curves cover the length of his body. He wanted to slip his hand beneath her shirt, feel the softness of her skin. He wanted to cup her breast in his palm, learn her shape, feel her bloom against his fingers, his tongue.

He couldn't do what he wanted, wouldn't have even if he could. He couldn't lean back because he couldn't lift his leg to the chaise, much less lead her off to his room. More importantly, he could feel the restraint slipping into her muscles, tensing her, pulling back.

He wouldn't push. She came willingly or not at all.

His thumbs brushed her cheeks, and he drew back before she could. Her eyes were dark as obsidian. Confusion and desire clouded the fragile lines of her face.

"You started to help me up." With the pad of his thumb, he traced her lower lip. "I think maybe that would be a good idea now."

She thought she nodded. She knew she moved back. By the time he was on his feet, she was sure there was enough strength in her voice to say good-night. But before she could, he kissed her again. The devastating assault on her senses made her feel soft, desired and nearly incapable of considering what it was, exactly, that she was doing.

It wasn't until after she'd watched him go inside and she'd headed in herself, that she considered how much better off she'd been before she'd known how it felt to be in his arms.

Chapter Nine

Alex's first thought when consciousness stirred was that she should have moved away from Chase when he'd given her the chance. Her second was that she'd overslept a full hour. He'd had her so agitated, so preoccupied, that she'd forgotten to set the alarm.

The only good thing about the morning was that Chase was taking Brent to therapy so she didn't have to worry about getting him up and moving. Other than that little silver lining, the day slid steadily downhill.

Every one of her morning appointments, which were backed up anyway because she was late, ran long. Her afternoon arthroscopy went fine, but her synovectomy went V-tach on her halfway through the procedure. The patient's pre-op testing had shown him to be a good surgical candidate, but a sleeper of a heart problem had her performing chest compressions before closing him up and shipping him off to cardiac intensive care instead of surgical recovery.

It was past seven that evening before she found a minute for a call to make sure Brent had made it back to the house. He had. He even answered the phone because he was on the other line talking to his parents and he assured her that he could fix himself something to eat since she was going to be late. While an emergency clavicle was being prepped, she stopped by Child Care to get a quick hug from Tyler and tell him he'd be having supper there, before heading upstairs to scrub.

If it hadn't been for the suffering of the patients involved, she would have been openly grateful for what the day was demanding of her. Having to think of everyone else didn't allow her any time to consider what had happened last night. And thinking about last night was something she simply didn't want to do.

Every time she did, she remembered what Chase had made her feel, the yearning that went soul-deep and tugged at needs that were easier, safer, to ignore than consider.

He was making her face those needs anyway.

He made her feel desired and feminine and it had been so long since she'd felt that way that her heart and her body ached for more. It was like pouring water on a dying plant, she supposed, though the thought that part of her was withering inside disturbed her too much to truly consider, so she thought about him, instead.

He was going through so much. He was in an unfamiliar town, torn between what had been and what now was and, whether he liked the idea or not, he could talk to her.

And he wanted her.

The thought alone was enough to bring back the ache he'd created. What she needed to remember, though, was that he was accustomed to taking what he wanted, then moving on. Love would never enter a relationship with him. He probably couldn't even recognize the emotion, much less return it. As long as she kept that in mind, and kept a little physical distance between them, she'd be fine.

It was always good to have a plan. Even if her plans did have a nasty habit of falling apart. But she was prepared to overlook that particular detail by the time she arrived at the house a little before eleven o'clock that night.

Except for the porch light and the stove light someone had left on in the kitchen, the house was dark. Quietly, so as not to disturb anyone, she slipped inside with a sleeping Tyler propped against her shoulder and quickly tucked him into bed. Within five minutes, she was in bed with him.

She didn't even remember her head hitting the pillow when she roused to the sound of her pager going off two hours later.

The digital clock she'd brought from her house glowed 1:22 in neon-green. The red digits on her pager were for the hospital's emergency room.

"Chase?" Alex dropped her athletic shoes on the thick hallway carpet and knocked quietly on the carved white door. "Chase, I need to talk to you. I need a favor."

Zipping up the gray sweatshirt she'd thrown on over her sweatpants, she listened for any sign of life inside his bedroom. She'd thought she heard a click, but rustling around as she was, she couldn't be sure.

"Chase?" she called again, voice low as she bent to grab a shoe. She pulled it on, balancing on one foot while she tied the laces and kept listening.

One shoe on, she reached for the other and was thinking about opening the door to poke her head inside when the brass latch turned.

The door swung inward. In the soft light from the lamp on the nightstand, she saw Chase lean back on his crutches. He was wearing nothing but bruises that were fading in places to a sickly shade of green, a pair of burgundy silk boxer shorts and the fixation device on his leg.

Jerking her glance to the six-pack of muscles corrugating his abdomen and past a set of beautifully formed pectoralis majors, she ignored the quick jolt low in her belly and tightened her grip on her shoe.

"I didn't mean for you to get up."

"Doesn't matter." His voice was heavy with sleep, but his blue eyes were sharp as they ran over her sweats and settled on her face. "What's going on?"

"A busload of kids went off the interstate."

"This time of night?"

"The paramedics told ER they were on their way from Canada to Disneyland." Her words were clipped, her professional defenses fighting to keep from thinking of all those children in pain as she pulled on her other shoe. "Sounds like the driver fell asleep."

Crouching to whip the laces into a bow, she glanced up and found herself eye level with the silky boxers. A feathering of dark hair fanned inward over his hard, flat stomach, merging to arrow beneath the silk riding low on his narrow hips.

The man had been far easier to take in a hospital gown.

"Tyler's only been in bed for a couple of hours," she continued, feeling a prickly sensation on the back of her neck as his glance skimmed her nape. "I hate to wake him if I don't have to. Would you mind listening for him in case he wakes up? He shouldn't," she hastily assured him. "And I'd ask Brent to do it, but he sleeps so hard I'm not sure what I said would even register. I can take him to Child Care. Tyler, I mean. But it would be so much easier on him if he could just stay here and sleep."

Chase could practically see her mind racing as she straightened. Even half-groggy from sleep himself, it was obvious that she wasn't wasting time getting herself together and out the door. A small sleep-crease marred the translucent skin of her cheek, her hair was tousled, looking more as if she'd styled it with her fingers than a comb and she wore no makeup at all.

He doubted she'd been out of bed any longer than it had taken to dress and run down the hall. He knew she hadn't been in bed more than a couple of hours, either. But thinking of Alex in bed conjured images guaranteed to wreck his sleep, and he'd wrestled the sheets enough for one night. Instead, he considered only that if Tyler stayed, it would be easier for the boy—and easier for her, too.

She apparently hadn't even hesitated to come to him. Unexpectedly drawn by the thought, not caring that it had been the only practical thing to do, he watched her give the pull of her sweatshirt zipper another tug.

"What do I need to do?"

"Just leave your door open so you can hear him if he gets up. I'll leave his door and the door to the kitchen open, too." She hesitated, glancing worriedly down the hall, then at her watch. "If he does get up, just tell him where I am and that I'll be back as soon as I can."

"I can handle that."

"I'm sure I'll be gone all night."

"That's okay."

"You'll leave your door open?"

He edged forward. The muscles in his shoulders rippled with the movement, biceps bunching as he brought himself a foot from the threshold. With the rubber tip of his right crutch, he nudged the door back against the wall. "Door's open."

"Thanks. And Chase, if I'm not back by breakfast, he can get himself a bowl of dry cereal."

"Dry cereal. Got it."

"And he can have juice. But only a juice box. He'll spill it if he pours it from the big carton."

"Juice box. No carton."

Behind the concern in her brown eyes, her mental wheels were spinning like tops. He could practically see them as she turned away, then turned right back around again.

"If anything happens and you need me, have me paged and I'll—"

"Alex," he said, his voice utterly flat. His hand snaked out, catching the back of her neck. "Stop worrying about it."

He tugged her forward. An instant later, his mouth closed over hers, cutting off the sound of her startled breath and threatening the stability of her legs.

He kissed her thoroughly, soundly, and when he lifted his head, she could have sworn his breathing was no steadier than her own.

A muscle in his jaw jumped as he grazed his thumb along her lower lip. But all he said was, "Go."

He had the sensation of being watched.

Dimly aware of light shining against the back of his eyelids, Chase threw his arm over his eyes and thought about burying his head under his pillow. Then he remembered he was on his back because of his leg and putting a pillow over his face didn't have the same appeal. He was used to sleeping on his stomach, sprawled across the bed, claiming it all for himself.

Until he'd been forced to change his sleep position, he had rarely given any thought to how he slept, or to the fact that he took up all the room. Since he made it a habit to never wake up with anyone else in his bed—the only sure way to avoid morning-after complications—it didn't matter.

Mostly what he thought about now was that he wasn't alone.

Shielding his eyes against the morning light pouring through the sheer curtains, he turned to meet a pair of blinking brown eyes.

Tyler was standing three feet from the edge of the bed. A spike of pale blond hair stood up from the back of his head. "Do you know where my mom is?"

"Uh…yeah. What time is it?"

Beneath the militant-looking turtles covering his flannel pajama top, Tyler's shoulders rose to his ears. "I dunno. But there's a six and a four and a one on the clock."

It was six-forty-one. Not quite the crack of dawn, but close enough.

"She must still be at the hospital," Chase said, since the little boy obviously couldn't find her. "She said you can have cereal."

"I'm not supposed to pour milk by myself. Mom said."

"Mom said, huh?"

The spike bounced with the little boy's confirming nod.

"Then, I guess you'd better not do it," he mumbled and elbowed himself up to throw back the sheet.

It seemed Alex had also said something about having the cereal dry. But as Chase dropped his foot over the edge of the bed, groggily noting that fewer body parts ached each day, he figured that was because she thought the kid would be getting it for himself.

Needing coffee, he motioned to the dresser. "There's a pair of running shorts in the third drawer. If you'll grab them for me and bring me that T-shirt on the chair, I'll go get us both fixed up. Okay?"

"Okay," Tyler echoed and marched to the dresser. "Is this one the third?"

"One down."

Tyler grinned. Spreading his arms to grip the handles, he tugged the drawer open.

Smiling too, something he never did before coffee, Chase hauled himself into the bathroom.

Ten minutes later, Tyler was on a stool at the island in the kitchen and Chase was edging himself and a mug of coffee down the counter. Carrying anything that he couldn't hold with his hand on the crutch grip was out of the question—which was why he'd had Tyler heft the milk from the fridge to the island and carry over the box of cereal and the bowl he'd handed him. Chase was on his own with the hot coffee, though. He didn't have to know anything about kids to know where it would end up if he asked Tyler to carry it and he'd told Alex not to worry about her little boy.

Alex trusted him.

The realization hit like a jolt from a live wire. She had to trust him. On some level, anyway. If she didn't, she never would have left her son with him.

He wasn't sure why that should matter as much as it did. He wasn't even sure what it was about the realization that touched him. But he'd just become aware of something else that felt equally profound.

He'd never in his life been responsible for another person until Alex had asked for his help.

"We never stayed with anybody before you," he heard Tyler mumble around a mouthful of pastel-colored puffs. "We always have people stay at our house. Wendy had a baby and she stayed with us. An' Dr. Sarji. But she talked different and I couldn't understand her."

In desperate need of coffee, Chase balanced himself to lift the mug. "She had an accent?" he ventured, making a careful swing from the counter to the island.

"I dunno." Tyler's shoulders lifted in another ear-reaching shrug. "An' now we have Brent, 'cept he's going home 'cause he's getting better.

"My mom makes people better," Tyler continued gravely. "'Cept she doesn't kiss owies on them. She only does that for me. I have one here."

He poked his elbow up in the air, showing off a bright blue bandage. "Griffin hit me with his truck." Tugging his pajama sleeve back down, he reached for his glass. "Can I have more milk, please?"

For a moment, Chase simply stared at the chalky film on the tumbler. Thinking he'd do better keeping up with the string of non sequiturs once the caffeine kicked in, he slid onto the stool beside Tyler, refilled the boy's glass, and picked up his coffee, cradling the steaming mug between his hands.

Breathing in the life-giving aroma of the fresh brew, he reverently sipped.

"Mom does that, too."

"Does what?"

"Closes her eyes and makes that sound when she drinks her coffee."

"What sound?"

"You know." The little boy closed his eyes and gave a long, deep sigh. When he opened his eyes again, he innocently turned his attention back to his oddly colored food. "That sound."

Chase bit back a grin. "What else does your mom do?" he asked, conversationally.

"She talks on the phone. An' she sings with me."

"Oh yeah?"

"Uh-huh. She knows all the words, too."

"Does she see anyone? A man, I mean?"

Tyler nodded. "Sometimes."

Chase's brow pinched. Not sure he liked the odd feeling

in his chest, not caring to consider what it was, he casually murmured, ''Who?''

''Griffin's dad. An' Lia's dad. We go to Pizza Pete's.''

Lia's dad. Tanner.

This time the smile formed. ''Anyone else?''

Tyler took a gulp of milk, shaking his head at the same time. Wiping his mouth with the back of his hand, apparently considering the subject either boring or closed, he set the glass down and said, ''Can I watch a video?''

''You didn't eat your cereal.''

''I'm full. Will you help me get dressed?''

''I thought you wanted to watch TV?''

''I do,'' the child said, looking as if he couldn't figure out why he'd think otherwise.

''I guess,'' Chase replied, sounding a little confused himself. ''Bring me your clothes. And a washcloth,'' he added, eyeing the half of the milk-moustache he'd missed.

Tyler mumbled an obliging, ''Okay.'' After nearly knocking the stool over when he jumped down, he scooped up the cat that had been peacefully licking its paws under a chair at the table and headed down the hall.

Suddenly skeptical, not wanting it to show, Chase turned back to his coffee.

Taking care of Tyler hadn't sounded like that big a deal at two in the morning. Listen for him. Feed him cereal. He could do that. All he'd really been thinking of anyway was that it didn't make any sense for Alex to have to hassle with the boy when she was in such a hurry already. Now, though, he was operating without a manual. She hadn't left any instructions beyond the cereal part.

Figuring Tyler would know what he needed to do—hoping, anyway—he glanced at the clock on the stove. The market was open in New York. He should be calling his broker.

Instead, he was pondering his first taste of just how much attention a child required.

He should also be thinking about the property he was in the process of buying near the hospital, deciding if he should fly his architect down to give him some preliminary sketches for a medical building or if he should hire someone local.

Instead, he was imagining Alex, sleep-tousled and sighing over her first sip of coffee in the morning—and wondering how she was holding up on so little sleep. He didn't know how she did it. Fixed people the way she did.

My mom makes people better.

He'd never dreamed he'd find a conversation with a four-year-old so intriguing.

There had actually been a strange logic to the child's seemingly disjointed statements. A creative sort of segue from one topic to the next that was remarkably intelligent, if a guy thought about it. But despite Tyler's chattiness, he hadn't revealed anything of substance that Chase hadn't already known—or suspected—about his mom.

Through the nurses at the hospital and his brothers, Chase had already known there was usually someone in need living in her guest room. And he knew from talking with Brent that Alex picked up the tab for some of her patients. The boy had told him his parents were only having to pay the hospital charges for the therapy. She wasn't charging at all for his office visits.

It sounded as if Brent's family didn't know she was probably making up a portion of what she didn't charge from her own pocket. A medical practice was a business and the other associates in it wouldn't take kindly to someone who wasn't bringing in her share.

He seriously doubted Alex ever saw what she did as a business, however. And, though no one who knew him would believe it, he was having a hard time thinking in terms of profit and loss himself lately. Alex was really good at taking care of people. She seemed to have a knack for zeroing in on a need and doing whatever she could to help. She knew *how* to help, too. But he was flying by the seat of his pants.

He'd just remembered he needed to wake Brent when Tyler walked in carrying his clothes, one shoe and a drip-ping-wet washcloth.

Battle stations, he mentally muttered and frowned at the trail of water drops on the floor. Figuring he'd just prioritize the way he'd seen Alex do and delegate the way he did, he had Tyler push a hand towel across the floor to mop up the water while he woke up Brent and got the teenager moving toward the shower.

By the time he heard the front door open ten minutes later, the shower was running, Tyler was dressed and sprawled on the family-room sofa with the television head-phones on and Chase was pouring himself a second cup of coffee.

"I'm sorry I'm so late," Alex said in a rush, tossing the newspaper she'd picked up from the porch onto the counter as her eyes swept the room for signs of her son. "I have to get back, but I know you have therapy in an hour. I'll get Brent moving while you get ready. Is everything all right?"

"Everything's fine."

Chase stood at the counter, crutches under his arms and the shirt he'd worn yesterday hanging over a pair of jogging shorts. He was barefoot, unshaven and looked as if he'd been dragged from bed, which he probably had been. When she met his eyes, her only thought before she jerked her glance toward the family room was that he had no business looking that appealing.

All she could see of her little boy over the sofa back was the top of his head and the black headset covering his ears. He was motionless, utterly transfixed by a curiously silent scene of careening cars and huge explosions. The carnage wasn't the sort of thing she normally let him watch, but she figured another minute of it wouldn't scar him too badly and headed for the coffeepot herself.

She'd be fine as long as she didn't slow down. Alex reminded herself of that as she reached past Chase and took a mug from the cabinet above them. Her body clock had already worked past its sleep cycle and now that it was morning, all she needed was caffeine and a shower and she'd be good for the rest of the day.

Most of it, anyway.

Chase hadn't budged.

Looking toward the biceps straining against the sleeve of his black T-shirt, she glanced past the stubble covering his jaw. She made it as far as the sensual line of his mouth before she decided she wasn't up to such close contact.

"I need coffee."

"I know. Here." Picking up her hand, ignoring the way she went still at his touch, he curved her fingers around his mug and took an empty one for himself.

"You don't have to worry about Tyler," he said, over the splash of coffee being poured. "He's already dressed. We had a small debate over whether a blue-striped T-shirt went with green plaid shorts and settled on tan and olive." The carafe slid into place with a quick click of glass against metal. "I explained that a man is usually better off to play it safe with fashion and save the risks for the stock market."

The faintest hint of a smile lit his eyes when he saw her breathe in the scent of her coffee and glance back up. But that light vanished as his glance swept her face. He wasn't checking her out so much as he was checking her over, and that made his thorough perusal incredibly intimate despite the matter-of-fact tone of his voice.

"He's washed, clothed and fed. Not necessarily in that order and mostly what he had was milk. Brent should be getting out of the shower any minute," he went on, sounding as if he were delivering a report. "He asked if we could hit a McDonald's for breakfast on the way to therapy, so that's what we'll do. All your bases are covered."

He had everything under control? "You dressed Tyler?"

With everything she had on her mind—the patients she'd left, the office calls waiting for her, the way he'd slowly, systematically robbed her of her senses last night—the thought that nearly everything she needed to do at the house was already done seemed too incongruous to comprehend.

She must have looked as baffled as she felt.

"We managed," he muttered. "I might not know much about kids, but I didn't break him or anything."

"That's not what I meant," she murmured, apologizing. He was feeling good about what he'd done. She hadn't meant to ruin that for him. "I just didn't expect you to go to so much trouble."

"It wasn't any trouble." Seeing her rub her temple, the defense left his tone. "He wanted to get dressed and I figured it would be easier for you if he was ready when you got here. There was no sense in you worrying about Brent, either."

She saw his glance cut to the family room. Seeing that Tyler was still occupied, he reached out and nudged back the bangs brushing her eyebrow.

"Take your coffee and go get your shower," he said, letting his hand fall. "I'll keep an eye on him until you're out."

Any other time, she might have marveled at how easily

he stepped in when she needed help. But as she stood there, fighting the fatigue she couldn't afford to acknowledge, all she could do was wonder if he knew how much it meant that he'd done something just to make things easier for her—and if he used that knowledge to his advantage.

Don't you ever suspect ulterior motives?

What she was thinking wasn't like her at all. She couldn't believe she was questioning a kindness. Yet, the more she tried to shake the thought, the tighter it clung. She knew what a cynic he was. She knew he believed people showed consideration out of obligation or to serve a purpose. She was where she was at that very moment because he'd felt obligated over her help with his brothers.

Not caring to consider what his purpose might be, just grateful for the help, she shoved the thoughts aside. She didn't have the time or the energy to worry about it right now. Needing to conserve both, she stepped away just as Chase slid his mug down the counter.

Seeing where he wanted to go with it, she reached for the mug herself.

"I'll get it," she murmured, and, avoiding his eyes, she set his coffee beside the newspaper. Moments later, aware of his speculative glance on her back, she took a quick detour to kiss the top of her son's head before heading for the shower to let hot water melt the knots in her neck.

Those knots had cloned themselves by the time she tucked Tyler into bed twelve hours later and traded her clothes for her favorite sleepshirt.

She hadn't talked to Chase when she'd come in. He'd been in the study with someone. A man in a suit, Brent had said when the boy had surfaced from MTV long enough to assure her that he'd had more than the package of chips on the counter for dinner.

The man was apparently leaving now, though. Brent had mercifully turned off the television and gone to bed to read when she had returned to the kitchen a few moments ago. In the blessed silence, she could hear muffled male voices drifting from the entry as she searched the kitchen cabinets.

She wasn't hungry. She'd downed a carton of yogurt on the run a few hours ago. What she needed was aspirin.

She was a doctor. She could write prescriptions for the most powerful painkillers available to modern man. And she would barter everything but her soul and her son for the synthetic derivative of willow bark.

She was on her sixth cabinet when she heard the front door close.

She'd just given up and headed for the sink to get a glass of water when Chase swung himself through the archway.

He stopped when he saw her, a mountain of hesitation in cargo shorts and an indigo polo shirt that made his eyes look as blue as a lake.

"I'd ask how you're doing," he said, his glance narrowing as he moved toward her, "but it's not necessary. I don't suppose you caught a couple of hours' sleep today, did you?"

She was as pale as a snowbank. Her eyes were rimmed with fatigue. "Unfortunately, no." Dragging her fingers through her hair, she turned to the sink with the empty glass she held. "I used to be better at this. I could go three days without sleep. Now, I'm toast after two."

Bright light bounced off the white porcelain, blinding as a strobe. Instead of reaching for the faucet, she reached for the light switch above the counter and flipped off the task light. With the glare cut by half, she filled the glass.

"You wouldn't happen to have any aspirin, would you?"

"Headache?"

"Killer."

"Come here."

Glancing toward him, she saw him prop his crutches against the counter and turn to lean against it himself.

"Come on," he said, reaching over to take the glass from her and set it aside. Grasping her wrist, he tugged her closer. "I don't have any aspirin, but this'll help. Turn around."

Somewhere in the back of her throbbing brain it occurred to her that letting Chase touch her probably wasn't a very good idea. She should just go to bed. Go to sleep. She'd felt worse than this before. She'd even been more exhausted than she felt right now, though she really couldn't remember being so tired since Tyler was an infant. But while she was wrestling with thoughts of what she should and shouldn't do, Chase was taking her by her shoulders and turning her around in front of him.

When he slipped his fingers up the back of her neck and told her to take a deep breath, she promptly gave up the battle.

"Breathe in more," he said, gently increasing the pressure of his thumb and fingers where they pressed low on the base of her skull.

Her shoulders rose as her lungs filled, the pressure inside her head seeming to increase by the second.

"Now out. Slowly," he murmured, working his fingers in tiny circles against the tight bunches of muscle.

She did as he said, her shoulders lowering by degrees as the air left her lungs, taking some of the tension with it.

"Again."

His fingers stilled as she complied, the firm, yet gentle motions continuing when she breathed out once more.

"Your muscles feel like rocks," he muttered.

She felt his other hand settle on her shoulder, but he didn't begin to knead with it as she thought he might. He just rested it there, his touch seeming almost protective as he continued working on her neck.

"It's from bending over a table for so long."

"It's not just from the last couple of days," he countered. "They're always this way."

Puzzled by how he'd know something like that, she started to look back at him.

Nudging her head right back around, he muttered, "Breathe."

There didn't seem to be much of anything he hadn't noticed about her. There didn't seem to be a muscle in her body that didn't respond to him, either. He was only touching a couple of centimeters of skin, but she could feel muscles loosening clear to the base of her spine.

"You're not on call this weekend, are you?"

"No," she said, closing her eyes as his hands slid together and he began to work his thumbs from her neck to a particularly sore spot between her shoulder blades. "I'm only on once a month."

"You can catch up on your sleep."

She would have told him that was highly doubtful. After all, she had a four-year-old. But the comment wasn't worth the effort. She'd rather spend her energy concentrating on what he was doing. And what he was doing felt like pure heaven.

His big hands splayed over her back, their heat seeping through the thin cotton of her shirt. Beneath his thumbs, knots were slowly dissolving and her thoughts were being drained of everything but the strength and sureness of his touch. He knew exactly what to do to make her body let go of the stress. He knew exactly how much pressure to apply, when to go easy because a spot was tender, when to stroke deeper, massage a spot longer.

By the time he'd worked to the small of her back, her

head had lolled forward and she should have felt as malleable as modeling clay.

She would have, too, but fatigue was slowly giving way to an entirely different sort of lethargy, and the faint clamor of warning bells drifted through her consciousness.

Chase's hands now curved her waist. They felt good there. Better than good. They fit around her in a way that made her feel very small, very female and very aware of the little licks of heat he was suddenly generating inside her. Until that moment, she hadn't realized how completely she'd given herself over to him. The instant she did, some of the tension he'd relieved shot to the surface.

With that quick jolt back to reality, she swallowed a groan.

"I can't do anything this weekend but look for an apartment." She turned around, picking up their conversation right where they'd left off. "I forgot that I need to look for a place to stay."

He hadn't let her go. She'd simply turned in his hands. Now, trapped between his legs, she watched his glance move quietly over her face.

"You don't have to go anywhere, Alex." Slipping his hands to her hips, he tugged her closer. "I want you to stay."

She opened her mouth, only to have her protest change course before she could utter a word about his offer. His thumbs were moving again, shifting the thin fabric of her shirt over her stomach, rubbing it against her skin.

"I can't do this, Chase." The man didn't play fair. She had no reserves. She was running on empty. And his hands were flexing into her flesh, ten points of fire that threatened to turn her sense of self-protection to ash.

"Do what?" he quietly asked, his eyes steady on hers.

"I can't get involved with you. Not this way." It was

fatigue. It was the way he looked at her mouth. It was the way he touched her. They all combined to make her legs feel as stable as Tyler's building blocks.

She touched her hands to his biceps, needing to lean, just a little.

"Why not?"

"Because you don't really want me."

One eyebrow shot up. Running his tongue over his teeth, he glanced down, then complacently met her eyes. "How many years did you study human anatomy?"

Her heart bumped her ribs. "That's not what I meant. I'm talking about why you want me. Or why you think you do. You're my patient," she murmured, feeling hopelessly inept at explaining something she wouldn't have even attempted to tackle had she had all her wits about her. "And I helped you with your brothers. That's how things started out, anyway. Maybe you're just confusing gratitude with attraction. Or maybe it's just convenience," she concluded, because every time she'd thought about how nice he'd been to her that morning, that was the thought that had trailed right behind it.

Even as she felt him go still, she couldn't help thinking that he'd lived his entire life with that same sort of distrust and suspicion. But while part of her finally understood how he felt, another part braced herself for his blunt honesty.

All he did was give her a slow, considered nod.

"There's something I want you to understand right now, Alex." The conviction in his voice was echoed in his expression. "I didn't invite you here to get you into my bed. And I certainly don't expect you to sleep with me in exchange for a room. As for the rest of it," he said, lifting his hand to her face, "I've never confused physical attraction with anything else in my life." With the tip of his finger, he traced the fullness of her lower lip, the heat of memory darkening his eyes. "I want you. If you don't want me, be honest and say so. Don't hide behind that doctor-patient argument." His finger drifted to the point of her chin. "We passed that long before last night."

It wasn't a question of want. It was a question of self-preservation. He hadn't been trying to seduce her into bed with the things he'd done for her. He didn't need to play that kind of game. He wanted her. Plain and simple. No deceit. No promises. Take it or leave it.

It would have been so much easier to leave it if he hadn't been touching her. She could be rational then. When she was away from him, she could think of all the reasons why falling in love with him was a really bad idea.

He must have sensed her struggle. Tipping her chin up, he lowered his mouth to within a breath of hers. "You don't have to answer me tonight."

His lips brushed hers once. Twice. Then his tongue touched hers, gently, slowly seeking entry. His kiss was long and deep, exquisitely tender, devastatingly intimate.

He breathed in her sigh as he curved a hand around her ribs. She drank in his groan when he cupped her unrestrained breast. That low, guttural sound filled her, vibrating deep inside her body as he taunted long-buried needs and feelings she wanted desperately to deny.

Only when she caught his wrist, did he raise his head. When he did, his breathing was as ragged as hers.

"It's okay," he whispered, smoothing her hair back from her face. "I'm not going to push." He skimmed his thumb over her temple, soothing the pain she'd nearly forgotten was there. "Not when you're this tired."

A wry smile touched his mouth as he nodded toward his leg. "I'm hardly in a position to carry you off to bed, anyway. When it happens," he whispered, brushing one last kiss over her mouth, "you'll have to take the lead."

Chapter Ten

You'll have to take the lead.

"We just can't thank you enough, Dr. Larson. I just wish there was some way we could repay you."

"You can repay me by making sure he keeps up his exercises," Alex replied, smiling at Glen Chalmers as she mentally shouldered aside the memories of last night. Those memories had tormented her all morning. It was midafternoon, and she still couldn't banish them. They played through her mind in a continuous loop; thoughts of how Chase had so skillfully eased the tension in her neck. Thoughts of how he'd kissed her, how he'd touched her. The husky certainty in his voice.

When it happens, you'll have to take the lead.

Not "if," but "when." And as if she would seduce him.

"Get him back over to see me in a month," she added, giving the thoughts another shove. She'd never taken the lead with a man in her life. She couldn't begin to imagine it happening now.

Glen and Maryann Chalmers sat across from her desk, Glen in freshly laundered coveralls and Maryann in a lace-bibbed floral dress. Two of their towheaded young children sat on the sofa beneath Alex's diplomas. Brent sat on the sofa's arm, holding the baby brother he'd sorely missed.

The Chalmers deserved her full attention. Chase was *not* going to distract her any more than he already had.

Raising his work-roughened hand, Glen thoughtfully scratched his jaw. "Berries will be coming on next month, Doctor. It's nigh-on to impossible to take half a day driving over here and back. We've only got the one vehicle and I need it in the field. Would it hurt him to wait a little longer?"

"It really would be better if I could see him," she gently stressed. "But if you can't get here then, come in as soon after that as you can. All right?"

"I could drive over, Dad," Brent offered. "I've got my license. I can buy Lawry Anderson's old Mustang. It's an automatic, so it's not like I'd have to shift or anything."

"That'd be a fine idea, son. But you don't have enough saved up to buy that car. He's wanting the moon for it."

"Yeah, but Chase…I mean Mr. Harrington," Brent corrected, since his parents apparently preferred he address adults formally. "He told me how to negotiate. We were talking about cars 'cause Tyler…Dr. Larson's little boy," he explained, "likes cars and I was telling him, Mr. Harrington, I mean, about the Mustang. He said Lawry has no reason to come down on the price because he knows how much I want it. Since there's nobody else bidding against me," he continued, slipping into the lingo he'd picked up from his new friend, "what I have to do is pretend I've found some other car I'm interested in more and when

Lawry starts thinking he could lose the sale, he'll start coming down on the price.''

A month ago, Alex wouldn't have believed the boy could string so many words together all at once, much less look so confident when he spoke. Even with his mom and dad, she'd noticed his diffidence.

Now, the boy sat with a romper-clad ten-month-old gumming a fistful of his shirt, sounding as if he could captain the debate team.

Maryann, her wispy, dishwater-blond hair scraped back in a ponytail, blinked at her son, then at her husband. Her husband just looked the boy over as if checking to be sure he was really his progeny.

"That would be the way to do it," Glen said, looking thoughtful again.

The Chalmers had known from the day after Alex's washing machine had sprung its little leak that their son was staying with her in the home of another patient. They knew the man's name and whatever Brent told them about him, but it had been apparent that Chase Harrington and his lifestyle were not known in the Chalmers' rural world.

They'd looked incredulous when Brent told them he'd gone through a McDonald's drive-through in the limousine that had dropped him and his suitcase at her office a half an hour ago. Now when the receptionist buzzed Alex and told her there was a man outside who needed to see Brent, they both started fussing with the children's clothes as if they were about to be presented to royalty.

They didn't get to meet Chase, though. The man who'd come to see Brent was a preppy-looking young man named Dave from a local car dealership who just needed to drop off the keys to the car he'd left in the parking lot.

"That car right there," he said, pointing through the slats of Alex's blinds to a brand-new black Mustang parked by a row of flowering hawthorn. "I was told to hand these to Brent Chalmers and to tell him to save his money for college."

"Who would...? Where did...? We can't accept that," Glen stuttered while Brent, dumbstruck, stared at the keys in his hand.

"You have to," Dave said, handing a packet of papers over to Brent. "Cash sale. Don't even know the name of the person who paid for it." He grinned at the kid grinning back at him. "Only name on it's yours."

Glen sputtered a little more as Dave walked out. Alex couldn't tell if the boy's father wanted to worry about why someone would bestow such an expensive gift, believe his son's good fortune or protect his own pride at not being able to produce the thing himself.

She couldn't quite tell what Brent was thinking, either. All he said was, "Man, I gotta call Chase."

But Chase told Brent he had no idea where the car came from.

Alex heard him herself because she put him on the speaker phone in her office so the Chalmers could hear the conversation, too. Chase did tell Brent, however, that it wasn't very often that something came without strings, so he might as well enjoy it. He then suggested that Brent be careful driving and asked him to give him a call when he came into town for his next appointment.

Neither Alex nor Brent bought Chase's denial. And because they didn't, neither did Brent's parents, but there was no way they could have their son decline the gift when the man wouldn't acknowledge that he'd given it—and the car was clearly, completely, Brent's. By the time they were off the phone and the Chalmers were trooping out of her office, Maryann was shaking her head and marveling at how something good had come from her son's awful accident, and

Glen was telling Brent that the two of them could take a couple of the kids with them in the Mustang and Mom could follow in their crew-cab truck.

Alex didn't realize how wide her own smile had been until she felt it fade along with the voices in the hall. She couldn't believe what Chase had done. Not just with the car, expensive as it had to be. It was what he'd done to instill some confidence in the shy young teenager that impressed her. He'd obviously spent time talking with the boy, taken him under his wing, drawn him out. The gift of time he'd given could have more far-reaching effects than anything he could possibly have bought him. And that, as he'd told him about the car, had come with no strings, too.

"Dr. Larson. Your next patient is ready."

With an absent nod toward the nurse in the doorway, Alex closed Brent's file and set it in her out box.

Strings. Even faced with a revealing glimpse of Chase's kindness, she was being reminded of his basic opinion of human nature. He didn't like strings. Not in business and not in his personal life. He was only now getting his first taste of family ties and even there, even though he wanted a relationship with his brothers, he resisted getting tangled too much. He'd yet to meet Kelly or Ronni, or his nieces and nephews.

And he'd made it clear last night there were no strings between the two of them. He wanted her. Apparently, in his mind, that was all that mattered.

She left her office, mentally downshifting to focus on her next patient. But even as she lifted the file from the box by the exam-room door, it wasn't her patient on her mind. It was the generosity of a man who kept insisting generosity didn't exist—and the nagging feeling that she was falling in love with him.

* * *

Had Chase been at the house that evening, Alex would have told him just how kind she thought he was for doing what he'd done—whether he wanted to admit having done it or not. But she didn't see him until she went to fish the newspaper from under a bush by the front door the next morning and ran into him as she walked back into the house.

She was studying the headlines, looking forward to actually sitting down with the paper and a cup of coffee, as she pushed the door open and stepped in.

Chase was on the other side, three feet from the four-foot-wide section of the double doors. The masterfully carved whitewashed wood collided with his shoulder, but it was putting his weight on his injured leg that had him hissing a breath an instant before he caught his balance with his crutches. Half a second later, he groaned.

"Oh, my…oh, Chase." The paper was at her feet, her hands clutching his stone-hard arms. "I had no idea you were there. Are you all right? Did you feel anything pop?"

Her glance worriedly scanned his face. She'd caught the quick flash of pain, the sudden paleness. Now she saw him tighten his jaw as he took a deep breath and opened his eyes to mutter something she was really glad Tyler couldn't hear from the family room.

"I thought you were leaving. I wanted to ask you something."

"I just went to get the paper," she explained, releasing one arm to look down at his leg. The response was automatic. Short of popping a pin, which would have had him writhing on the floor, just looking wouldn't tell her a blasted thing. "How does it feel?"

"It's fine."

"Come on, Chase. I saw—"

"It's fine," he insisted, sounding more determined now

than anything else. "It hurt worse the other day when I bumped it in the shower."

This time Alex closed her eyes, shaking her head as she straightened. Somehow, certain patients managed to heal in spite of themselves. Certain patients handled discomfort better, too. Except for where his bruises were turning chartreuse and the pink scar high on his cheekbone, his color was already back to normal.

"What did you want to ask me?"

A minute ago, Chase's entire focus had been on business. The pride he'd felt over taking care of the boys the other morning and the protective feelings that had come when he'd found Alex in the kitchen looking like warmed-over death that night, were even more foreign than the emotional upheaval he'd already been dealing with. Those feelings had felt far more dangerous. Far more difficult to understand. He'd needed normalcy. He'd needed familiar ground. He'd needed work.

In the last twenty-four hours, he'd arranged the meetings he needed to move on the project he'd conceived in the hospital. The possibilities, the details, the pure fun of taking all the pieces and merging them into a workable whole filled him with a blessedly familiar energy. The adrenaline of a pending deal pumped in his veins. It was better than a drug. Better than sex.

He'd thought so at one time, anyway.

In the space of seconds, Alex had jarred every productive thought from his head.

It wasn't her fault that she'd nailed him with the door. She hadn't realized he'd come chasing after her. She was totally responsible, however, for the way his body hardened. Her soft, small hand curled around his arm and every breath he drew brought her light, fresh scent. He knew exactly how she could relax with his touch. How she tasted. How her gently rounded breasts fit in the palm of his hand.

The thought nearly made him groan. Mercilessly, he banished it. It shouldn't be possible that she could have such an effect on him seconds after his body had so impolitely reminded him that he couldn't put his weight on his leg. But there was no denying that she did.

Seeing the sudden hesitation in her expression, he had the satisfaction of knowing she couldn't deny his effect on her, either. The quality of her concern seemed to shift, her lips unconsciously parting as awareness snapped between them. He'd made it clear enough that he wanted her. With his cards on the table, she either played her hand or folded.

A fine tension hummed in the air as her fingers slowly slipped away.

"I need the name of a caterer," he said, not caring for the feeling that there might be more to her withdrawal than bad timing. This was neither the time nor the place to continue last night's discussion. Cartoon voices filtered from the family room. Tyler could come tearing in any minute. "I have half a dozen people coming here in half an hour and Gwen's plane is late. I need coffee now and lunch brought in, but she won't be here in time to get it ordered and delivered. Who would you call for something like that?"

Snagging back her hair, she bent to pick up what she'd dropped. When she straightened, tucking her plastic-shrouded paper against her navy sweater to cross her arms, all he could see in her lovely face was concentration. He recognized it by the two tiny lines that formed between the soft wings of her eyebrows.

"For lunch?" The only thing she'd ever had catered was Tyler's last birthday party. Cakes-'n-Clowns wouldn't be what he had in mind. "What do you want served?"

"I don't care. Sandwiches or a couple of salads would be fine. I just want it plated and on the table in the dining room so it's ready when we break for lunch."

He wanted it in the dining room. The table in there was travertine marble. The chairs were upholstered. The room was formal with a capital F. He wasn't talking tuna fish.

"I can go to the deli—"

His eyebrows slammed down. "I'm not asking you to do it," he growled. "Just tell me who to call."

"I'm trying to," she muttered back. "There's a gourmet deli in the shopping center at the bottom of the hill. If you call in your order, I can pick it up."

"I'm not having you running around for me on your day off. I'll have it delivered. But that only solves part of the problem."

"It solves the biggest part," she pointed out, seeing no reason why she couldn't help with the rest of it. "The only thing I have to do today is meet that lady you set me up with to pick out my carpeting. I'm meeting her at my house instead of here. I'll find some linens and put the food on plates and have them on the table before I leave.

"The name of the place is La Charcuterie," she told him, watching him battle with the idea of having her do his assistant's job. "You make the call, and I'll start the coffee. How many people do you have coming?"

It was plain enough that he realized hers was the easiest solution to his problem. It only took him ten seconds of frowning at her before he said there would be eight, including him and Gwen. His lawyer, three members of the city planning commission, the owner of the old Taylor building and the owner's Realtor. Tonight, he'd be meeting again with the architect he'd had dinner with last evening.

"What are you putting together?" she asked as he followed her into the kitchen to make the call from there.

"Medical offices," he told her, then added that he wasn't sure if he would renovate the old building or raze it and put up a new one. And that was only if he could get the property for a decent price.

All he was doing now was seeing if the project was feasible. He told her that while she put on the coffee and he flipped through the phone book to get the number he needed. Then, after he'd made his call, he mentioned that he'd meet tomorrow with an architect Tanner had recommended to get a different perspective on the project. He liked having options.

It was obvious to Alex that the amount of work required just to see if the idea would work was incredible. It was obvious, too, that Chase thrived on it. There was an intensity about him as he spoke, a gleam in his eyes and an aura of energy that probably had the opposition swallowing hard whenever he entered the room. It was an aura of power, confidence and a hint of the warrior cloaked in the guise of a businessman. By the time he got around to telling her that he wanted Tanner's construction company in on the deal, she had no doubt that it was the logistics of the battle he enjoyed as much as the outcome.

He lived for the negotiations. The challenge.

He'd even passed on the most basic trick of the trade to the young man who'd gone home yesterday.

She'd set a thermal carafe by the coffeemaker and Chase was beside her closing the bag of coffee when she finally voiced the thoughts that had been nagging at her since the Chalmers family had left her office.

"You know," she began conversationally. "What you did for Brent was awfully nice. I'm just not sure I completely understand why you told him you didn't know where that car came from."

Though he hesitated for an instant, he kept his attention

on the tabs he was folding on the narrow brown bag. "Because I don't."

It was her turn to pause. "Chase, there's no way—"

"Listen," he muttered, setting the bag by a row of copper canisters and looking right at her. "I don't know where it came from."

Disbelief flashed in her eyes. A moment later, distrust moved in. It was the distrust that had Chase biting back an oath. He could handle seeing anything in her but that. "My lawyer took care of everything. I told him what I wanted and he handled the details."

"That's semantics."

That was true. But her tone held softness. "Let it go. Okay? The kid needed a car."

So he'd bought it for him, she thought. Just like that.

But then, she reminded herself, just like that, when she'd needed a place to stay, he'd offered the house. And when he'd learned that Ryan needed help raising the rest of his funding, he'd started calling his friends.

Watching the defense tighten his jaw, wondering what else he'd done that he didn't want anyone to know about, she realized she wouldn't be surprised at all to learn now that he was the anonymous benefactor of an orphanage, that he funded scholarships or that he'd decided to bail out the rest of the hospital project himself.

If he hadn't already.

The stray thought suddenly tugged at her with the same odd certainty she'd felt when she'd first begun to suspect who Chase was. As far as she knew, Ryan and Ronni still didn't know where the huge anonymous donation for the building fund had come from. She just remembered that a cashier's check for five million dollars had arrived with a note congratulating them on their upcoming marriage—right about the time Chase had learned about his brothers.

He said he'd seen a picture of Ryan in a newspaper article about the lost funding.

"People should start getting here any time now. Thanks for taking care of this for me," he said, having clearly dismissed what they'd been talking about a moment ago. "I don't know what I'd have done without you."

She'd done nothing more than help out the way he had with Tyler and Brent the other morning. She might have told him that, too, had her need to understand him not been so acute. Every layer he so reluctantly revealed was covered by yet another, years of self-protection piling upon themselves like blocks hiding the heart of a tomb.

"Chase?"

"Yeah?" he muttered, just as he started to move away.

"Do you know anything about a donation Ryan received as an engagement present?"

His eyes pinned hers a little too quickly. Standing three feet from her, the sunlight flooding the room picking out the threads of silver near his temples, he looked very much as if he wanted to do what he'd done a moment ago. Look her in the eye and lean on a technicality.

He also looked as if it didn't please him that he couldn't.

"It's easier when people don't know about some things, Alex."

"Easier?" She stepped closer, her glance darting toward the family room. Tyler's feet still dangled over the end of the sofa, forty-eight colorful inches of cartoons keeping him transfixed.

She lowered her voice anyway.

"Chase," she said, in the same flat tone she usually reserved for her son when he was being particularly obtuse. "I can understand why you wouldn't have wanted your brothers to know what you'd done before they met you." He would never have known if they'd accepted him for himself or because of his money. It didn't take a psych rotation to figure that out. "But what harm can come from people knowing how kind you are?"

"Because I didn't do it to be kind. I just did it because the need was there. And that's not the reputation I want."

She blinked up at the mountain of pure masculine conviction staring back at her. The thought that he wanted the reputation the public had of him, that he wanted to be known as ruthless and demanding, was incomprehensible to her. But there was no mistaking his certainty. Or how his guard slipped into place. Though he remained towering over her, she could practically feel the subtle distance edging between them. He was no more comfortable with what she'd just discovered about him than he had been any other time she'd ventured too close to the parts of himself he needed to protect.

It was because he needed to protect himself that what she thought she couldn't understand finally made sense. If people knew what he cared about, that made him vulnerable. And that was the one thing he didn't want to be.

It was his vulnerabilities that she loved.

The realization coincided with the refined peal of the doorbell. The sound was too soft to be startling, but her hand flew up to cover her heart anyway, the motion purely protective.

"I'll get it!"

"That's okay, sport," Chase called out, as Tyler's head popped up over the back of the sofa. "That's for me. I'll take care of it.

"Look," he said, resignation cloaking him when he turned back to her. "For what it's worth, Ryan already figured it out. He and Tanner know. Now you. We keep this between ourselves. Okay?"

* * *

"I was beginning to think they were going to keep him all to themselves," Ronni admitted, studying Chase's back as he leaned on his crutches beside Tyler and Griffin at a video game. "Either that, or that he was a figment of Ryan's imagination."

Alex and Ronni sat across from Kelly in the middle of the chaos of Pizza Pete's. A din filled the crowded, colorful room, the cacophony a blend of electronic games, noisy children and a squeaky-voiced teenager booming out pizza pick-up numbers on a microphone. The only reason the women were having a conversation that didn't deal with the hospital, the new wing or Chase's project was because the men had taken off with the kids as soon as everyone had finished eating.

"There was always some excuse not to get together," Ronni continued, "but every day I'd hear that Ryan had lunch with Chase, or that he'd run into him with Tanner, or that Chase had called to tell him he'd lined up another donor for the wing." She shook her head, her moss-green eyes widening. "You can't believe how much Chase has raised," she elaborated, clearly excited for her husband's sake. "It's millions. I mean, he's brought in almost all of what they'll need to finish. And that's after what he…"

Enthusiasm dipped as suddenly as it had escalated. With a quick glance at Kelly, who immediately dropped her attention to the paper plate in front of her, Ronni tried to cover her near-slip with a smile for Alex.

"I mean, after all he's been through," she concluded, turning her save into a total change of subject. "I have no idea where he gets his energy. But I want some of it. He really is making a remarkable recovery, isn't he?"

"Better than I would have anticipated," Alex replied, watching Chase balance himself so he could help Tyler get a better aim at whatever it was they were trying to blast, evade or conquer.

Her heart tightening a little at the way Tyler grinned up at the big man, she turned her attention back to Ronni, who'd finally given up on civvies and was now into maternity wear, and Kelly, holding the blue-eyed, button-nosed infant who would soon become her daughter. It was apparent from their exchange a moment ago that both women were now privy to the source of the mysterious donation.

Considering how close Ronni and Kelly were to their respective men, Alex would have been surprised if they hadn't known. It was just as apparent that they had also been asked to keep quiet about it and, like her, would tuck the information away with the thousand other bits of confidential information physicians knew but never discussed.

"The guys sure seem to be getting along well." Her back to the game area, Kelly lifted Lia's carrier to the table and tucked her in so the baby could see what was going on. "But I was kind of surprised that Chase didn't seem more interested in the pictures. Tanner said he's really been curious about their parents. I don't think he said more than two words the whole time they were looking at that album."

Alex had noticed that, too. Only, to her, it hadn't been lack of interest that had made him seem so distracted. What she'd seen had looked more like withdrawal.

"I think the kids have him a little overwhelmed." She offered the excuse as she pushed back her plate, her appetite nonexistent. "They were all wanting to look, too."

"They just didn't want to miss anything." Busy eyeing the lone slice of pizza to survive the meal, Ronni missed the curious glance Kelly shot Alex. "It seemed odd that there weren't any of Chase in there," she said, clearly debating whether or not she should add the calories. "But he was only six months old. There probably weren't many to begin with."

Reaching down the table, Alex picked up the brown faux-leather photo album from where the men had left it. "Where did this come from?" she asked, opening the cracked cover. The pictures were old and many of the corner mounts had come off, leaving pictures loose. There were a few spots, too, where mounts remained, but snapshots had been removed.

It was the only record of their past the men possessed.

"Ryan's caseworker gave it to him when he turned eighteen." Caving in to her cravings, Ronni picked up the slice of Pete's Supreme and plopped it on her plate. "They'd had so many caseworkers over the years and she…that last one I mean," she clarified, "told Ryan that the file seemed a little incomplete to her. Like things were missing, but she couldn't tell what. He didn't think much of it at the time, but the guys now figure that the Harringtons bribed the original caseworker to remove any trace of Chase when they adopted him." She picked off a slice of onion. "Ryan had told Chase about the album and Chase wanted to see it. That's why Ryan brought it tonight."

That must have been why Chase decided to come this evening, Alex thought, turning to another page of smiling faces. She hadn't talked to him in days. His meetings had gone on into the nights, and in the mornings it had been Gwen who'd come to the kitchen to take him coffee within minutes after arriving from her hotel.

This is quite typical, the very formal and efficient woman had said. *Once Mr. Harrington has decided to move on something, he does nothing else until the details are completed. It can be rather taxing if a person's not used to it, but I can't imagine him working any other way.*

He'd been holed up with Tanner and the architect when she and Tyler had left for Pizza Pete's—which was why she'd been so surprised when he'd come in with Tanner shortly after everyone else had arrived. He'd held her glance for only a moment before his attention was claimed by introductions, but that brief contact had affected her as surely as his touch.

"I can't tell if you two had an argument, or if you're still in denial."

At Kelly's observation, Alex's attention shifted from the pages.

"I opt for denial," Ronni piped in, popping a slice of pepperoni. "He doesn't look at her like a man who knows he's messed up. Or one who knows he's right. It's more like he's...I don't know," she murmured, prying up another pepperoni slice, "...imagining her naked or something."

"You're right," Kelly agreed as Alex's mouth fell open. "It's probably denial. I just can't tell if they're denying their relationship to us or to themselves."

Alex frowned. "No one's denying anything to anybody. Chase and I are just...we're sort of..." What? Friends? "We're just helping each other out."

"Excuse me?" Kelly arched an eyebrow. "Look me in the eye and tell me there's no chemistry between the two of you. He zeroed in on you like a heat-seeking missile the minute he walked in here. People don't have to speak to communicate, you know. I've delivered enough evidence of that over the years. Which reminds me," she said, opening her purse and reaching for Alex's. "Here." Taking two small gold packets from her bag, she slipped them between Alex's pager and wallet. "I know you haven't been involved with anyone in a long time, and I can't blame you for wanting to be cautious, if that's what's going on. But it never hurts to be prepared. You know how I preach to everyone to use these things.''

''For Pete's sake, Kelly...''

''So, back to this denial thing,'' she continued, overlooking the way Alex rolled her eyes as she handed her purse back to her. ''We've had considerable experience with Malones. I'll admit this one is a bit of an enigma, but is there anything we can help you with?''

Alex didn't hand back the condoms her irrepressible gynecologist friend dispensed with abandon. She didn't answer her, either. Ryan and Chase were headed for the table, the two four-year-olds darting and weaving between the tables ahead of them.

Right behind them came the rest of the crew. When the men had headed for the games with the kids, Chase had stayed with Tyler and Griffin. It was the only age group there that he knew.

His glance caught hers even before he stopped behind Kelly, but she was spared her friend's knowing looks by the clamor of kids wanting to stay longer and adults reminding them that it was a school night.

''Mind if I catch a ride home with you?'' he asked.

Except for those few minutes with the family photos, there had been a deceptive ease about him all evening. She could see that mask cracking again now, though. He was ready to leave. Had been for a while from the strain she saw in his smile when everyone started saying their goodbyes and gathering their things. She just hadn't realized how tightly he'd been holding himself together until an hour later—when he thought there was no one else around.

Chapter Eleven

Tyler chattered all the way home in the car. He'd still been at it when Alex ushered him into the house ahead of her and Chase, but Chase had seemed to welcome the diversion of her little boy's constant questions about the electronic games they'd played. He'd actually talked far more to her son than he had to her. But then, her little magpie had talked enough for both of them. Tyler had continued his running commentary about how Chase had helped him zap the Black Raptor all the way to his bed. Then he'd fallen asleep within a minute of his head hitting his pillow.

As late as it was, Alex should have crawled in with him. Instead, thinking Chase had gone out to the patio because the lights out there were on, she headed out to see if he was all right.

He wasn't on the patio. She could see him, though. The way the house wrapped around the pool, he was clearly visible through the wide, open sliding-glass door to his bedroom. Still dressed in his white dress shirt and jeans, he sat on the edge of the big bed in the cream-colored space, staring at something in his hands. He wasn't moving. He just sat in the pool of light from the brass lamp on his nightstand, his dark head bent and his shoulders bowed as if the weight of his thoughts were simply too much to bear.

From the conversation at dinner, it was obvious that he was becoming an important part of his brothers' lives. As uncertain as she'd suspected he'd felt about how they would accept him, and with his acquisition having gone so well, she would have thought he'd be feeling wonderful tonight.

What she saw instead, was a man in pain.

When he tossed aside whatever it was he held, and put his hands over his face, she wasn't sure she'd ever seen such dejection.

She felt like an intruder. This was private. This was a man stripped of the armor he'd built around himself. There was nothing protecting him now. Part of her knew she should turn around, slip back into the house, pretend she hadn't seen. He'd hate knowing how vulnerable he looked. He'd hate even more that she'd seen him that way. But there was another part of her that held her there, freezing her feet to the flagstone when he pushed his hands up through his hair and he lifted his head.

Bleakness carved his face. That desolation ran soul-deep, seeming to engulf him in a weariness she couldn't begin to comprehend. In her loneliest moments, she'd never felt the ache he caused her to feel as she watched him glance once more at what he'd discarded.

He couldn't seem to leave the pictures alone.

Even as Chase lifted his head, his glance drifted to the photographs he'd tossed onto the bed. He'd gone outside a while ago just to get away from them. He'd thought the cool air would clear his head, that maybe Alex would come out after she'd tucked Tyler in and he could distract himself with conversation. But being with Alex hadn't seemed like a good idea in the mood he was in, so he'd come back in and found himself staring at the photos again.

He'd had them for nearly three months now. Yet, they hadn't really meant anything to him until he'd seen where they'd once been.

Or maybe it had been everything going on around him that had put the fading snapshots into perspective.

He took a deep breath, forced it out in a rush. He needed to shake this. He needed to focus on something other than the images of the attractive young couple with their little family of three. Anger would be good. Anger he could deal with. It was familiar. The ache in his chest was not. The cold rage of resentment should have been easy to access. Heaven knew he'd buried it often enough for it to be inside him somewhere. But he didn't want to feel. He didn't want to think. He was tired. Lacking an acceptable alternative, he might as well go to bed and seek the oblivion of sleep.

Reaching for his crutches, he pushed himself upright and moved to the door. His own image reflected back at him from the wide expanse of window glass. The elegant room glowed softly behind him. It was the open portion that had his attention. Through it he could see the wavering illumination of the pool lights, the dark silhouettes of shrubs and trees—and Alex, slender and graceful in the casual calf-skimming dress she'd worn earlier that evening, moving from the pool to walk toward him.

Her expression held bated concern as she approached. Her soft smile when she drew to a halt only magnified it.

"I saw the light on," she explained, crossing her arms against the evening chill. Clouds had rolled in with the evening, turning the air damp. "On the patio, I mean. Tonight seemed a little hectic,'' she said, as if offering him an excuse for his preoccupation when they'd arrived at the house. ''I thought maybe you'd come out to do what you'd tried to do before.''

He knew exactly what she was talking about. The last time they'd met on the patio he'd been trying to relax. But, even then, he'd been trying to escape.

''Maybe I was,'' he muttered, torn between wanting her there and wishing she'd go away. His glance skimmed her bare arms. She'd obviously come after him as soon as she'd done whatever she'd had to do with Tyler. She hadn't even bothered to grab a sweater.

Touched by that, he stepped back when he saw her shiver.

''Come on in. It's cold out there.''

Alex shivered again as she stepped past him, as much from nerves as from the cool night air. The bleakness she'd sensed in Chase lurked beneath the mantle of control he'd slipped over himself even before he'd seen her. But she was more aware of his big body behind her when she turned to roll the door closed. As the glass slid into place, she saw his reflection towering behind her, his tall, powerful physique dwarfing her completely.

Their eyes met in the mirrorlike glass, his jaw tightening. But when she turned, he was already swinging his crutches around and moving away.

''It was a little crazy,'' he admitted, speaking of the chaos she'd mentioned a moment ago. ''I'd never been to a place like that before.''

''A place that noisy?'' she ventured.

''A place for families.'' Muscles bunched and shifted tensely beneath his shirt. ''I never realized it could be like that.''

''Like what?''

"The kids. The parents." Even though he'd stopped, his knuckles were white as he fisted the crutch grips. "They were really having a good time."

He stood at the foot of the bed with its oyster brocade comforter and carved Italian headboard. The double doors beyond the dresser that led to the hall were closed. The way he glanced toward them made her think he wouldn't mind if she just kept going right on through them.

Because she'd moved with him, she could now see what he'd been looking at a while ago. She even recognized the pictures. The people in them anyway. Except for the baby. The photos were of the Malones, various combinations of Ryan and Tanner with their parents and an infant. The baby would have to be Chase. But, as she, Ronni and Kelly had noted, there'd been no photographs of him in Ryan's album. Anyone looking through it wouldn't even have known he'd existed.

An edge entered his tone when he saw what had her attention. "The investigator said those were apparently offered to Elena and Walter when they adopted me. They were in the file of the attorney who handled the adoption. They only took the ones of me alone."

"I see," Alex murmured, gathering the pictures to look at them. The photos she'd seen a while ago had been of his family up to when Ryan was about three years old. Those she held were of the boys with a pretty, radiant young woman holding a baby a few months old. Another with the boys piling leaves on a handsome, grinning man seated by that same dark-haired baby propped up in a wheelbarrow. "It's no wonder you got so quiet when you were looking at the album."

The pictures had been lifted from their places just as he'd been plucked by Fate from the loving family depicted in them. But it was what he'd said about the gathering tonight that hinted at why he was having such a hard time with these pictures now.

Seeing his little nieces and nephews with their parents, he was truly beginning to understand what it was he had missed.

"They're just pictures," he muttered, trying to dismiss their import.

"They're part of your past."

He made a sound that was half resignation, half derision. "My past is a joke. Things were lousy for my brothers, but at least they weren't living a lie. They knew who they were and where they'd come from. I spent nearly half my life trying to figure out why I couldn't make the people I thought were my parents care about me."

Bitterness sliced through a paper-thin layer of composure. "I was nothing but a possession for my mother and less than that for the man I thought was my father. I tried everything I could to earn his acceptance. But no matter what I did, it was never enough. I was never good enough," he grated, jamming his chest with his finger. "But then I couldn't ever be because I wasn't really his son. So don't talk to me about my 'past.'"

He stood for a moment, big, angry, his impossibly blue eyes boring into hers. Clearly displeased with himself for losing control, or with her for having tested it, he lifted the tips of his crutches and started to turn away.

She reached for him, catching his arm. "Chase. Please." She could practically hear his defenses slamming into place. Not good enough, he'd said. As if there was some flaw in him, some fault of his own that had made it impossible for the people who'd raised him to care. "I'm sorry. I know tonight was hard for you. I wanted to help. Not make it worse."

"I'm not one of your charity cases," he insisted, bricking up his emotional wall before she had it crumbling completely. "I can handle this myself."

Alex stepped back, crossing her arms so quickly there was no way he could have missed the protectiveness of the position. She knew tonight had been a strain. She knew he'd been pushing himself. She understood that his physical condition was still less than optimum, no matter how badly he wanted to believe otherwise.

The rationale did nothing to relieve the rejection that stung like a slap.

"I'm sorry I bothered you," she murmured, and started for the door.

She'd taken two steps when she heard him swear. She'd made it the width of the king-size bed when she heard him moving behind her.

"Wait. Please," he added, making her think the oath had been directed more at himself than at her.

She felt his hand touch her shoulder. Glancing around, she saw him draw back to grab his crutch. It wasn't worth having him break his neck to get her to stop, even though she wasn't as adverse to the thought as a physician probably should be.

"You didn't deserve that." He had no business striking out at her. She was the only one who understood what he was trying to cope with, who knew how badly he was handling everything. That was probably why he got as defensive with her as he did. She knew him too well. Saw all his flaws. Yet, she seemed to suffer him anyway.

"Don't go," he asked, cursing the hurt he'd put in her eyes. Cursing himself for having put it there. He lifted his hand to her face, more relieved than he wanted to admit when she didn't pull away. "You said it yourself. It was a rough night. But I have no business taking it out on you."

His apology disarmed her. With her arms locked over

the achy knot in her stomach, Alex watched the shadows move through his face. She'd bumped an emotional bruise and he'd lashed out in pain. That pain was still visible even as he slipped his fingers along her jaw and let his hand trail away.

He'd asked her not to leave. As he leaned on his crutches to catch her by the shoulders and slowly pull her into his arms, she all but forgot why she'd been about to go.

He needed to be held. She realized that the moment she slipped her arms around his waist and felt his arms tighten around her. She felt him draw a ragged breath, his hard chest expanding against her breasts. Some of the strain seemed to leave his body when that breath slowly shuddered out and he buried his face in the side of her neck.

Her hand came up to cup the back of his head, her need to offer comfort as great as his need to seek it. He was so solitary in so many ways. Yet, he'd let himself reach for her. That alone told her how badly he needed her arms. And that alone kept her right where she was when, long moments later, the tension shifting through him changed quality and she felt his lips graze the skin of her neck.

The sensation began as a feeling of softness, a little thread of warmth that turned to a trail of heat as he nuzzled a path from the curve of her shoulder to the sensitive spot behind her ear. His fingers slipped through her hair and he tugged her head back so he could carry that debilitating caress to the hollow of her throat. Her pulse fluttered there as he worked his way up to settle his mouth over hers.

It had never occurred to her to move away. The arm at her back tightened as he turned with her in his arms, his crutches falling with soft thuds against the carpet as he sank to the edge of the bed. Caught between his legs, her hands settled on his shoulders and he skimmed his kiss to her chin, her throat, the soft swells of her breasts. She felt his breath, hot and moist through the thin cotton of her dress as he nuzzled first one tightening bud, then the other.

She was sure he felt the tremors he shot through her. His hands spanned her waist, tightening as if he knew he needed to hold her upright. She whispered his name, the sound part sigh, part plea. But not until he felt her knees sag against the mattress did he tip back his head.

His eyes glittered like blue diamonds on her face.

"Have you ever seduced a man before, Alex?"

Her heart was already pounding. The intent in his expression nearly made it stop. She thought she whispered, "No." She knew she shook her head.

"Do you want me to show you how?"

In the back of her mind, sanity warned that she would regret giving her heart to this man. With his hands moving over her hips, his thumbs dipping low on her stomach and her pulse clamoring in her ears, she barely heard that faint voice of caution. It was too late for warnings anyway. She was already in love with him. He made her feel more alive than she had in a very long time. And she needed that as badly right now as he needed her.

He'd told her she'd have to take the lead. "Please," she whispered.

In the low, golden glow from the lamp she saw his features go taut. The gleam in his eyes turned feral. "You'll have to be on top."

She swallowed, the thought of straddling his hard body jolting her to her core. "I know."

Watching her closely, he lifted her hands from his shoulders and moved them to the front of his shirt.

"Then, the first thing you have to do," he said, his voice dropping to a husky rasp as he guided her fingers to his buttons, "is get rid of this."

Her hands were trembling. She didn't realize that until

he let them go. He made no move to help her. He just sat on the edge of the brocade-covered bed, his glance drifting to her mouth when she took a breath and began slipping buttons through holes. When she reached his belt and the waistband of his jeans, he leaned back a little for her to tug out his shirttail.

The taut muscles of his shoulders felt hard as stone when she slipped her hand under the crisp white fabric and drew it down his arms. His skin gleamed like hammered bronze in the soft light.

She knew how beautifully his chest was formed, how the muscles of his flat stomach rippled, how the swirl of dark hair arrowed beneath his belt. There was just something about knowing she was free to touch him that made her knees feel even weaker than they had moments ago.

"Now," he said, catching her wrist as the shirt hit the floor. Reaching for her other hand, he drew them both up to his face. "You kiss me."

His fingers slid from hers to circle her waist once more. With the heat of his hands searing into her, the faint rasp of his nighttime beard sensitizing her fingers, she leaned forward and hesitantly lowered her head.

She felt him open to her the instant her lips touched his, but he waited until the first tentative touch of her tongue before he let his tangle with hers. Even then, he let her take the lead. He tasted hot and faintly of mint and she found herself growing bolder, leaning closer as her fingers threaded through the softness of his hair.

In the quiet of the room, she heard a faint rasp as he moved his hand down her back, opening the zipper of her dress. When she lifted her head a moment later, he slipped the loose garment from her shoulders.

"Drop your arms," he urged, and let the dress drop to a puddle at her feet.

The instant the fabric had fallen, her hand crossed her chest. Frowning at the automatic way she'd attempted to cover herself, he snagged her by the hips. The forward motion forced her hands to his shoulders to keep herself from losing her balance.

"Don't." His hot glance raked from the stark white lace covering the small mounds of her breasts to the enticingly high-cut legs of her sensible cotton briefs. "You have nothing to be self-conscious about. Not with me."

It had been five years since she'd been with a man. Five years since she'd been reminded of how inadequate she was in certain areas of her anatomy. But Chase scattered those thoughts with the flick of his fingers. Skimming the lace away, he shaped her with his hands, the hunger in his face relieving insecurities he'd scarcely given her time to consider.

She couldn't believe how beautiful he made her feel when he told her she was perfect and closed his mouth over her, groaning with the way she bloomed against his tongue. She couldn't believe, either, how easy he made it for her to do what she never thought she could have done and play the aggressor with him. He emboldened her. He freed her. And by the time he let her go to move back on the bed, he'd systematically attacked every defense she possessed.

Together they eased his leg up, and he edged back to the pillows so they could deal with his belt and his jeans. The safety pins holding the split seam of his denims were a challenge. But she managed to get them unfastened and to get his pants and boxers over the EFD. The clothing had barely hit the floor before he leaned over to take a condom from the nightstand. A moment later, he'd curved his hand around the back of her neck to bring her back with him, and he told her he could take it from there.

"My turn," he murmured, and kissing her breathless,

stripped off the last bit of fabric she wore and pulled her on top of him.

His long hard body seared her softer curves, her stomach quivering at the feel of his turgid length pressed to her. She drank his moan at that contact, then nearly moaned herself at the loss when he tore his mouth away and hooked his hands under her arms.

As if she weighed nothing at all, he drew her up his chest. His mouth brushed the pulse pounding at the base of her throat, the soft skin between her breasts. He shifted her then, catching her nipple in his mouth, and the sensations he created nearly sent her up in flames. He traced that arc of fire to the other side, ministering there until she nearly whimpered with need. Whispering her name, he told her how he'd ached to do exactly what he was doing now. And did it all over again.

He had every nerve in her body vibrating when he guided her back down. His tongue plunged into her mouth on the way, carrying her into a dark swirl of mindless sensation as his hands swept over her, molding, exploring. She could taste his need, feel his raw, unmasked hunger. He'd unleashed that same hunger in her, tapped into a place she'd never known existed. She didn't just feel alive with him. He made her feel essential. He made her feel a feminine power that told her she was as vital to him at that moment as the very air he breathed.

He'd thought he could hold out. He'd thought he could take the torture a little longer. He'd told himself he'd reached for her only because she'd looked so hurt by what he'd said. But he had known even then that he'd needed to feel her in his arms. He'd thought if he could just hold her for a minute, he would be all right. He'd needed the calm he sometimes felt when she touched him.

Need.

He didn't trust the word. Want, he understood. That was all this was. This mind-numbing desire boiling his blood. The calm had come over him long enough for her scent to fill him, for her softness to beckon him. And all he'd wanted from that instant on was to lose himself inside her.

That was all he wanted now. Holding out was no longer possible.

He urged her small, supple body upward, hooking her by the waist to guide her back down. Burying his head against her shoulder, he gritted his teeth against the exquisite sensation of gloving himself in her heat, then trapped her face between his hands when her breath hitched and swallowed her welcoming sigh.

Beyond that, there was no thought. There was just her and what she made him feel—and the overwhelming sensation that he was racing toward something that he needed with every fiber of his being.

He should turn off the light. The thought occurred to him, vaguely, as he smoothed back the strand of Alex's hair tickling his cheek and drew the sheet to her shoulders. It was two o'clock in the morning. They'd fallen asleep, only to awaken and make love again, under the covers this time, and drift back off.

He wasn't sure what had wakened him now. The tickling, maybe. She lay curled against his right side, her long leg draped over his good one, her head on his shoulder and her hand curved against his chest. Her breathing was deep and even.

She shouldn't have felt so good there. He was sated, sleepy, and his whole body felt as relaxed as hers. He should have been waking her, telling her what time it was so she could go on to her own bed. He always woke up alone.

It was because he felt so relaxed that he closed his eyes, tucked his cheek against the top of her head and ignored the light. He'd never before felt the peace he did at that moment. He was sure it wouldn't last. It would probably even be gone the next time he awoke. But for now, it was there. And he just wanted to hold her.

Chapter Twelve

Alex's house still wasn't ready. It had now been a month since the water damage had forced her from her home, but a delay with the drywall contractor had caused a delay with the painter who couldn't start until Monday. It would be the middle of next week before the mess would be gone.

Chase had mentioned that little circumstance while he'd piled pasta on their dinner plates that evening. Because the subject had come up between Alex's pleased comments about the report she'd received from his therapist about his progress and Chase's reminder that he had a meeting tomorrow night with his architect, the latest development with her house had merely sounded like a minor detail—rather than the postponement of the inevitable.

For the past two weeks Alex had been dreading the day she no longer had an excuse to stay under his roof. She and Chase had melded into each other's lives with an ease that would have been frightening had she allowed herself to truly think about it. When he was busy, she brought dinner home or put something together herself. When he wasn't tied up with business, he cooked for them, then he and Tyler would watch videos or CNN while she reviewed a file or took a call or—once—while she slipped into a long, hot bath. There had been a few times when his day had run long; others when she'd come in late. But no matter what the day had brought, or how late the evening had been, they spent their nights in each other's arms.

He was an incredible lover. He was a wonderful friend. To her and to her son. Yet there was still a part of himself he held back from her.

With the news about her house, she didn't yet have to face what she might or might not mean to him. But that day inched inexorably closer. And every day she fell a little more in love.

Make that every minute, she thought, as she stopped in the doorway of Chase's study.

The room was an expansive space of empty built-in bookcases and a space-age-looking arc of slate desk that Gwen had equipped with nearly every office gadget known to man. Behind the desk loomed a black leather chair that looked like the command seat for a space shuttle.

Chase sat in that chair in front of the computer, a cobalt-blue golf shirt stretching across his broad shoulders. Tyler leaned against his side, his little hand on the computer's mouse. When he'd seen Chase wearing a blue shirt this morning, he'd run back to his room and changed into the baggy blue T-shirt that now sported a slash of yellow fingerpaint from a project at Child Care.

Smiling, her glance moved between the dark-haired man's compelling profile and the concentration screwing up Tyler's little face.

"Hey," she murmured, walking past a table stacked with documents.

"Hey, yourself." His smile intimate and easy, Chase sat back and rubbed his chin. "We're playing Monopoly."

"Yeah, Mom. I'm gonna get Park Place!"

"Good for you."

Chase splayed his big hand over Tyler's cornsilk hair, ruffling it good-naturedly. "We're having a little trouble keeping our money straight, but we're working on it."

"He's only four," she pointed out, watching her grinning little boy rub his chin the way the big man had done. "Isn't there something in there a little easier?"

"A man is never too young to acquire real estate."

"Yeah, Mom," Tyler repeated. "I'm an ogle."

"Mogul," Chase corrected, smiling at his protegé.

Tyler grinned back, basking in the man's attention.

Alex wasn't quite sure what it was that tugged at her heart just then. It was as clear as a test tube that her son adored Chase. The man was as patient as a saint with him and she'd felt more than a little gratitude for the way he'd answered countless questions about cars and bugs and spiders. She knew Tyler needed male influence. That was one of the reasons she was so grateful for Ryan's and Tanner's presence in their lives. She just hadn't realized how attached Tyler was becoming to Chase until she saw him standing in the shirt he'd put on to match Chase's, mimicking the man's motions and grinning up at him as if the guy had invented the earth.

Suddenly uneasy, trying to hide it, she held out her hand to her budding tycoon. "Come on, sweetie. Chase said he had some things he needed to do, and you need to feed your pets and get your bath so I can get to the work I brought home."

"Aw, Mommy. Do I hafta?"

"I already made my calls." Turning in his chair, Chase murmured something to Tyler that had the boy looking utterly resigned. A moment later, Tyler had tucked his tongue in the corner of his mouth and was clicking on the icon Chase had pointed out. "I'll supervise the bath while you review your files. Just give us a minute to shut down the computer, okay?"

Maternal instincts jerked hard. "That's okay. I'd rather bathe him myself. I haven't seen him much today," she explained, immediately softening her tone and her refusal of his offer to help her out. "But thanks."

Chase's brow pinched, his glance holding hers long enough for her to know he'd caught the defensiveness in her tone. It seemed to him that she'd been a little edgy tonight. She had been ever since he'd told her about the call he'd received from her agent about her house. Between Tyler whining because he'd been hungry and the phone call she'd had to take right after he'd told her he'd be late tomorrow evening, he'd figured she was just preoccupied with any of the dozen things she usually had on her mind. Now, though, seeing the way she glanced so quickly from him, he had the feeling it wasn't work on her mind.

He had the feeling he knew what was, though, and he wanted to set her mind at ease. Now just wasn't the time.

"Okay, sport," he said, scooting Tyler toward his mom. "Bath and bed. We'll take up where we left off tomorrow."

The little boy made it to the end of the desk before he turned right back around, walked up to his side and leaned in for a hug. Without even thinking about it, Chase hugged him back and lifted his hand for Tyler to "high five." Another hug and he was walking toward his mom, wiping his nose on the hem of his baggy shirt.

It was a fair indication of how distracted Alex was that she didn't groan at what her son was doing. She was too busy feeling protective, and wondering where along the line she'd forgotten to be wary of how natural Chase looked with her son. It was bad enough that the dreams she'd been afraid to consider had slipped past her guard. She didn't want her son suffering the loss of those nebulous hopes, too. He was too young. Too innocent.

Tyler, as usual, was one step ahead of her—and his chatter made it apparent he was already thinking along the very lines she was trying to avoid. Chase was all he talked about while they fed Tom, the gerbil and the goldfish, and during his bath and while she dried and dressed him and tucked him into bed. He told her that Chase said he was having a model built of his new building and that he'd take Tyler to see it if it was okay with her. He told her he wanted to build buildings like Chase. He wanted to get crutches like Chase. He wanted to be just like Chase.

"How about you being just like you?" she asked, smiling at his earnest little face as she smoothed the sheet under his chin. "I happen to love you the way you are, you know."

"But don't you love him, too?" he asked, perplexed.

Yes, she thought. I do. "I love a lot of people," she said, copping out. "But I love you best."

"But he's neat, huh?"

"Yes, sweetie. He's neat." She kissed his freckled nose. "Now go to sleep."

"Mom?"

"What?" she asked, reaching past the goldfish bowl on the white oak nightstand to turn off the light.

"Griffin has a dad. Can I have one, too?"

Oh, Tyler. "Maybe someday."

"Can I call Chase Daddy?"

She flicked off the light, using darkness to hide the way she must certainly have paled. "No, sweetheart." Her voice was hushed, her touch gentle as she stroked her son's soft cheek. "It's different with you and Griffin. Ryan is Griffin's father. Chase is your...friend."

"Oh."

Just like that. Oh.

She whispered good-night to him then, and he mumbled "'Night," around an expansive yawn, snuggling deeper into the blankets as she moved to the door. But what he seemed to have accepted with relative ease only compounded the concern that had formed in her chest a while ago—until she realized she really didn't need to worry about Tyler getting any more attached to the man than he already was. The problem would take care of itself when she moved back to her house in a few days.

An hour ago, she'd dreaded that day. She still did, only now the need to protect her son had added ambivalence to the mix of emotions she dealt with on her way into the kitchen with her briefcase.

Work demanded that she push aside that confusion of feelings, however. She had two files to review before tomorrow morning's surgeries.

By the time she'd fixed herself a cup of tea, she'd cleared her mind of everything but that nagging concern for her little boy. Forcing her focus to her patients, she managed to put even that on hold when she reached for the first file and settled herself at the island.

She was still sitting there, her head bent in concentration, when Chase came through the archway an hour later.

"I thought you were still with Tyler."

Glancing up, she saw him look from the open file in front of her as he maneuvered himself to stand behind the stool she occupied.

Balanced on his crutches, he curved his hands over her

shoulders, zeroing in on the spots he knew were tightest.
"You could bring that to bed, you know."

"I needed to concentrate."

"Meaning you can't concentrate in bed?"

"Not on an infected femoral nonunion."

"I'm not sure I want to know."

"It's what you could have had if your bones hadn't knit
so beautifully and the antibiotics hadn't worked."

"Knowing that," he murmured, brushing his lips along
the side of her neck while his thumbs dissolved her knots,
"I wouldn't be able to concentrate, either."

She didn't know how he did it. In the space of seconds,
he could have the tension draining from certain places only
to have her tightening in others. All he had to do was start
working on her neck. And kissing her.

"How much longer will you be?"

Reaching forward, she closed the file. "I just finished."

"Then my timing's good. I want to talk to you. About
what I told you about your house."

His hands suddenly slipped away. A moment later, he'd
pulled out the stool beside her with the tip of his crutch
and sat down facing her, his injured leg extended below
the hem of his tan shorts and one boater-shod foot planted
on the low rung.

Except for the hum of the refrigerator, the room was
silent.

Alex wasn't sure her heart was even beating. His glance
skimmed her face as he reached out and trailed his fingers
along her jaw. The touch was familiar, something he usually did just before he drew her into his arms. But this time,
he just edged her knees around so that she faced him and
picked up her hand.

"When I told you what your agent said," he prefaced,
"I got the feeling you might think you have to leave just

because your house is ready. You don't have to go, Alex. I want you and Tyler to stay.''

She'd gone completely still. She knew she was waiting. She just wasn't sure if she was waiting to figure out how she was supposed to respond, or waiting for words she hadn't dared hope to hear.

He gave her no clue as he sat watching the confusion play over her face. Apparently, that was all he'd intended to say.

Caution stole through her stillness. He'd leased the house for three months. That had been nearly two months ago. ''How long do you plan to stay in Honeygrove?''

His glance fell to where her hand rested limply in his. With his thumb, he brushed over her knuckles, then looked back up. ''Another month. Until the dedication of the new wing.''

A hollow ache settled in her stomach as she slowly slipped her hand away. ''You're going back to Seattle then?'' she asked, amazed by the evenness of her tone.

''That's where I live, Alex. This is just temporary.''

They were talking about the house. But she knew he was talking about them, too. He wasn't asking her to go with him. He wasn't saying he wanted them to keep seeing each other after he'd gone. He wasn't even making polite noises about seeing her when he returned to see his brothers. All he'd said was that he wanted her to stay with him now.

Stool legs scraped lightly on the floor as she turned with all the grace she could muster and stepped away to pick up her cup. The agitation creeping through her demanded movement. The ache in her chest demanded distance. ''My staying here was temporary, too,'' she reminded him, refusing to let him see that ache. ''I need to go home when the house is ready.''

She could feel his eyes on her back as she dumped the remaining tea into the sink.

"Why?"

The honest puzzlement in the question had her staring at him blankly.

"Why can't you stay?" he prodded. "You're comfortable here, aren't you? I know Tyler is."

Comfort had nothing to do with it. "Tyler's part of the reason I need to go." The biggest part. "It's probably easier for you having us here, but it will be easier on him in the long run if we stick to the original plan."

"Easier on me?" he asked, his tone suddenly, deceptively, quiet.

She wanted to be fair. She'd known from the beginning how Chase protected himself, how he wouldn't let himself care too much. She had no one to blame but herself for letting her heart overrule her head.

"I know the past couple of months have been hard for you, Chase. And I know you've been trying to find your way between two very different worlds. I can't even imagine what your life must have been like before," she admitted, because her only contact with it had been Gwen and in some ways, the woman intimidated the daylights out of her. "But I don't want my son being part of your experiment with domesticity, if that's what's going on here. I don't want him getting any closer to you than he already is."

For a moment, Chase said nothing. He just sat with one arm resting on the shiny white island, his hand dangling casually over the side and his eyes narrowed on her face.

"We'll overlook the part about the experiment," he said, his voice deadly calm. "But I asked you to stay because I like having you here. If there's something else going on, just say it. Don't use your son as an excuse."

"He's not an excuse. I can handle knowing you aren't always going to be there," she told him, being as reasonable and honest with him as he'd always been with her. He'd never once made a promise. Never once led her to believe they'd have anything beyond what they had at that moment. "But I'm not going to have him wondering what's wrong with him that you didn't care enough to always be there for him. That's what he'll eventually do, too. He's already looking at you as if you were his father."

"I doubt that," Chase muttered.

"Don't. An hour ago he asked if he could call you Daddy."

The request had clearly shaken her. It caught Chase just as unprepared. But, then, he hadn't been prepared for her to say she wouldn't stay, either.

If she wanted to go, he wouldn't try to stop her. She was right about how difficult things had been—until the last couple of weeks anyway. But the life he was living here wasn't the life he would return to, and he'd known from the beginning that he was going back. He'd accomplished what he'd come to do. She knew that.

"So, how do we handle this?"

The edge in his tone put caution in hers. "I'm not sure what you mean."

"I'll still be here for a month."

"If you're asking if we'll still see each other, I'm sure we will. You have an appointment at my office for an X-ray next Tuesday."

He recognized the mask of composure she wore. He'd seen it often enough when he'd been in the hospital. It was her professional shield, the one she hid behind so her feelings didn't get involved with whatever it was she had to do. She was shutting down, shutting him out. As expert as he was at the tactic himself, he had no trouble recognizing it at all.

Hating the way she'd withdrawn from him, his glance slipped to where her fingers absently rubbed the single pearl at the base of her throat.

"And Tyler?" he prodded, knowing she couldn't keep the mask on for long when it came to her son.

Her fingers stilled. Looking at him as if he simply didn't get it, she crossed her arms over her pink oxford shirt. "You know how hard it was not being able to get your father's affection," she reminded him, needing him to understand the impact he'd had on her little boy. "I won't have Tyler going through that kind of pain."

The thought that he would do something like that to a child was incomprehensible. But it jerked at his defenses anyway.

"I'm out of his life just like that?"

"You're going to be out of it anyway."

"So, what do you plan to do?" he countered, not totally sure why he was pushing. "Have a constant stream of people moving in and out of his life so he doesn't have time to get attached to anyone? Or is it yourself you're protecting?"

She spun on him, composure cracking. "You ask me to stay with you, to sleep with you, and in the next breath you tell me you're still moving on next month." She was wrong, she couldn't handle knowing there was no future for them. She couldn't be with him knowing she was about to become a thing of his past. "You don't want to be part of my life so you have absolutely no business questioning how I live it."

She hurt. The hollow spot felt as if it were ripping apart, exposing her heart to this man who refused to invest his own.

"I'm not going to do this." Turning away, she pushed her fingers through her hair, took a breath, calming herself. "I'm not going to say things I'll have to regret. I knew we'd be over eventually and now we are. Let's not make it any worse than it has to be."

She had no idea what Chase would have said. Or if he'd have said anything at all. The telephone rang, mercifully taking her attention from the blue eyes staring at her back when she turned away to snatch it up.

It was the hospital, but long before she'd concluded the call, Chase had left her in the kitchen and headed for his room.

She slept with Tyler that night. And even though there were unpainted walls and furniture piled everywhere, she and her little boy moved back home the next day.

She heard from the associate in her office who took Chase's appointment for her that Tuesday, that he was going back to Seattle and that he wanted his records transferred to his personal physician.

From Ronni, she heard that he left the following week.

The dedication of Honeygrove Memorial Hospital's new wing took place at noon on the first of September. The day was bright and clear, the air warm. The wide swath of concrete fronting the new building's main entrance was packed with local dignitaries, private citizens and members of the hospital board and staff. The press had taken up a command post near the refreshment table on the lawn and the mayor was presently waxing eloquent from a dais by the main entrance.

Over the occasional pitch and screech of the PA system, Alex heard the man speak of the debt of gratitude the community owed the Malone brothers; Ryan for his campaign to replace the embezzled Pembroke Trust funds, Tanner who kept crews working at his own expense while those funds were being raised and Chase Harrington—whom everyone now knew, thanks to the media, was a Malone, too—for raising the last of the money needed to complete the project. Because of their contributions, the new construction was being dedicated as the James and Cecilia Malone Memorial Wing, in honor of their deceased parents.

Alex stood at the back of the crowd, listening to the applause and wishing fervently that Ryan would hurry up and make his speech so she could get back to her office.

Chase was up there. Somewhere. She'd caught a glimpse of him near the dais a few minutes ago, which was why she'd moved to the back of the crowd. Knowing he was so close made it harder by the second to stay.

She'd known he'd be there. Kelly had told her he would. And she'd thought she could handle seeing him. But she'd been wrong. That brief glimpse had been enough to undo an entire month's worth of mental lectures about how the heart was just a muscle that would heal like any other torn and damaged body part. All she had to do was give it time. But it would never heal if she didn't protect the wound. Seeing him had ripped it wide open again.

She couldn't believe how she'd missed him, missed talking to him, just being with him. She'd even missed worrying about him, crazy as that sounded to her at the moment. He was still on crutches, would be for another month, but the ease of his movements when she'd seen him a few minutes ago made it apparent that he was staying on top of his therapy.

"Alex."

She knew it was physiologically impossible for her heart to slide to her throat. It just felt as if it had at the sound of that disturbingly familiar voice. It even seemed to tighten there when she felt his hand touch her elbow.

Willing composure into place, she turned around.

Eyes as blue as sapphires locked on hers. In the instant before she realized the bruises were gone, she saw hesitation wash his beautifully molded features.

She was sure she was the only one who saw that less-than-totally-confident trait. Even on crutches, his aura of wealth and power was unmistakable. His dark hair was meticulously cut, his navy suit impeccably tailored. Neat little tabs held his sharply creased slacks closed over the fixation device. His tie was silk. The tack, gold.

Before she could say a word, his glance cut to the people on either side of them.

"Can we go someplace else?"

His voice was low, but the rich depth of it had the woman beside her looking up. Laying her hand over her heart, the middle-aged matron blinked and promptly elbowed her companion.

With more elbows signaling a celebrity in the midst, it wasn't going to take long before dozens of eyes would turn their way. The people knotted ahead of them were already looking from him to her, which made it a tad difficult for her to pretend he wasn't there. Two of her colleagues were openly staring.

Pushing her hands into the pockets of the lab coat she wore over a mocha-colored sheath, Alex gave him a nod. Moments later, they were moving away from the crowd and the booming public address system.

Another round of applause filled the air.

"How's your leg?" she asked because she needed to say something and, like it or not, she really wanted to know.

"It's good. My doctor said my surgeon is a genius."

Her smile felt strained. "Thank him for me."

"I will." Moving with an athletic ease that no man on crutches should possess, he glanced along the side of the new building, its glass facade a stark contrast to the main building's brick. With another group of people walking toward them, he nodded toward an unmarked doorway farther down the new structure. "It'll be quieter in there."

"Chase, I don't have time—"

"Two minutes," he said, when she hesitated. "Just give me two minutes. Okay?"

There were too many familiar faces around for her to protest without causing a scene. Figuring capitulation the better part of valor at the moment, she opened the door since it was easier for her to get it than for him, and followed him inside.

This part of the new wing still housed packing crates. The air was filled with the smells of the putty-gray paint on the long hallway's wall and the darker institutional gray carpet. Construction was finished, but not all of the building was occupied.

Chase had obviously known that. The metal door closed with a solid thunk, shutting out the outside sounds. With even their footsteps muffled as he turned to face her, Alex was very aware of the sudden, heavy silence.

He stood in front of the wall, a mountain of masculinity in designer gabardine.

"This isn't where I wanted to talk," he said before that silence could grow deadly. "I was going to phone you after this thing was over today, but I know you saw me a while ago. When you took off, I was afraid you might not take my call."

Nerves jumping, she crossed her arms. She didn't know if she'd have taken his call or not. "What did you want?"

He looked a little apprehensive, which wasn't like him at all. He also looked a little defensive, which was. She figured that was only fair, considering that she felt that way herself.

"I wanted to apologize."

She found it easier to look at his tie tack.

"For what it's worth," he said, sounding a little more tense than he liked when he realized she wasn't going to help him out, "you were probably right about what I was doing. The experimenting, I mean. I just want you to know it hadn't been conscious."

"That's supposed to make me feel better?"

She posed the question quietly, but the hurt was there, still on the surface, still too fresh.

He had the heart to wince, the furrows at the corners of his eyes deepening. "I never meant to hurt you, Alex. Or your son."

He was trying. She had to give him credit for that. Heaven knew she'd met lesser men. And since he was apologizing, the gracious thing to do would be to accept it. From a purely selfish standpoint, she figured it would be easier in the long run. Chase would undoubtedly be in Honeygrove on occasion to see his brothers and check on his building project and it was entirely possible that she would run into him now and again. The last thing she wanted was the world—or Chase—to think she hadn't gotten over him. "Just let it go. Okay? That's what I'd like to do."

"Can I convince you not to?"

"Not to what?"

His eyes held hers, probing, searching. She wasn't sure what he saw there other than the hurt she was doing a lousy job of hiding, but whatever it was seemed to give him the encouragement he needed. "Not to let it go."

There was a hint of uncertainty in Chase's deep voice, and something that sounded a little too much like a plea.

"Don't do this," she whispered. It had always been too easy for him to push her away, only to pull her back again. Too easy. And too unfair. "I can't—"

"Don't say that." He snagged her by the shoulder as she stepped back, needing to stop her, needing to touch. "I don't want to lose you, Alex.

"Please," he said, wondering at how still she'd gone. "Just listen to me. Okay?"

There was caution in her nod, and a look in her eyes that bore an unsettling resemblance to disbelief, but at least she wasn't bolting. She wasn't pulling back from him, either. Encouraged by that, desperately needing to believe some of what she'd once felt for him remained, he leaned against the wall, tugging her with him.

With one hand on her shoulder, he curved his other at the side of her neck. "I've had a lot of time to think," he told her, praying he'd find the right words. He'd wanted to take her someplace romantic, someplace where the atmosphere would aide his cause. The way she'd turned from him a while ago, he feared this was the only chance he'd get.

"You know how messed up the last several months have been," he began, because she, more than anyone, had understood what he'd struggled with. "I'd always known something was missing in my life, but I thought I'd figured out what it was when I found my brothers. They're part of it, Alex. But I didn't really understand what was missing until you showed me."

He brushed his thumb along her jaw, relieved by how she allowed the touch, amazed by how, sometimes, just touching her could calm him.

"I've always had money," he said, his tone matter-of-fact. "And people are constantly after me for whatever they can get. But you taught me how good it feels to give. Not money. But time." His thumb stilled. "No one ever needed me just to be there for them before."

It was the intangibles that had mattered. Watching Tyler

for her. Rubbing her back. Helping her out when he could. It was the time he'd spent with the little boy he sorely missed, the feeling of accomplishment when the child had finally grasped the concept of adding two numbers. It was helping with Brent and feeding the cat and being able to turn to her for help with all the emotional chaos he'd dealt with.

They'd worked together. They'd shared. They'd been there for each other.

"There's something else you taught me," he told her, needing her to understand just how hard his life would be without her. "I'd finally learned how to relax, but only when I was reading to Tyler or answering those mind-boggling questions of his." The skin beneath his fingers felt warm and as soft as silk. "Or touching you.

"I've spent years going after things I wanted. I just never knew what I needed. I do now. I need you," he said, his certainty a sharp contrast to the subtle tension filling him. "I just need to know what *you* want."

Alex swallowed, tried to speak. All she could do was stare at Chase and shake her head in disbelief. Knowing him as she did, she didn't doubt a word he said. It was too hard for him to open up, too hard for him to make himself vulnerable. But it seemed he'd just pushed all his cards to her side of the table. She just didn't know what she was supposed to do with them.

"What I want?"

"From me. You never told me."

She'd been afraid to. She'd been afraid to open the dreams that wide.

"Whatever you want," he said, his voice husky and low as he cupped her face. "Whatever I have. Just ask, Alex, and it's yours.

"What?" he asked, watching the suspicious brightness shimmer in her eyes.

She shook her head as she touched her hand to his chest and felt the strong heavy beat beneath the crisp white cotton.

"This is all I want."

He glanced down to where the tips of her fingers rested against his heart. When he looked back to her, realization had washed the tension from his face.

He turned to prop his crutches against the wall, then leaned against it again. "You've already got that," he told her, drawing her into his arms. "What else?"

"That's all," she said, scarcely able to believe he was holding her. Minutes ago, she'd thought she would never again know the strength of his arms, the warmth of his touch. "If I have that, I have everything." Swallowing past the knot in her throat, she whispered, "I love you."

She wanted him. Just him. Not because of who he was or what he possessed but because she loved him. The knowledge filled him with wonder—and made his heart feel a little too full for his chest.

"I love you, too, Alex." He touched her cheek, her hair. "That's what I'd wanted to tell you tonight. You see," he continued, slipping his hand between them to reach into the watch pocket of his pants, "there's something else I want." He picked up her hand. In his, he held a platinum band graced with a two-karat solitaire. "I want us to live here and be a real family," he explained, slipping the ring onto her finger. "I want you to be my wife and I want Tyler to be my son. And if you ever feel the urge to be a mom again, I wouldn't mind having a daughter, too."

She edged back a little, looking from the diamond sparkling on her finger, needing to see his face. Overwhelmed, all she could do was search his eyes with her heart in hers as he threaded his fingers through her hair.

She didn't know if she rose to meet his lips or if he lowered his head to meet hers. It didn't matter. There was need in his kiss, and possession and protectiveness and a heady jolt of pure, unadulterated desire. Alex felt them all as he molded her body to his, holding her as if he'd never let her go. She kissed him back with that same heat, letting him know she needed him as badly as he needed her.

Not until he'd altered her breathing and drained the strength from her knees did he lift his head. When he did, his smile was devastating. "Am I to assume we have an agreement?"

She smiled back, her eyes bright and slightly bewildered as she gave him a nod. "Oh, I think so," she teased. "I just have no idea how I'll manage a baby along with everything else."

"It's we who'll have to manage. And I'll tell you what," he said, intent darkening his eyes as he lowered his head once more. "Since we need to go out there with my brothers in a few minutes, let's just close the deal now and we'll negotiate the details later."

Epilogue

"I can't believe you pulled this together so fast, Alex. I gave up trying to get anything planned. That's why Tanner and I finally just did a close-friends-and-family ceremony, too. But this…" Kelly glanced around the living room of what had been the Pembrooke estate—before Chase had bought it for his new family last month. Lavish garlands of white roses were draped over the marble mantel, the sideboard and twined around railings and pillars. Tall white candles glowed everywhere. Outside on the patio, where twinkling lights had been wrapped through and around every tree, the strains of a string quartet underscored the buzz of seventy guests laughing, mingling, talking. The cake, a fabulous tiered confection with icing that looked like poured satin had been flown in from San Francisco and awaited the bride and groom on a silver cart by the pool.

"This," Kelly repeated, snagging a crystal flute of Dom Pérignon from a passing waiter, "is amazing."

"You didn't have Gwen." The silk organza of Alex's simple white gown rustled as she took a flute, too. She hadn't worn a veil, only small pearl combs holding her hair back above her ears. "I've told you before, the woman intimidates the daylights out of me. We never could have pulled this off without her."

"Well, she has excellent taste." Ronni, looking as if she were about to deliver any minute, held out her plate of hors d'oeuvres. "I tell you, Alex. The ceremony was lovely. And you look fabulous. But that caterer is truly inspired. I almost wish Ryan and I were getting married again just so I'd have an excuse to use him. Try a crab puff."

"I know what you mean," Kelly agreed, helping herself to one of the delectable morsels, "but now that the three of us are married there are no weddings to plan." She paused, suddenly looking terribly thoughtful. "You know," she said, pondering, "the three of us all just married within the past few months. And last year, there were three nurses at the hospital who'd signed some sort of pact to never marry doctors and they all got married within months of each other. It almost makes me wonder who's next."

"Who's next for what?" The groom, looking drop-dead gorgeous in his Armani tuxedo, walked up behind his bride and curved his arm around her waist. "I hope I'm not interrupting a consultation. You're looking pretty serious over here."

"It's definitely a critical subject," Alex informed him.

"Someone's future is at stake," said Kelly.

Ronni, chewing, simply nodded gravely.

"Can whoever it is survive without my wife for a minute?" he asked his sisters-in-law as he tugged Alex toward the entry. "I need her for a consultation of my own."

"Oh, I think so." Kelly grinned. "You look as if you have something pretty critical on your mind."

"She's right," Alex echoed, glancing at the determined set of her husband's jaw. "Where are we going?"

"In here." Leading her down the wide hall, nodding to a knot of guests who'd congregated there to admire the new art now hanging on the walls, he ushered her into his study, which happened to be the first room they reached without anyone else in it. "I know we need to get back to our guests in a minute, but there's something I need to do."

"What's that?"

"Thank you," he said, pulling her to him.

"Thank me? I'm not sure what for," she replied, looping her arms around her husband's neck, "but I certainly like the way you're approaching this." She tipped her head, her eyes shining. "What did I do?"

Drawing her closer, Chase lowered his head toward hers. "You said 'yes.'"

*   *   *   *   *

A NOTE FROM THE AUTHOR

Dear Reader,

If this is your first visit to Honeygrove Memorial Hospital, welcome! If you're already part of the Honeygrove family, it's good to have you here!

When Susan Mallery, Christine Rimmer and I first talked about writing a trilogy together, we had no idea that our project would take on a life of its own. I had such fun working with these two talented women that I was delighted when our editors asked us to continue the series.

To work out the new details, Chris and Susan flew to Arizona where we spent one long, intense and extremely productive weekend at my home. We pondered, debated, paced, laughed, groaned and paced some more. By the end of that weekend, we had everything we needed to get started: the wonderful Malone brothers, my fabulously rich and secretive Chase Harrington and three dedicated female physicians with the sorts of dreams and hang-ups familiar to any woman who has ever loved, lost and loved again. So, after rewarding ourselves late that last night with a great old movie (a romance, of course), Susan headed west, Chris headed east, I headed upstairs and we went to work on the characters we had assigned ourselves.

As with every Special Edition, each book in Prescription: Marriage is a complete story in its own right. Each is the story of a powerful man and a strong successful woman who discovers how much better they are with each other than they can ever be alone. These are tales of people dedicated to healing, to friendship and to family. To family, most of all.

I love the time I spend in Honeygrove. I hope you did, too.

Take care,
Christine Flynn

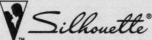

If you enjoyed what you just read,
then we've got an offer you can't resist!

Take 2 bestselling love stories FREE!

Plus get a FREE surprise gift!

THE FORTUNES OF TEXAS

Membership in this family has its privileges…and its price. But what a fortune can't buy, a true-bred Texas love is sure to bring!

On sale in March…

The **Heiress** and the **Sheriff**

by STELLA BAGWELL

Sheriff Wyatt Grayhawk didn't trust strangers, especially the lovely damsel who claimed to have no memory yet sought a haven on the Fortunes' Texas ranch. But would Wyatt's mission to uncover Gabrielle's past be sidetracked by the allure of the mysterious beauty?

THE FORTUNES OF TEXAS continues with **LONE STAR WEDDING** by Sandra Steffen, available in April from Silhouette Books.

Available at your favorite retail outlet.

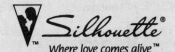

Silhouette®

Where love comes alive™

MONTANA
MAVERICKS
Big Sky Brides

Legendary love comes to Whitehorn, Montana,
once more as beloved authors

Christine Rimmer, Jennifer Greene and Cheryl St.John

present three brand-new stories in this exciting anthology!

Meet the Brennan women:
SUZANNA, DIANA and ISABELLE

Strong-willed beauties who find unexpected
love in these irresistible marriage of
covnenience stories.

Don't miss
MONTANA MAVERICKS: BIG SKY BRIDES
On sale in February 2000,
only from Silhouette Books!

Available at your favorite retail outlet.

SILHOUETTE'S 20TH ANNIVERSARY CONTEST
OFFICIAL RULES
NO PURCHASE NECESSARY TO ENTER

1. To enter, follow directions published in the offer to which you are responding. Contest begins 1/1/00 and ends on 8/24/00 (the "Promotion Period"). Method of entry may vary. Mailed entries must be postmarked by 8/24/00, and received by 8/31/00.

2. During the Promotion Period, the Contest may be presented via the Internet. Entry via the Internet may be restricted to residents of certain geographic areas that are disclosed on the Web site. To enter via the Internet, if you are a resident of a geographic area in which Internet entry is permissible, follow the directions displayed on-line, including typing your essay of 100 words or fewer telling us "Where In The World Your Love Will Come Alive." On-line entries must be received by 11:59 p.m. Eastern Standard time on 8/24/00. Limit one e-mail entry per person, household and e-mail address per day, per presentation. If you are a resident of a geographic area in which entry via the Internet is permissible, you may, in lieu of submitting an entry on-line, enter by mail, by hand-printing your name, address, telephone number and contest number/name on an 8"x 11" plain piece of paper and telling us in 100 words or fewer "Where In The World Your Love Will Come Alive," and mailing via first-class mail to: Silhouette 20th Anniversary Contest, (in the U.S.) P.O. Box 9069, Buffalo, NY 14269-9069; (In Canada) P.O. Box 637, Fort Erie, Ontario, Canada L2A 5X3. Limit one 8"x 11" mailed entry per person, household and e-mail address per day. On-line and/or 8"x 11" mailed entries received from persons residing in geographic areas in which Internet entry is not permissible will be disqualified. No liability is assumed for lost, late, incomplete, inaccurate, nondelivered or misdirected mail, or misdirected e-mail, for technical, hardware or software failures of any kind, lost or unavailable network connection, or failed, incomplete, garbled or delayed computer transmission or any human error which may occur in the receipt or processing of the entries in the contest.

3. Essays will be judged by a panel of members of the Silhouette editorial and marketing staff based on the following criteria:

   Sincerity (believability, credibility)—50%
   Originality (freshness, creativity)—30%
   Aptness (appropriateness to contest ideas)—20%

   Purchase or acceptance of a product offer does not improve your chances of winning. In the event of a tie, duplicate prizes will be awarded.

4. All entries become the property of Harlequin Enterprises Ltd., and will not be returned. Winner will be determined no later than 10/31/00 and will be notified by mail. Grand Prize winner will be required to sign and return Affidavit of Eligibility within 15 days of receipt of notification. Noncompliance within the time period may result in disqualification and an alternative winner may be selected. All municipal, provincial, federal, state and local laws and regulations apply. Contest open only to residents of the U.S. and Canada who are 18 years of age or older, and is void wherever prohibited by law. Internet entry is restricted solely to residents of those geographical areas in which Internet entry is permissible. Employees of Torstar Corp., their affiliates, agents and members of their immediate families are not eligible. Taxes on the prizes are the sole responsibility of winners. Entry and acceptance of any prize offered constitutes permission to use winner's name, photograph or other likeness for the purposes of advertising, trade and promotion on behalf of Torstar Corp. without further compensation to the winner, unless prohibited by law. Torstar Corp and D.L. Blair, Inc., their parents, affiliates and subsidiaries, are not responsible for errors in printing or electronic presentation of contest or entries. In the event of printing or other errors which may result in unintended prize values or duplication of prizes, all affected contest materials or entries shall be null and void. If for any reason the Internet portion of the contest is not capable of running as planned, including infection by computer virus, bugs, tampering, unauthorized intervention, fraud, technical failures, or any other causes beyond the control of Torstar Corp. which corrupt or affect the administration, secrecy, fairness, integrity or proper conduct of the contest, Torstar Corp. reserves the right, at its sole discretion, to disqualify any individual who tampers with the entry process and to cancel, terminate, modify or suspend the contest or the Internet portion thereof. In the event of a dispute regarding an on-line entry, the entry will be deemed submitted by the authorized holder of the e-mail account submitted at the time of entry. Authorized account holder is defined as the natural person who is assigned to an e-mail address by an Internet access provider, on-line service provider or other organization that is responsible for arranging e-mail address for the domain associated with the submitted e-mail address.

5. Prizes: Grand Prize—a $10,000 vacation to anywhere in the world. Travelers (at least one must be 18 years of age or older) or parent or guardian if one traveler is a minor, must sign and return a Release of Liability prior to departure. Travel must be completed by December 31, 2001, and is subject to space and accommodations availability. Two hundred (200) Second Prizes—a two-book limited edition autographed collector set from one of the Silhouette Anniversary authors: Nora Roberts, Diana Palmer, Linda Howard or Annette Broadrick (value $10.00 each set). All prizes are valued in U.S. dollars.

6. For a list of winners (available after 10/31/00), send a self-addressed, stamped envelope to: Harlequin Silhouette 20th Anniversary Winners, P.O. Box 4200, Blair, NE 68009-4200.

Contest sponsored by Torstar Corp., P.O. Box 9042, Buffalo, NY 14269-9042.

ENTER FOR
A CHANCE TO WIN*
Silhouette's 20th Anniversary Contest

Tell Us Where in the World
You Would Like *Your* Love To Come Alive...
And We'll Send the Lucky Winner There!

Silhouette wants to take you wherever
your happy ending can come true.

Here's how to enter: Tell us, in 100 words or less,
where you want to go to make your love come alive!

In addition to the grand prize, there will be 200
runner-up prizes, collector's-edition book sets
autographed by one of the Silhouette anniversary
authors: **Nora Roberts, Diana Palmer,
Linda Howard** or **Annette Broadrick**.

DON'T MISS YOUR CHANCE TO WIN!
ENTER NOW! No Purchase Necessary

Silhouette®
Where love comes alive™

Name:

Address:

City: State/Province:

Zip/Postal Code:

Mail to Harlequin Books: **In the U.S.**: P.O. Box 9069, Buffalo, NY
14269-9069; **In Canada**: P.O. Box 637, Fort Erie, Ontario, L4A 5X3

PS20CON_R